THE HAND THAT FEEDS

GIL MASON SERIES
BOOK 8

GORDON CARROLL

D1534020

PROLOGUE

The sound of blood dripping brought me awake. It wasn't loud, really. The consistency of the pattern did the trick—a steady, *drip-drip-drip*. I opened my eyes, feeling the pain in my ... *well* ... pretty much everywhere. The car was destroyed, but the airbags and crumple design had saved my life, at least for now. I could see I wasn't out of the woods yet—pun intended, since I was literally *in* the woods. Hanging upside down and held in place by only the restraining tension of the seatbelt, I looked around as best I could and saw that the car and I were stuck in a tree somewhere above the ground.

It was night and incredibly dark, but shafts of moonlight and stars shone through the branches. I reached for my belt-buckle knife, a small two-inch job with a sharp point and double razor edges. The movement shifted the car's balance ever so slightly. Branches snapped, giving way, and suddenly we were falling. The front end canted at an angle, and the crushed passenger side hit a branch about the thickness of my forearm that punched through the window, showering me with glass.

Holding my breath, I waited as the metal groaned like an old man getting out of bed. Small cubed chunks of safety glass pittered and pattered and tinkled about as the twisted block of metal shifted and slanted until it came to terms with gravity for a holding place.

It was impossible to gauge how high I was through the needle-covered branches. I might be ten feet or a hundred off the ground. I remembered the impact and the spin. I remembered the free fall for ... *how long I couldn't say* ... the thought of falling off a mountain and dying has that effect. A second impact was immediately followed by the airbag punching me hard in the face. I blacked out and eventually woke up here. And then everything came rushing back to me. I suddenly remembered *why* I was here.

I craned my neck as carefully as possible as I looked into the backseat.

Empty.

It shouldn't have been.

"Max?" I called. "Pilgrim?"

My blood was doing that annoying dripping thing again.

"Pilgrim?" I yelled louder. I noticed that all the back windows were shattered, and fur was scraped on pieces of glass along the side. It looked like Pilgrim's. *And there was blood.* I clenched my teeth, breathing hard. "Max? Toby?"

Nothing.

I reached for the buckle knife again, slowly this time. Sliding it free, I placed one edge along the shoulder strap. The knife would make short work of the strap, and I'd be free, but I'd have to be careful not to let my weight upset the precarious balance. Just before that became an issue, I heard the branch give way again. It sounded like a gunshot and could prove to be just as deadly.

The world upended as the car slipped forward, crashing through tree limbs in a storm of splinters that rained through my once spectacular Escalade, showering and slicing and battering my face as I dove toward the unforgiving earth.

It took a while.

I wasn't ten feet off the ground—I can attest to that much, at least. Probably not a hundred, either. Split the difference, maybe.

Lucky I hadn't cut the seatbelt, or I probably would have been crushed.

Either way, the impact did the trick, and out I went again.

Drip-drip-drip ... the sound woke me up once more.

And, again, there was pain.

This time we were out of the tree—both me and the car—only the car, what was left of it, was kind of propped up against the trunk. I was hanging forward by the seatbelt, almost like before the fall.

It was so dark.

Nearly black.

Everything hurt even worse than before.

"Max? Pilgrim? Toby?" My voice sounded hoarse and dry. I tried again, louder.

But there was no answer—only the night and the wind and the swaying trees.

I was alone.

1

Leaf added two logs to the giant stack of firewood piled outside the massive cathedral that served as the Assembly's meeting hall, mess hall, worship hall, and all-around gathering place. He squinted up at the winter sun as it threatened to set behind the higher mountains to the west and saw the top of the One Tree rising through and above the steepled glass ceiling.

Under his breath, he chanted the sacred incantation taught to him by the Gardener and the mothers. Everyone was required to repeat the sacred incantation when they saw the One Tree. It had taken him time to learn it, but he now knew it by heart. There were three incantations: two prayers, and the one word of power. He had learned them all.

Memorization came easy to some of the children, but not to Leaf. Mother Willow scolded him when he forgot things, reminding him that although he was nearly seven, many of the five-year-olds were better at it than he was.

It wasn't that Leaf didn't try—he did, he really did. But he was easily distracted, especially during lessons. Even the threat of Mother Willow's lash couldn't always hold him to his tasks. He'd felt the bites from her branch on four separate occasions—one lash the first time, two the second, three the third, and so on. He was trying as hard as he could to not let it get to five.

The four lashes had bled and hurt so bad he thought he'd pass out. His mother—his real mother—tended to him after each beating, soothing the wounds with water, balms, gentle words, and even gentler kisses. She never chided him for his lack of skills.

Each time he had begged her to take him away from the Assembly, but she just shushed him and told him not to speak of such things—that the Gardener heard all, saw all, knew all, and that they had to accept this new life now that his father had died. She told him the Gardener was his new father, that he was father to them all, and that they must obey him in all things.

Leaf often cried for her to stay the night with him, but she wouldn't. She couldn't. She had duties—cleaning, cooking, making things to sell. For a time, she had been assigned to the kiln pit, where the heat and labor were nearly unbearable, but recently, the Gardener had promoted her. As one of his new wives, she was moved and given new duties. Leaf didn't understand the new duties, and when he asked, his mother wouldn't talk about them. He thought they must be hard, though, because she had bruises, and sometimes she would limp and cringe at loud sounds.

They had been with the Assembly for almost a year now—so long that he sometimes had difficulty remembering life before. But he did remember some things. His father had been tall and strong and loving, and his mother had laughed all the time. Toby remembered being tossed in the air by his father and rolling around on the floor with him.

He remembered being happy.

But then his father went to fight in the war. He stayed away for a long time, and when he came back, he was different. His father acted like everything was fine, but Leaf knew something was wrong. It reminded Leaf of how he felt when he tried to memorize things. His father tried, but it wasn't the same—it wasn't real. And then his father went back to war, and he died.

His mother had been seeing other men by then, even before his father died. She called them her BFFs and told Toby they were just nice men.

But they weren't nice.

They came and went, some staying for a week, others just a night. One of them kicked Toby. The man was smoking something nasty smelling, and when Toby gave him a mean look, he kicked him hard in the leg. His mother punched the man and chased him out of the house. She promised Toby she'd stop seeing the men, but she didn't, and soon she was smoking the nasty-smelling cigarettes and drinking all the time.

After a while, she started seeing Jimmy. Jimmy was better than most of the men. He hardly ever got drunk, and he never hit or kicked Toby. In fact, he didn't pay much attention to Toby at all, which was better than hitting or kicking.

One day, his mother got really drunk, threw up, and had to go to the hospital for a few days. Afterward, all three of them loaded up the car and drove far into the mountains to the Assembly. His mother told him this is where Jimmy lived, and they would live here now, too. In this new place, she would be away from the drugs and the alcohol, and they could live better lives. Pure, good lives. Jimmy had been trying to get them to move here for a long time, and now it was the *right* time. She needed this. *They* needed this. If they *didn't* do this, she would die.

Like his father had died.

She said they could be happy here like they used to be.

And they were.

The Gardener met them, hugged them, told them how wonderful it was that Jimmy had brought them. The Gardener told them he had seen them in a vision and had sent Jimmy to find them. He gave them new names. His mother was now Starflower, like a superhero, and Toby—he was Leaf. The Gardener told Leaf that one day he would grow to be a mighty tree.

The Assembly gave them easy jobs to do, and everyone was so nice. Before long, the people in the Assembly began to feel like one big family. His mother gave up the drugs and the alcohol overnight—a miracle.

The Gardener told them about the aliens who had visited him and his planting of the One Tree. He taught them the special incantations, the chants, and the word of power. He showed them the sacred scrolls he was writing, which would soon replace all the world's false teachings—the Bible, the Koran, the Talmud, the Rigveda, the Satkhandagama, and the Satanic Bible.

The Gardener said that all religions were corrupt, but his writings would cleanse and unite them. The truth of his teachings would be incontestable, and everyone would believe. He said that the chosen few, those of his Assembly, would rule the cosmos because of their belief and devotion. Jimmy, Teresa, and Toby, along with the rest of the Assembly, would rule with him.

The sun dipped lower, outlining the One Tree.

How pretty it was.

Leaf took in a deep breath of the clear, brisk mountain air. He looked at his small, ungloved palms and saw the callouses they were developing. The logs were heavy and rough, but he was getting stronger like his mother had gotten stronger. Life here was not as easy as it had seemed in the beginning, but it was better than when his mother was drinking and better than her being with the men.

He missed Jimmy—*West Wind*—his Assembly name. Leaf hadn't seen him since his mother's promotion. But he had gotten to know many of the boys, and most of them were nice.

Turning to get more logs, Leaf saw the Gardener standing a few yards away. He hadn't heard him, but the Gardener was like that—big, *giant really*, handsome, with big muscles like Maui in the movie *Moana*, only the Gardener didn't have a power hook. He didn't need one.

The Gardener smiled at him, his white teeth shining against his bronze skin. He walked up to Toby and laid a massive hand on his shoulder.

"You're doing well, Leaf," he said, smiling down at him. His hand moved from Leaf's shoulder to his head, gently rubbing his hair. "I think," the Gardener paused, "yes, yes, I think you might be ready." The Gardener rubbed his shoulder. "Ready for a promotion."

Leaf grinned, his heart swelling with pride.

How happy his mother would be.

2

"You've got a customer," said Yolanda, my secretary, as I walked in, flanked by Max and Pilgrim. "I told him there was no way to know how long it might take you to show up, you working whenever you want and all, but he was so nice and polite and handsome, unlike most of your Marine friends, and said he'd be happy to wait."

I looked toward my office and saw a flat-top burr barely cresting the top of the high-backed leather chair on the client side of my desk.

"Who is it?" I asked.

"He said his name is Kirk Sinclair, but for me to call him *Pappy*. I love nicknames. They're so cute. And doesn't it just fit him perfectly? He's so handsome and masculine."

I looked back at her. She was grinning, scrunching her shoulders, and holding her hands under her chin like a schoolgirl. It made me feel a little sick to my stomach. After a mental head shake, I walked into my office.

"Gunnery Sergeant Sinclair?" I said, grinning. "How are you, sir?"

Smoothly spinning the chair to face me, he stood. I hadn't seen him in years, but he looked exactly the same, except for a few new wrinkles and scars. Fifty years old, skin as brown and tough as leather, broad shoulders, narrow hips, about the same height as my five-ten—*lighter though*—maybe one-eighty. He was an exact proto-type of the *lean-green-fighting-machine* Marine. I'd done more than a few missions with him over several campaigns in the wars.

He was, and is, the most dangerous man I've ever known.

Picture a taller, tougher version of the actor Robert Conrad, who played James T. West in the old western secret agent series *The Wild Wild West*—the same guy who did the commercials daring people to knock the Eveready Battery off his shoulder. Back in the day, while Conrad was doing a commercial in Greeley, a couple of UNC (University of Northern Colorado) football players started taunting him about the whole battery thing. Big mistake. According to local legend, Conrad put them both in the hospital.

They were lucky it was Conrad and not Pappy. He'd have put them in the ground.

"Sir?" said Pappy, grinning. "Son, I *work* for a living."

"It's not the rank," I said, grinning back, "it's the age. I was raised to respect old people."

We shook hands. I would have hugged him, but Pappy's not the hugging sort.

"You never change," he said. "Always joking, always making cracks. How many times has that gotten you into trouble?"

"None I can think of," I said.

"Right," said Pappy. "I seem to remember a Samoan in a bar out in Twenty-Nine Stumps who took offense at something you said and threw you through a wall."

Looking up towards the ceiling, I said, "I don't think I remember it happening exactly like that, but thanks for pulling him off me."

"That was a good fight," he said, reminiscing.

I shook my head. "Again, that's not exactly how I remember it, but yes ... yes, it was a good fight."

We both laughed.

"So," I asked, "is this a personal or professional visit?"

"Both, but mostly business."

"Well, please, have a seat, and let's see what's what."

I walked around my desk and saw Pappy turn toward Max and Pilgrim, who still stood where I'd left them.

"Who do we have here?" he asked, reaching down and petting Pilgrim's head.

Pilgrim licked his fingers and nuzzled up against him.

Max just watched.

"That's Pilgrim," I said. "He's the nice one."

Pappy's eyes swiveled to Max. "Which means this one isn't?"

"Not so much," I said.

Max stared into him.

"Oh, yeah, I see it there," said Pappy, not looking away. "You as tough as you think you are, boy?"

Max didn't say anything. He just kept staring.

"You a Marine dog?" asked Pappy.

"Uh, Gunny," I said, "you might not want to do that. Not with him."

"Stand down, Sergeant," he said to me without moving his gaze from Max. "I can fight my own battles."

For the first time, I wasn't sure who I was more afraid for—Pappy or Max.

"You really all that?" asked Pappy, his voice low and even.

I was about to try and step between them when Max sat and started licking himself as if the gunny wasn't worth bothering over. Now I was really scared. No one disrespected Pappy. *No one.*

Pappy placed both hands on his hips, leaned his head back, and roared with laughter.

I don't think I'd ever seen him laugh like that before.

Scary.

Pappy turned to me, tears in his eyes.

"He really is all that, isn't he?" he said.

"Yes, sir, he really is," I said, thinking we might all make it out of this alive.

"A real tough dog," he said. "But are you a *Devil Dog?*"

The term *Devil Dogs* stuck after the WWI battle of Belleau Wood in 1918. When Marines were ordered to attack a hill while wearing gas masks, the Germans referred to them as *Teufel hunden*, or *Devil Dogs*, the vicious, wild mountain dogs of Bavarian folklore. Even though Max was never officially in the Marines, I think the name fits.

"He is," I said. "I can attest to it numerous times over."

"I value your opinion," said Pappy, giving me half a glance, "you know I do. But when it comes to character, I make up my own mind." He turned back to Max and pointed a finger.

Max stopped licking and looked back at him.

"You strike me as hard," said Pappy to Max. "Still, we'll have to see about you." Pappy pointed the peace sign to his eyes, then back at Max, telling him he'd be watching.

Max went back to licking.

Pappy gave Pilgrim another rub, then sat down, smiling at me.

"How do you like the PI gig?" he asked.

"Pays the bills."

"Yeah, like you care about that."

"Gotta feed the dogs," I said.

"Maybe I can help with that. I got a job for you."

"Let's hear it, Gunny."

"First off, it's not gunny anymore. It's Master Sergeant."

Standing up, I reached across the desk, extending a hand.

"Congratulations! How did that happen?"

He just shook his head, taking my hand and shaking.

"It wasn't my idea," he said, "I can tell you that. Command forced my hand—either promote or retire. They plan to make me take a desk job."

"That sounds like Command," I said. "Still, congrats."

"Yeah, thanks. Anyway, since there isn't a good war going on right now, I decided to take some vacation time to clear up a few matters."

"Matters," I echoed. "And that brings you to me?"

"It does," he said. "I'm making a tour of the states, taking a few personal items and stories back to the families of Marines who died under my command. Keeping some promises."

Nodding, I said, "I understand."

"One of my Marines, a corporal, got hurt bad by an IED. Came real close to dying. He lost a lot of blood and was in an induced coma for months. Then there were surgeries, recovery, and more surgeries. After all that, he was discharged, unable to serve due to his injuries. Turns out his wife left him some months before he got blown up. They have a kid together—boy, about seven. His wife sent him a Dear John email, then took off. Left no forwarding address, just a PO box for his government checks to land. When he got out of the hospital, he went looking for her ... her and the boy. No luck, though. I thought maybe you could help."

"Is he vengeful?" I asked.

"Vengeful?"

"Is he looking to hurt her? To pay her back for dumping him?"

The Gunn ... *Master Sergeant* ... shook his head.

"No, nothing like that. He's a good man. Gentle like. He just wants to have contact with his kid."

"You sure?" I asked. "I wouldn't want to see anyone get hurt."

"I get it," he said, "but no, I'm sure. He wouldn't hurt them."

"Did he try the PO box? That's the first place I would start. Stake it out, and when she comes to get her checks ...."

"He got his last checks at the VA when they processed him out. But he did try at the PO box. Said he found some old junk mail—no checks. Looked like it'd been a while since she'd been there. "

"Where's the PO box?"

"Here in Colorado," he said. "Somewhere in the mountains. He and the woman were originally from Idaho, but they were stationed in Cali while he was deployed to the Pit. She moved here when she left him. He only knows that because of the PO box, though."

"Okay," I said. "I'll find them. I'll need to meet with him to get the details."

"Good," said Pappy. "I'll have him set up an appointment. I'll be in town for a few days. Send the bill to me."

"Bill?" I grinned. "What bill?"

He gave me serious.

"What about the dogs having to eat?"

"They're getting fat," I said.

"The nice one, maybe. The other one? I can count his ribs."

"He's fat on the inside," I said, looking over at Max.

He looked back and let out a burp. I just shook my head.

"You don't get to be the only good guy on this," I said to Pappy. "Let me help."

Nodding, he stood. "Thanks, Gil. You're a good man."

"I know you are, but what am I?"

"Oh, right," said Pappy, "that weirdo with the red bow tie and the kiddie shows. I remember. You should remember the big Samoan who didn't like jokes."

Everyone's a critic.

"You have any info on her so I can get the ball rolling?" I asked.

"Just her name and DOB," said Pappy.

"It's a start," I said.

Pappy handed me a paper with what little information he had, then reached down to rub Pilgrim's head one last time. He looked at Max and gave him the snake eyes with the fingers again, letting him know he was watching.

Judging.

Max didn't move—just watched back.

I held up the folded note he'd given me with her information, "You know you could have texted this to me."

"Something wrong with paper?" he asked. "You don't know how to read cursive anymore?"

"No, Master Sergeant," I said, smiling and shaking my head, feeling as though I was talking with Max. "Paper's just fine." At least he didn't burp at me or start licking himself.

Pappy nodded and held out his hand.

"Thanks again, Gil," he said. "It's very generous of you."

I shook it, feeling the strength in that grip.

"My pleasure, Pappy. Should take me about forty hours tops to find her. Piece of cake."

I was never more wrong in my life.

3

Max stood next to Pilgrim as the Alpha shook hands with the man—stayed where he was as Pilgrim went to him —smelling and licking and letting the man rub him. Outwardly, Max looked the same as he had when he entered the room, but inwardly he was ready to attack.

To kill.

Pilgrim was either too old or perhaps too *different* from Max to recognize the danger. The Alpha had allowed the man to get far too close, which probably set Pilgrim's mind at ease.

But the Alpha could sometimes be foolish.

He didn't always see what he *should* see, smell what he *should* smell, hear what he *should* hear. Sometimes, the Alpha was weaker than he should be as the pack leader.

This man was not someone to take lightly.

This man was not of their pack.

This man should be killed here and now.

Max would do it—he wanted to—for the *safety* of the pack. But he could sense the Alpha had no intention of killing the man, and that meant he did not want Max to kill him either.

Foolish.

Danger was danger, and this man was dangerous—to all of them. And then the man turned his attention to Max. Spoke to him. Challenged him with his eyes.

Almost too much.

But the Alpha was to be obeyed—for as long as the Alpha *was* the Alpha.

Max was not afraid of the man. Max was only afraid *for* the pack—more so now than ever before. Now that the pack was what it was.

More.

Viper and the pups.

His pups.

So, if the man tried to hurt the pack, Max would end him. Until then, Max would watch.

Closely.

~

BILLY WALKED through the door just as Gil and Pappy were nearing Yolanda's desk.

"Morning, everyone," he said cheerfully. "This guy an old Marine buddy of yours, Gil?"

Gil palmed a hand toward Billy. "Pappy, this is my intern, Billy Carlino."

"Intern?" said Billy. "You mean partner, right?"

"Best I can do," said Gil, imitating Rick Harrison from *Pawn Stars*, "is possible *future* partner."

Billy grinned and extended a hand toward Pappy.

"I get no respect," said Billy, stealing a line from Gil, who stole it from Rodney Dangerfield. "Nice to meet you, old timer."

Gil's face went pale. He shook his head imperceptibly at Billy, trying to warn him.

Billy saw the signal but didn't pick up on it.

Pappy didn't shake hands, just gave a little smile.

"Hey, I'm just joking," said Billy. "What? Did you guys serve together back in WW1?" Billy laughed at his own joke.

Gil's face went paler.

"I thought Gil here was old," said Billy, still not picking up on Gil's terror. "But wow, I mean, doesn't the army have an age limit or mandatory retirement at some point?"

Gil stepped up.

"Billy," he said, his hands shaking slightly, "this is Master Sergeant Kirk Sinclair."

"Master sergeant," said Billy. "That sounds pretty high up for a soldier. What's after that, like, god or something?"

"Close," said Gil. "Sergeant major comes after master sergeant. God's two ranks higher."

"Ha!" said Billy, pointing at Pappy. "Old as you are, pal, I'd a figured you would have topped out already. What happened? Get busted down a few times?"

Gil started to say something, but before he could, Pappy grabbed Billy's pointing finger, bending it back and down.

Billy reacted as a true MMA cage fighter. He spun with the move to ease the pressure and then came back with an elbow. But somehow, his arm was blocked, his legs swept, and he felt the tip of a blade poking sharply into his armpit. Pappy's legs circled Billy's waist, heels notched into his hip sockets. Pappy's other arm cradled Billy's throat in the nook between bicep and forearm.

Billy instantly tapped with his free hand, signaling surrender.

"What's that supposed to mean?" asked Pappy from behind. Pappy was on his back, still curled around him, while Billy was belly to ceiling, stretched out, looking up at Gil.

Pappy pushed down with his heels and legs, restricting the blood supply to Billy's brain.

"I surrender," grunted out Billy. "Tapping is the universal sign for surrender."

"Yeah?" said Pappy, "Well, disrespect to a Marine is the universal sign for *I want to commit suicide*. And, Son, I don't take prisoners."

"Don't kill him, Pappy," said Gil. "Please. It would cause me a lot of trouble."

"Fine," said Pappy.

Billy started to relax, feeling the knife ease out from his underarm, but then Pappy stretched, and everything went black.

When he awoke, Yolanda was applying a cool, wet cloth to his forehead.

"What happened?"

"You two boys were wrestling," said Yolanda, "and you fell asleep." She shook her head. "Pilgrim was licking your face. I shooed him away. I'm surprised at you, Billy." She chinned toward Gil, who was on the phone in his office. "I expect this kind of thing from that one, but from you?" She shook her head.

Billy reached under his arm and felt the torn silk of his shirt. No pain, though, and when he looked at his fingers, no blood.

"Who was that guy?"

"Pappy Sinclair," said Yolanda. "And he's a very nice man. You shouldn't have been being a smart aleck like that."

"I was just ... goofing around."

"Well, sometimes goofing around gets you a spanking." Yolanda removed the cloth, and Billy sat up. "He didn't hurt you, did he?"

"No," said Billy, "only my pride."

"Good. Take your paddling and learn from it. Some people don't take to smart-alecking. Next time, be respectful of your elders."

"Yes, ma'am," said Billy, getting to his feet. "Speaking of which, I better go talk to Gil."

4

The Gardener walked through the Assembly's grounds, talking to his people. They belonged to him, and he loved them. Like his gifts, the people were his birthright, bestowed back on him from the Visitors—the aliens—who had held them for him from his past life.

The gifts—his visions, strength, and ability to bend others to his will—had always been his. They did not belong to the Visitors and never had. They were his and his alone. It had always been so. The Visitors had simply kept these gifts in waiting until the time of his arrival.

The Gardener had been reincarnated a million—a billion—perhaps a trillion times, but this life would be his last. *This* life was eternal. This life would prove to be the most important of all his lives. The time had finally come to reclaim his rightful power over matter, time, and life itself.

In past lives, he had been like God the Son, who came as baby Jesus, having divested himself of his heavenly powers, making himself of no reputation, taking the form of a bondservant, and coming in the likeness of men. The Gardener had existed for a millennium in such a state, waiting for this time, this life. And now he could do anything—*everything*.

Some nights he would sit at his desk, rearranging objects, moving their molecules, their atoms, their energy. He would turn his electric pencil sharpener into a lamp, his bed into a chair, the wife he was sleeping with into a mouse. Nothing was beyond his ability. His every wish, whim, or command was a mere thought away.

But it hadn't always been so. Poverty had been this life's first birthright. Before the Visitors came and before he recovered his powers, he had learned what it was to struggle for survival. It wasn't until that strange night, the night he almost died, that he came to understand his true purpose. The purpose of the One Tree. Now that he had embraced it, there was no turning back.

It had taken time for his gifts to mature—he'd had to grow into them—but the visions had spoken to him from the beginning. And he'd listened. He'd followed them. He *always* followed them, knowing they were from himself, from himself in the future. Knowing they would lead him to the right path. And as he listened and followed, he gradually understood the importance of his calling.

Everything had happened before, and it was about to happen again, but this time, *this last time*, it would turn out right. The way he had always intended—the way it had to be.

And when it was over, he would recreate the universe in *his* image. It would be paradise, nirvana. All thoughts, all actions, all emotions would consist of him. And through his perfection—his mind, his soul, his thoughts—he could achieve true oneness. But first, when the time was right, everyone else would have to die. Until then, all served his purpose.

Grinning, he motioned to Sandstone to hand him the axe he was using to cut down a tree. It was close to sunset, and dinner would soon be ready in the Assembly hall. From the looks of it, the two men were going to be late.

"Gardener," said Sandstone as he handed him the axe. Sandstone used to be known as Jason Murdock until the Gardener recognized his true personality. Jason had been married to Shannon, a beautiful, shapely woman with red hair and green eyes. The Gardener had taken her as one of his wives a year after their arrival.

Thinking of her now, he knew he'd call for her later that night. It had been a long time since they'd been together. He had many more wives now, nearly a thousand, spread over several continents. The number of wives he'd claimed rivaled the greatest men in history.

He took a moment to reflect on the total number of followers he'd gathered. There were close to thirty thousand worldwide, and that number was growing exponentially. All of them, except those embedded in specific places, were required to make a pilgrimage to the One Tree every five years. Not all at once, of course. The Assembly's meeting hall and surrounding buildings could only accommodate three hundred pilgrims and permanent residents at any one time.

The Gardener had managed to position converts in most branches of government and the military. He had made pathways into so many different entities that he had to keep some of them secret, even from one another. There were members in various secret societies, as well as the CIA, DEA, FBI, and ATF. They kept him appraised of local, state, and even global operations. And when the time was right, they would do as he commanded.

Yes, everything was coming together exactly as he knew it should.

Taking the axe, he slipped off his jacket, exposing his bulging biceps, his shoulders stretching the silk of his blue shirt. The crispness in the air didn't bother him in the least. Both men stepped away from the tree, and the Gardener finished their work with three strikes. The men clapped and grinned, thankful the Gardener had blessed them with his time and effort. Sandstone never showed any regret or opposition to having lost his wife to the Gardener's decree.

Also, as it should be—it was an honor, after all.

The Gardener spoke with them for several minutes before moving along. He came to a great swath of open field, void of crops now that winter was almost upon them. The harvest on the Assembly's grounds had ended, but acres of other crops were growing in greenhouses outside the gates.

Money poured in from around the world—his followers donating their wealth, little or large. And once they'd given up all their possessions, they spent the rest of their lives working to grow the Assembly.

Wealth for wealth's sake meant nothing to the Gardener, but he understood that money was power, and power was necessary to complete his work. And so, he harvested the riches and resources of his people like the crops they were, all the while utilizing his gifts to transform them into the weapons of change he needed. The Assembly was now worth nearly half a billion dollars, and within two years, it would double. And within five—*within five*—he would be ready.

The scrolls would be finished.

The barren field left him feeling a little sad. Fresh produce reminded him of his native Hawaii—avocados, star apples, dragon fruit, pineapples, passion fruit, and many others. For a moment, he considered transforming the barren soil into a lush forest of fruits and vegetables—*perhaps more.*

He could change winter to spring. *Should he do it? Negate the cold months the world over?* Almost, but no, he stopped himself. The time was not yet. Instead, he knelt and scooped up a handful of the cold dirt.

Colorado was a desert, unlike Hawaii, but it provided vast, remote areas that offered a sense of seclusion and privacy. It had majestic mountains, forests, and wide-open spaces that lured religious cults like flies to dung—Heaven's Gate, The Twelve Tribes, and Love has Won, to name a few.

He'd done his research. Colorado had a history of attracting individuals and groups with alternative spiritual beliefs. Its cultural openness made it more conducive for finding followers receptive to unorthodox ideas—metaphysical concepts, occult teachings, Eastern mysticism, psychotherapeutic techniques, and healing power lifestyles.

Boulder, the New Age Athens, as one local astrologer dubbed it, was home to "experts in balancing and aligning energies," "past-life regression specialists," "life and growth empowerment professionals," "neurolinguistic programmers," "planetary assistance teachers," "soul mergers," "channelers," "rebirthers," "crystal healers," "interior voice and past existence interpreters."

And so, his Assembly—*tiny at first*—was largely ignored, allowing it to grow to its current size. And now, like the One Tree, it was too big to remove. Nothing could stop it or him.

The Gardener felt the transformation against the palm of his hand. The dirt was gone, replaced by a bright red strawberry. He smiled at it and took a bite, tasting the fresh, cool, wet promise of summer.

He would win. The miracles proved it.

LADEN by two thick plastic bags, heavy with trash from the children's dorms, Toby smiled and waved at the men cutting the trees.

"Hey, Leaf," said Sandstone, smiling and waving a gloved hand.

That's not my name, he wanted to shout but instead smiled back, pretending not to care. Since the Gardener had hurt his mother, Toby hated the name Leaf more than ever. He hated all the fake names but knew he would be punished at the One Tree if anyone found out.

He'd finished his other chores early, and after disposing of the trash, he would have time to play with the other kids before dinner— Tag, Kick the Can, Hide and Seek, or maybe Red Rover. Toby liked Red Light Green Light best. He was too small to break through the line in Red Rover and too slow to outrun the bigger kids in Tag.

The dumpster was a long way from his dorm, and halfway there, his arms became too tired to hold the bags off the ground. He dragged them for about twenty yards but then picked them back up, afraid they would tear or split, spilling their contents. If that happened, he'd never get done in time to play.

Sweat moistened his forehead as he reached the enclosures surrounding the dumpsters. Flipping the lids back, he hoisted them in one at a time.

While walking back to the dorm, he saw the men who had felled the tree making quick work of chopping it into fireplace-sized logs. Then he saw the Gardener, standing and looking out over the rutted empty fields. It was too late in the year for crops—before long, snow would cover the dry dirt.

Beyond the Gardener, the sun was beginning to dip below the mountain ridge, splashing the sky in brilliant reds, purples, and yellows. It reminded Toby of a painting he had once seen with his mother and father in a museum.

The temperature was dropping as quickly as the sun, but the Gardener had his jacket draped over his shoulder, not seeming to feel the cold. Toby felt it, though. Shivering, he pulled his coat collar up around his neck, even though he had been sweating just a few minutes before.

Toby hated the Gardener now. He knew he shouldn't think like that. It was wrong and dangerous, and the Gardener might read his thoughts, but he couldn't help it. Not since that night—the night the Gardener hit his mother. His mother hit the Gardener first, but still, he was big, and his mother was small. He didn't hit her with his fist, the way Sagebrush hit Toby sometimes, but it was still hard and made a loud slapping sound.

That's why Toby bit him.

The Gardener hit him then, almost knocking him out. And that made his mother fight harder. The Gardener punished her then—punished them both.

Even after the balms and bandages, Toby's back still hurt. His mother worried about him. The night before, he'd removed his coat and shirt to show her he was okay, but he could see she was still worried.

Toby didn't tell her about the other things the Gardener had done to him. He knew she'd be angry with the Gardener if he did, and he didn't want her to be kept away from him any longer than she already had. The Gardener wouldn't let her come home yet, but maybe soon. Toby figured she was still being punished. Refusing the Gardener anything was unthinkable, let alone hitting him. And so he hated the Gardener, no matter how dangerous it was.

As Toby watched, the Gardener knelt, picked up some dirt, and shifted it in his hand. After a few seconds, he held it to his lips, opened his fingers, and took a bite.

Toby forgot all about the game of Red Light Green Light he'd hoped to play. He forgot about his mother and the whipping he'd taken. Turning, he hurried back to the dorm, as quiet as possible, until he'd put distance between himself and the Gardener, afraid the Gardener might realize he'd seen.

As young as Toby was, he understood something was very wrong. The Gardener had stood there, eating a handful of dirt, smiling as though it was the best thing he'd ever tasted.

5

Through the glass doors of Gil's office, Max watched as the man took Billy to the ground and rendered him unconscious. Max could have broken through if he wanted to, but he didn't really care for Billy anyway—he'd considered killing him several times himself. Still, the ease with which the man took the younger, bigger Billy down proved Max's estimation of the older man.

He was dangerous.

But the Alpha had let him live and leave. As soon as the Alpha opened the doors, Pilgrim ran out and started trying to play with Billy, licking his face and tugging at his arms, but Yolanda had swooped in, caring for the unconscious Billy.

Max watched the Alpha, who went behind his desk and started working on the computer.

Good, *he* didn't seem to care much about Billy, either.

Max walked to his bed and went to sleep.

∼

I STARTED by placing the name and DOB Pappy had given me into about a dozen data banks—NCIC, credit history, DMV ... *others.*

Before he disappeared, my friend Kenny, *Mr. Universe*, had loaded my computer with high-tech algorithms that did things I couldn't begin to understand. Within minutes, the entire history of Teresa Carr-Ramirez started appearing before me on the monitor. She seemed an open book.

Like I told Pappy, piece of cake.

Billy walked in, looking sheepish but otherwise okay. Pilgrim came in alongside, then pounced on his bed, slobbering a rubber toy.

"You have tough friends," he said.

"You pick the wrong people to fight," I responded.

"Fight? I was just joking around?"

"Okay, you pick the wrong people to joke around with," I said.

"Who was that guy? And why didn't you warn me?"

"First off," I said, "I did. I shook my head at you—gave you *the look*. That should have told you not to mess with him. You ignored it. And second, he's the Marine Corps' secret weapon."

"Then why didn't you help me?" asked Billy, looking a little butthurt, like I'd betrayed him.

"Some lessons are best learned experientially," I said. "And ... I didn't want to get killed."

"You could have at least sicced Max on him."

"I didn't want Max to get killed either," I said.

Billy crossed his arms, giving me frustrated.

I held up my hands. "What part of *secret weapon* don't you get?" I asked.

"Seriously?" he lifted his arm, poking at the hole. "He ruined my shirt. This thing cost three hundred bucks, and I don't make enough these days to go throwing them away."

"There's an old saying—*beware old men in a profession where men die young.* Consider yourself lucky," I said. "You ever hear of Dan Daly?"

"No," said Billy.

"Smedley Butler?"

"Nope."

"Carlos Hathcock?"

"Doesn't ring a bell."

"Chesty Puller?"

"She a stripper?"

I about came out of my chair.

Billy held his hands up, backing away. "Joking," he said. "No, I don't know any of them."

Regaining self-control, I sat back down. "How about ... Major Payne?"

"*Yes,*" said Billy. "Him I've heard of. That super tough Marine guy in that movie ... with the little engine that could ... *but, Bubba, you ain't got no legs.* Yeah, I know him. I love that guy."

I just shook my head, although it was hard to argue because even though Payne was fictional, I, too, loved him. And he did exhibit Marine spirit to a T, which is why I threw him in as an example.

"*Girl Scouts,*" I said using my best Vizzini impression from *Princess Bride*, "all of them, next to Pappy."

"Even Payne?" he asked.

"*Especially* Payne," I said, "since he isn't even real. All the others I mentioned are true Marine Corps legends."

"Easy, easy," said Billy, holding his hands up again. "I get it. Okay, he's tough."

"No," I said, "you *don't* get it. You're barely scratching the surface of getting it. If you had even an inkling of how many people Pappy has fought, the battles he's won, the men he's killed, the men he's saved, the blood he's spilled, you would be ... you would be ..." I was pointing, and somehow, I was on my feet again.

Billy was doing that *holding-his-hands-up* thing again.

"Okay, okay, easy now, big guy, I get it. Secret weapon, right?"

I took a breath—*in through the nose, out through the mouth*—closed my eyes, opened them again, and sat back down.

"Exactly," I said, "secret weapon."

"You really respect the guy, I see that," said Billy.

"No ... I mean, yes. I respect him, but more than that ..." I looked into Billy's eyes, "of all the men I've ever known, he's the *only one* who scares me."

~

ABOUT AN HOUR LATER, I saw Max standing at the glass doors separating my office from Yolanda's area. Billy was working on a case I'd briefed him on at the makeshift desk I'd had brought in for him. A few minutes later, I saw Tina enter from the hallway. Billy saw her too. She was holding a carrier. Billy waved, smiling. Tina waved back, tossing him a wink as she opened the carrier for Yolanda to have a look inside.

Billy got up, and so did I. He opened the door, and instantly Max was at Yolanda's desk, watching. Yolanda pulled a puppy from the carrier and rubbed it all over her face, kissing, scrunching, and laughing as the little Mal licked and bit, making adorable growling sounds.

"Aren't you just the cutest thing in the world?" she said, laughing like a schoolgirl.

This particular pup was an exact miniature of Max in color and markings.

Mewling and growling came from the carrier where the other puppies jealously pawed at the little locked gate.

Billy hugged Tina, and she kissed him on the lips, brief but intimate.

"You two are so cute," said Yolanda. "Just like this little guy."

Tina looked at me, maybe a little embarrassed. I smiled and hugged her, letting her know I was perfectly fine with the exchange. To be honest, their being together took a huge load off my shoulders. Tina is a K9 handler for the Colorado State Patrol, and we'd dated once—her idea. But then we got into a massive gun battle with a very bad man from my past and his army. Tina took a bullet and almost bled out. I did some nasty things to the man who shot her, and after that, she saw me in a different light. And once she met Billy, any interest she might have still held for me quickly faded.

"Names or owners picked out yet?" I asked.

Tina grinned, looking at Max. "Well, since *he's* the stud that started all this, I guess the traditional observance is that you get pick of the litter."

I hadn't expected that. "Wow," I said.

"Unless you don't want one," she said.

I hadn't even thought of it. Another dog ... no ... a *puppy* ... a *Malingator puppy!* Did I want to take on that responsibility right now?

"I absolutely want one," I said.

Tina laughed. "Sucker," she said. "I knew it."

"I want one, too," said Billy. "For Irmgard. If both of you will help me train it."

"I'm in," I said.

"Me too," said Tina, beaming love at him.

"I want this one," I said. "The one Yolanda's holding."

"Just like that?" asked Tina. "No testing? No slumber party? No nothing?"

"I've seen enough in the past few weeks," I said. "He's Max's mini-me, only cute and fun."

Max's eyes swiveled toward me as if he knew I was talking about him.

I looked down at him. "You ain't cute, and you sure ain't fun. Thor gets that from Viper."

"Thor?" said Tina. "You already named him?"

"Fish or cut bait," I said. "I'm not slow like you. Real K9ers are decisive." I reached out and stroked the little guy's melon. "Isn't that right, Thor?"

In response, he turned, snapping at my finger, barely missing.

"Not *fast* enough, little Thunder God, but we'll fix that soon. How long before you'll let them go?" I asked.

"Pretty soon," she said. "Couple of weeks ... maybe sooner."

"Works for me," I said.

"Me too," said Billy. "But nobody says a word to Irmgard. I want it to be a surprise."

"Only if you promise I can be there when you spring it," I said.

"Ditto," said Tina.

"It's a promise," said Billy, wrapping an arm around her.

They stared into each other's eyes, and I wondered just how serious this thing between them was becoming. I'd known Billy to be a bit of a womanizer in the past. I'd have to check his intentions soon. If he was just playing Tina, that wouldn't sit well with me.

It wouldn't sit well at all.

6

"I want you to pick for me," said Billy.

We were at Ramon's on Kipling and Colfax, my favorite Mexican restaurant. Dino's sat right next door, my favorite Italian restaurant. They were both owned by the same family and were Colorado treasures.

"You sure you don't want to do that with Irmgard?" I asked.

"Yeah, I know that would be cute and all, but I want to make sure we get the *right* dog. That's more important to me. And you're the expert's *expert*. Besides, I know her—she'd love any puppy that comes from Max."

"The *right* dog?" I asked.

"Yeah. Tough as Max—*a killer*—but sweet and totally protective of Irmgard."

I saw his eyes glaze over and knew he was remembering when Ryan Floss held a gun at Irmgard's head. Floss was the leader of a skin-head biker gang that kidnapped Billy's daughter, Irmgard. Billy adopted Irmgard after helping me rescue her from Germany following the murder of her father. Ryan Floss was a bad man. Billy killed him.

"Okay," I said. "I'll pick for you. But you have to stay consistent with the training."

"One hundred percent," he said, "Scout's honor." He held up three fingers and then genuflected. I just shook my head.

My therapist, Rick, walked in, bracketed by two young men— early to mid-twenties. They came to our table, and I shook Rick's hand. We'd been waiting for them before ordering. I introduced Billy to Rick, and they shook hands, Rick looking Billy up and down.

"So, you're the Billy Gil's been telling me about."

Billy looked at me, eyes squinting, one eyebrow raised. "Probably," said Billy, "what did he say?"

"I can't tell you," said Rick, "doctor-patient privilege."

"You told him I was a nut-job, didn't you?" said Billy.

"I know you are, but what am I?" I said, grinning.

"We're all nut-jobs," said Rick. "The tricky part is narrowing down what kind of a nut you are."

"Who are your friends?" I asked.

Rick pointed at the taller man first. "This is Wayne Lederman. The other one is Jules Harrow. They're both interns and will be studying under me for the foreseeable future."

Everyone shook hands, and then they all sat down.

I looked at Lederman. "So, what's your story?" I asked.

"We're both pursuing careers in mind medicine," he said.

"Mind medicine?" I asked.

"Dealing with the brain pan," said Harrow, tapping at his temple. "Therapy, psychoanalysis, psychiatry, psychology, moods, behaviors, cognition, perception ...."

"Like I said," Lederman interrupted, "mind medicine."

Harrow broke in, "Specializing in different fields."

"Sort of," said Rick.

Both of the interns turned sharply to Rick. "Completely," they both said in unison.

Rick laughed, shaking his head and taking a corn chip from a basket on the table.

"What kind of nuts are *they*?" I asked.

Rick dipped the chip in the salsa, hitching his head at Harrow.

"He's Myers-Briggs, and he's Enneagram."

"I have no idea what you just said," I shrugged.

Rick laughed. "These systems are a holistic approach to understanding how and why we act in given circumstances. Traditional psychiatry doesn't put a lot of stock in either Enneagram or Myers-Briggs, but I believe in a more encompassing approach to healing—like including chiropractic techniques along with traditional medicine and surgery in repairing the physical body. Why not the same for the mind?"

Looking at Rick, Lederman spoke up. "Doctor Leo is a revolutionary in psychiatric medicine. What he's doing with us, opening the door and letting the disciplines merge, could well impact the entire future of treating mental illness. Enneagram is, at its root, a system of personality typing that assists the therapist in understanding how a person interprets life, helping them to organize, develop, and manage their emotions to better cope with the world."

I gave them both puzzled. "That really doesn't help," I said.

Rick crunched the chip. "It's touted as a system to understand why, *internally*, you do what you do, and helps you to come back into balance—smooth your rough edges."

"Oh," I said.

"Whereas," said Harrow, "the framework for Myers-Briggs was first developed by Doctor Carl Jung in 1913. He postulated that people are either introverts or extroverts and that virtually all their behaviors can be ...."

I stopped him with a raised hand and looked at Rick.

Rick was about to take another bite but checked himself. "Basically, a test to show how other people see you."

"Okay," I said.

"I get it," said Billy. The Emmy thing tells you what you are on the inside, while the Bridge thing tells you what you look like on the outside."

Both interns looked insulted, but before they could say anything, Rick interrupted, "You got the names wrong, but the idea right."

Picking up a chip, Billy gave a small fist pump.

Lederman turned to Harrow. "A definite eight," he said.

"An *ESTP* eight," said Harrow.

"What's that?" asked Billy, around a mouthful. "Sounds like some kind of race car, or motor oil, something slick and fast."

Rick shook his head, grinning. "I wouldn't encourage them," he said.

"Well, without getting too technical, the letters ESTP, in the Meyers-Briggs system, stand for extroverted, sensor, thinker, perceiver. ESTPs are usually analytical, outgoing, enthusiastic, and logical. They are energetic and action-oriented—able to deftly navigate obstacles and handle difficult situations," Harrow said, energized by the opportunity to explain.

"On the other hand," added Lederman, "Enneagram eights are motivated to be self-reliant, strong, and independent. Type eights are caring, positive, playful, truthful, straightforward, generous, and supportive."

Rick rolled his eyes, but neither of the interns took note. The waitress stopped by, and we all ordered. Once she left, I turned to Rick.

"You wanted to meet?" I asked.

"I did," he said. "It might seem a waste of time, and if you don't want to take on the job, I'll completely understand."

"Job? You mean like detective work?"

"I do," he said.

"Who's missing?" I asked.

"Not a who," Rick said, "a what. It's my tree."

Grinning, Billy looked up from scooping salsa onto a chip.

"Now, who's a nut?" he said. "Hey! A nut tree! I like that."

"Definitely an eight," said Lederman, "wing seven."

"Not too healthy either," said Harrow. "Way far from center."

"On that, we agree," said Lederman. "Big-time extrovert too."

"Yes indeed," said Harrow.

"Please go on, Rick," I said.

"It was a gift from my father," said Rick. "He was a huge *Karate Kid* fan. We used to watch it over and over together when I was like ten. Anyway, when I was going off to college, he gave me a Juniper Procumbens Tree."

Excited, I said, "You mean the little bonsai tree Mr. Miyagi gave to Daniel?"

"Exactly, that tree," said Rick, also excited. "I've kept it all these years, carefully pruning it, shaping it, infusing it with my emotions and anxieties, my hopes and dreams. It's been my sounding board, my shoulder to cry on, my confidante." He stopped and sat back, looking a little embarrassed. Shrugging his shoulders, he turned to either side where the interns sat.

"I think I understand," I said. "The tree was the symbolic representation of your father. You couldn't tell him everything. What son can? And, for the first time in your life, he wasn't there. So you, away from home and alone, feeling lost, the tree became, to you ... your father."

I popped a dipped chip into my mouth and saw everyone else staring at me like I had something on my face. Both interns looked at Rick. Rick's eyebrows drew down, his head canting to one side.

Billy said, "Wow, that was deep."

"Right," said Harrow. "Like the puppy in *John Wick*. A gift from his dead wife to help keep him on track."

Lederman wagged a finger. "More like the dog in *Zombieland*," he said. "Woody Harrelson's character internalizes his son's death, deflecting his loss into the projection of a dog rather than his child. Still painful, but infinitely less so than losing his son."

"Or Toto in Wizard of Oz," said Billy, offering no explanation while eating another chip.

Both Harrow and Lederman looked at him. I shook my head again, raising my eyebrows.

"I ... I never thought of it like that, Gil," said Rick.

I grinned, pointing a finger at him. "My sessions with you are paying off," I said. "So, what happened to the tree?"

"Someone stole it," said Rick.

"Stole a tree?" asked Billy. "How desperate do you have to be to steal a tree?"

"It was a really nice tree," said Harrow.

Rick handed over his phone, its cover photo a picture of the bonsai.

"That *is* a nice tree," I said. "Just like the one in the movie."

"Still," said Billy, "it's a tree." He handed the phone back. "Then again, doc, you *do* work with crazies."

"We don't call them crazies," said Rick. "Your boss is one of my patients."

Billy turned to me. "I rest my case. You don't get much crazier than him." He laughed, scooping another chip into the salsa. "Besides, who'd steal a tree except for someone with some screws loose?"

I would have shaken my head again, but my neck was getting sore. "How long ago was it stolen?" I asked.

"Sometime last week," said Rick. "I've had a busy schedule; a couple of interviews, an article for a medical journal, an emergency patient, my regular list ... and these two."

Both Harrow and Lederman nodded in unison.

"Security feeds?" I asked.

"Some of my patients are phobic about cameras."

"See?" said Billy, "Crazies."

"Sixes," said Lederman. "They don't trust surveillance."

"INFJs and INTJs," said Harrow. "Introverted intuitives don't like to be exposed or seen."

Nodding, I said, "I'll need a list of your patients—when they were there, what they were there for, why you are seeing them, home addresses, phone numbers, dates of birth."

Rick held up his hands, face cringing.

"I ... I don't think I can give you any of that," he said. "Again, doctor-patient privilege."

"I won't tell anyone," I said. "And it's not like this is going to the police. I know you better than that."

"No, no, of course not. But still, it just wouldn't be ethical."

Billy snorted. "Yeah, like that matters," he said.

"It does to me," said Rick.

"It does to us, too," I said, giving Billy a dirty look. "Okay, tell me this, have any of your patients quit coming to you since you last saw the tree?"

Billy sat up straight. "That's a good question," he said.

Both Harrow and Lederman agreed.

"No," said Rick.

Billy, Harrow, and Lederman seemed let down.

"Could you at least tell me if there are any kleptomaniacs in your group?" I asked.

The three stooges looked back and forth between them, weighing the quality of the question.

Rick shook his head, smiling. "I couldn't if there were," he said, "but no, there aren't."

"Have you checked your office thoroughly to see if anything else might be missing?"

Curly, Mo, and Larry again exchanged looks, each wearing exaggerated facial expressions.

"I did," said Rick, "but I haven't found anything else missing. Of course, I might just be overlooking something."

"Okay," I said. "Gather up anything you ethically can about any of your patients who might have had access to the tree in the time frame. I'll want to talk to your secretary, too."

"I already asked her," he said.

"Your asking her and my asking her might be two different things," I told him. "Therapists are good at getting certain types of answers, while detectives are good at getting others."

"I'll make her available to you," he said.

"One last thing," I said. "Try and give me a little extra on this emergency patient you mentioned. I'm not saying to break your rules or go against your conscience but put in everything you can."

"Why him?" asked Rick.

"Because he's new," said Billy, catching my drift. "The other wackos were coming to you before, and nothing happened to the tree. New guy comes, and presto, tree's gone."

I just nodded.

"See?" said Billy, grinning and looking at me. "I'm getting this whole PI thing."

The waitress arrived with our food.

Harrow and Lederman spent the rest of the meal analyzing the waitress, other customers, and Billy—most of all, Billy. And by the end of dinner, they seemed to have him completely mapped out.

And it was pretty funny.

7

Toby watched as the Gardener and the adults walked in. Once they were seated in the bleachers of the sanctuary, two more walked in—Toby's brother, River, between them. River, who was once called Ishmael, was older, nearly twelve, while Toby was only six and nine months. River wasn't his real brother, but they were considered brothers of the One Tree.

River had done a bad thing.

Toby was scared for him. He loved River.

The two men brought River to the foot of the One Tree. The One Tree grew at the far end of the sanctuary and stood nearly sixty feet tall. The two lowest branches were thick and about nine feet off the ground. Thick ropes with attached loops were draped over the branches.

River was scared too—Toby could see it. He was trying to act brave and walk straight, but Toby could see how pale his face was and that his legs were trembling.

One of the men secured River's wrists to the rope on one of the branches, stripped his shirt off, pulled the rope tight until his toes barely touched the ground, and walked away. Toby wanted to cry, but crying wasn't allowed. He wanted his mother, but she wasn't here. The Gardener had taken her away after the night of the fight. Toby could only visit her in secret.

The Gardener stood and walked to the table, where he selected a wooden rod. There were many. The one he chose was long, thick at one end, stretching to a fine point at the other. It, like all the others, had been clipped from the One Tree—because the One Tree knew.

Like the Gardener, it knew everything.

The One Tree had *taught* the Gardener, retrieving the stored knowledge from past lives the Gardner himself had entrusted to it for just such a time. This final time. The last reincarnation.

And now, the One Tree would teach River. Teach him to not be bad. Not to run away.

Little Toby felt his chin start to quiver, his eyes to water. Clenching his fists, he fought to stay strong—strong and straight and tall, like the One Tree, like the Gardener.

But it was so hard.

River was more than just his brother—he was his best friend. His protector. He and Timber.

The Gardener turned to the assembly, flexing the rod between his hands. He swished it through the air, making a whistling sound that hurt Toby's ears. He had heard that sound before—heard it and felt it. That sound, and the other sounds.

The screams.

Toby had to pee, but no one was allowed to pee while knowledge was being revealed. Everyone had to watch. Everyone had to learn.

The Gardener laid the rod back on the table and took up the Scroll. The Scroll was made from the One Tree's wood, so its truth was undeniable. No false words could mark its surface. No wrongdoing could come from the One Tree. The One Tree had defeated the *other* tree. All the assembly knew the story. The mothers read that story every night to the children.

The Gardener read from the Scroll. Toby didn't understand most of the words, but he knew what they said would be bad for River. The mothers had told them the beatings from the branches of the One Tree gave knowledge, just as the Gardener's words gave knowledge, just as the Gardener's *touch* gave knowledge, gentle or harsh. *Good and evil.* Knowledge, all knowledge, was good in its way, but it could be misused. River had misused his knowledge of the Assembly's grounds to try and escape.

When the Gardener finished reading from the Scroll, he carefully rolled it and set it back on the table. He took the chosen rod into his hand.

The Gardener was strong, like the One Tree—the strongest of all. No one could defeat him. No one dared stand against him.

Moving close to River, the Gardener whispered something into his ear. Toby could not hear what was said, but as the Gardener stepped away, Rivers' legs buckled.

Toby couldn't help it—he closed his eyes as the wood whistled, tears spilling. One of the mothers standing beside him gripped his neck, digging her nails into his skin. Toby opened his eyes, the tears still running.

Below, as the One Tree's wood sang its promise of pain, River screamed and screamed.

EDWARD RAMIREZ SAT across from me. Billy had rolled his chair over, too. Ramirez was maybe five-nine, thin, *very thin*, with dark eyes and darker hair. There were scars along his right jaw stretching up to his ear. He'd limped painfully walking in—*the IED*—but he didn't use a cane or crutches.

Good for him.

We'd only been back from lunch with Rick and his sidekicks for about an hour when, just after two, Mr. Ramirez showed up. He hadn't called Yolanda to make an appointment, but I guess if my son were missing, I'd skip the formalities too.

We'd exchanged the usual Marine Semper Fi greetings, talked

about how Pappy had saved both our lives, and then got down to business.

"So," he continued, "you think you can find them?"

I laid out what I already had. "Close to a year ago, in an unincorporated county southwest of here, your wife, Teresa, maiden name Carr, last used her credit cards at a gas station. Around the same time and while in the same general area, her cell stopped pinging."

"What does that mean?" he asked.

I shrugged. "Well, since she told you she was leaving you not long before that, and since you were actively trying to find her, it's highly possible she doesn't want to be found."

He slumped. "I just want to see my son, make sure he's okay. I mean, I want to find her too, but if she doesn't want to be with a crip ... with *me*, that's her choice. But my son, she can't keep him from me."

"I'll need your joint bank account information," I said.

"Sure. Teresa cleaned it out before she sent me the email."

I'd already read the email and saved it to my files—the equivalent of a Dear John letter in today's technological world. Can't say it looked like it hurt any less.

"So, what's next?" he asked.

"Next, I go old school, which means hitting the pavement. I'll check out the gas station—see if anyone remembers her or your son. Who knows, maybe they'll have security footage. Not likely after this long, but possible. Then I'll canvass the area—talk to local law enforcement, other PI stuff."

"Can I tag along?" he asked.

"I understand why you'd want to," I said. "But I'll get better results alone. People tend to talk more openly one on one."

"I wouldn't slow you down," he said, "if that's what you're worried about."

"It's not," I said. "If people have seen her or remember seeing her, she might have told them a cover story in case you came looking."

"Cover story?"

"Like maybe you're abusive or trying to kidnap her son—something like that. People on the run don't paint themselves as the bad guys."

"Oh, yeah, that makes sense," he said.

"Which brings up a point. I've checked you out pretty thoroughly, and Pappy vouches for you, which goes a long way with me, but you need to know—and I mean this in the strongest, most dangerous way I can put it—if Pappy and I are wrong about you, and you hurt her or the boy ...." He was looking at me, listening intently. I dropped my mask and let him see what was really there, deep down. "... I'll kill you. And worse, I'll make it hurt."

His face went a little pale, but he nodded. "I get it. Pappy told me stories about you—some of the stuff you did. I mean, I had to do stuff too. I took out my share of bad guys, saved a few Marines, but nothing like what Pappy told me about you. So, I do get it. You walk the walk of the talk you just talked. But you have nothing to worry about. I'm only alive because of my son. I should be dead. And even then, everyone said I'd never walk again. But I *am* walking—to find him. That's why I'm walking. You understand?"

"Yes," I said. "I won't bring it up again. I just needed us to be on the same page. No surprises."

Ed head-bobbed Billy. "He going with you?"

Billy nodded and started to speak, but I cut him off.

"No, he's got another case to work on. It'll be just me, like I said. Well, me and the dogs."

Ramirez turned, and Pilgrim took it as an invitation to come over for some attention. He limped a little on the way. Max was sleeping— at least, I think he was. He could be faking, plotting the best way to kill all of us.

Ed Ramirez smiled and rubbed Pilgrim's head. "I used to have a pointer when I was a kid," he said. "My dad named him Dumpster 'cause he was always getting into the trash. I loved that dog. Cried like a baby when he died." He looked at me. "I want that for my son. For him to be able to love and be loved like that."

I opened my desk drawer, took out one of the coins I use as a business card, and slid it across to him. They cost more, but they last forever. The head side is stamped with a Shepherd silhouette inside a six-point sheriff's star encircled with the phrase, *Keeping the wolves at bay*, while the flip side says *Blessed be the Lord my Rock, who trains my hands for war, And my fingers for battle. Psalms 144:1.* Ed took the coin, we discussed a few last details, and then he left.

Billy didn't look happy. In fact, he looked mad. "What do you mean I've got another case? What case? How am I supposed to learn this job if you do it all solo?"

"Wax on, wax off," I said.

"What?"

"You need to remember—I'm Mr. Miyagi, you're Daniel LaRusso. You don't start by learning the Crane Kick. First, you must learn to wash the car, paint the fence."

"What's that supposed to mean?" asked Billy, raising his eyebrows and hands.

"Youth," I said. "Homework for tonight—watch all three Karate Kid movies. And watch them with Irmgard. She can explain them to you. After that, watch the new series, but do it on Vid Angel—you can cut out the cussing."

"Funny," he said. "So, what's this major case you're assigning me?"

"Really?" I said. "After the clue I just threw?" I shook my head. "You have a tree to find."

MAX WATCHED from under his lids as the three men talked. The Alpha, of course, was safe—*for now, at least.* The puppies complicated things. They raised up old feelings, emotions, and drives he'd thought he'd come to terms with. Max was *their* alpha, Viper's alpha. But the Alpha was *his* alpha.

It rankled him—caused him confusion. Brought up the old conflict.

Billy would be easy. Max knew his moves—how to dodge, where to strike. This new man, with the limp, was different, broken. He would be slow, unable to react in time to save himself. However, Max sensed something deeper in him. A strength, courage. Still, it wouldn't be enough. Max would kill him if the need arose. Max knew exactly how to kill them all.

Except maybe the Alpha.

Maybe.

8

Tina sat on her living room floor, needle-sharp puppy teeth punching through her uniform pants and sleeves as easily as a sewing machine.

"Ow," she said as Thor got hold of the meaty portion of her hand just below the pinky. She rolled him gently, laughing at his awkward tumble, but had to pull her hand back as he recovered and was right back at her. "Yeah, you're Max's all right. No doubt about that."

Her amused smile faded. She'd thought her department would welcome her raising the pups to act as replacement dogs when the time came to retire the agency's K9s or if one was wounded on the job. Instead, she'd been informed that the entire unit was being re-evaluated after an incident where one of their K9s had injured a burglar. Tina had reviewed and helped investigate the case herself, and everything was completely justified.

Yes, the burglar had sustained serious injuries from the K9, but it was his fault. He should have surrendered. And he shouldn't have punched the two troopers, run, or pulled out a knife. The guy was a career criminal with a rap sheet full of bad life choices. But the media had decided to take up his mantle in their most recent bid to defund the police. They were running a series about supposed police brutality, using this case as an example.

Tina was a little afraid the entire unit could be disbanded. If that happened, she feared for the K9s. Technically they belonged to the State of Colorado, and if the K9 unit was dissolved, they could do with them as they pleased. In the past, most departments let the handlers have first refusal, meaning that if the handler wanted to keep the dog, it would be retired to them. But in the current climate, many agencies considered the liability too significant and looked at other options. The other options weren't good—rescue or worse.

The worst was euthanasia. Agencies feared that dogs trained to attack humans, even under the most controlled circumstances, might do worse in *less than controlled* circumstances. And in America, where anybody can sue anybody over anything or nothing at all, a release of liability just didn't cut it anymore.

One of the pups, the runt of the litter, bit Tina on the bottom. She jumped and grabbed the little girl up. Holding the hooligan close and rubbing noses, she inhaled the wonderfully familiar smell of puppy breath. The rest of the group swarmed. Her uniform, which she'd donned for court that morning, would be a mess. *Who cares?* she thought. *That's what dry cleaners and lint brushes are for.*

Tina's wounds were mostly healed—at least the outside ones. She'd been back to regular duty for a while now. Well, not exactly *regular duty*. Since Viper became pregnant and then was on maternity leave caring for the pups, Tina had been *pushing a radiator*—aka driving patrol—when there were no K9 training classes. She'd been making some good busts, but nothing beat catching bad guys with her girl. She'd gotten into a foot pursuit the previous week, chasing a kid who took off after shooting his girlfriend's dad in the neck. He took off as Tina pulled up, hopping a fence and disappearing. Tina played cat to his mouse, going right after him.

No cover, no dog.

That knowledge hit home about three backyards over, and the scene on the Royal Gorge Bridge played through her mind—the bullet ripping into her, the weakness, and the shock of massive blood loss. Gil kneeling over her, mechanically shoving gauze into the hole —his eyes focused with a frightening blankness.

Blindly, she hopped another fence and landed in a bush on top of the suspect, who screamed for her not to kill him. Tina cuffed and searched him. The gun was gone. An officer eventually found it in the middle of the yard where the suspect dumped it when he first started the run.

Tina turned him over to another officer, returned to her car, and while sitting behind the wheel, the shakes took their turn with her. They were most likely the aftereffects of the adrenaline rush. Mostly.

But not all.

She knew that. In her heart, she knew.

It was stupid to run after him. Tina would have read any of her K9 handlers the riot act if they did what she had just done. The smart thing, *the correct thing*, would have been to stop as soon as she lost sight of him, set up a perimeter, wait for K9, and let them track him down with a gaggle of SWAT officers in tow—and maybe a helicopter overhead using thermal imaging.

Yeah.

She was lucky he hadn't been lying in wait with the gun. The thought made her shudder—made her consider her own mortality. The girlfriend's father lived, the bullet somehow missing all the major arteries, veins, and bones. The kid turned out to be a soldier from Fort Carson, angry at his girlfriend for breaking up with him and blaming the father. The girl later told Tina she'd fallen for an Air Force cadet she liked better and that her father had nothing to do with the breakup.

Young love.

The swarm was gaining on Tina—crawling, jumping, nipping, adorable grunts and growls, accompanying bites, and head shaking. The thought of letting any of them go hurt her heart. One made it up her pant leg and latched onto her calf.

Enough.

She shook them all free—no easy task—and stood, leaving them to flow around her ankles, howling their displeasure at her leaving the game. Viper lay a few feet away, watching, thankful for a few minutes of respite.

"That's what you get for fooling around," said Tina, smirking. "Never trust those men."

As if on cue, the pups abandoned Tina en masse and rushed to their mother, going for milk. Viper licked their heads as they nursed, curling protectively around the group. The whole scene hit Tina's heart even harder. It made her think about ...

She shook her head. *Whoa, where had that come from?* She'd heard about baby fever before but never actually experienced it. Until—*now?*

And that, of course, made her think about Billy.

SARAH PUT a line of vials on the refrigerator shelf, shaking her head at the small assortment of sandwiches, fruit, and drinks that sat a few shelves down. How anyone could store their foodstuff in the same area that held the fluids and other items this cooler had was beyond her. It reminded her of the morticians, coroners, and their assistants who could eat beside dead bodies while performing autopsies and embalming procedures.

Ugh.

The thought made her squeamish—not to mention that she found it completely unprofessional. If a defense attorney found out, it could jeopardize their work—evidence preservation, chain of custody, contamination, etc. She'd complained verbally and in writing, taking it as far up the chain of command as she could. Sarah was head of her department, but the director of CBI, a short, abrasive alcoholic named Arthur Weeks, overruled her.

Tossing her latex gloves, she thought about Gil. Things had been going very nicely between them. They spent most evenings together, eating, watching movies and shows, walking the hills, playing games, talking—getting to know each other on a different level. The physical part was good, too, slow, easy, kissing, and cuddling. Gil was letting her in.

Sarah understood the conflict. He felt guilt over Joleen, worried he was betraying her memory. But Sarah knew better. He was really conflicted about the idea that letting himself live would somehow make Joleen, in his mind and heart, and soul, *dead*. It was easier to live half a life in that quasi-state of unsureness than to accept that Joleen was really gone. But now that Sarah and Gil were together, she was determined to show him what being alive was truly about.

The miracle for her was that since they'd been together, her feelings of being dirty—*unworthy*—had vanished. Instead, she just felt —*good*. Right. She was exactly where she was supposed to be, doing exactly what she should be doing. She'd never been happier.

Sarah's cell vibrated. It was Gil.

"Well, if it isn't Superman himself," she said, smiling.

"Hi, Lois," said Gil. "You aren't tied up on a train track, are you?"

"Stuck scraping and preserving epithelium samples next to my colleagues' lunches and snacks, so, pretty close."

"Yummy."

"Exactly," she said. "What did you want for dinner?"

"Yeah," said Gil, "that's sort of what I was calling about."

"I already don't like the sound of it," she said. "Is a meteor about to crash on Metropolis or a tsunami about to hit a tropical island?"

"Nothing so exciting. Just a missing woman and boy."

Sarah sobered. "Oh, I'm sorry. Are they in danger?"

"No," said Gil, "I don't think so. Just a domestic case where she left her husband while he was deployed, and he wants to have parental rights re-established."

"That's sad," said Sarah.

"It is. I've got to go out of town for a few days—hopefully less— but I won't be here for dinner tonight."

"That's also sad. But I knew the game before I signed up. Dating a superhero has its downside."

"You sure you're okay with it?" he asked. "I know it's short notice."

"I'm fine," she assured him, "you go and save the world, Underdog. I'll be here when you get back."

"Wow," said Gil. "You sure you're okay with it? I just went from Superman to Underdog in like thirty seconds."

"You think it's bad for you?" said Sarah. "I went from Lois Lane to Sweet Polly Purebred, and she's a dog."

"Don't be defaming dogs," said Gil. "Max might hear you, and he has a major crush on Polly."

"Not bird nor plane nor even frog," laughed Sarah, "just little old you, Underdog."

"You do that way better than Wally Cox. I'll miss you."

"I'll miss you too," said Sarah, "so get back here fast."

"I'll find the girl and the boy, then bring Sweet Polly a toy," Gil tried to imitate Andre the Giant's accent from *The Princess Bride*.

"That's terrible," Sarah chuckled.

"Everyone's a critic."

"That doesn't rhyme at all."

"Said the analytic," finished Gil.

"Oh, stop," Sarah joked.

"While on top," said Gil.

Laughing, Sarah told him, "Goodbye."

"With a salami sandwich on rye," said Gil.

Sarah clicked off, shaking her head. Her cell vibrated again. Expecting to see Gil's avatar, she was surprised to see what she saw instead. The name threw her brain into a fog, but it wasn't her boyfriend, Underdog. Rather—it was Kenny.

Mr. Universe.

9

I showed a picture of Teresa Carr-Ramirez and her son, Toby, to the clerk at the gas station where Teresa had last used her credit card. I'd done the same thing at the last five stations, *just in case*, and, like the other five, I got nothing. The clerk, a pretty nineteen-year-old named Pam, with braces, medium-length brown hair, glittery makeup and green lipstick, studied the pictures as though I were giving her a quiz.

"Wish I could help," she told me, shaking her head. "But I only started here a couple of months ago. Besides, a zillion people come in and out from the highway—just like you. Never seen a real private eye before, though. Is it like in the movies? Shootouts? Spying and fights and car chases?"

"It's exactly like that," I said. "Just this morning, I was going seventy-five down the street chasing bad guys."

"Did you shoot them?" she asked, looking excited.

"No, but I spied on them."

She shook her head. "You're just goofing. Seventy-five's the speed limit on the highway."

"Well, I *thought* about spying on them," I said. "What about your security cameras? Do you keep the footage here on the premises?"

"Maybe," she said. "It's all in the back office on a rack. My manager, Sally, told me never to touch it—that it does everything all by itself. So, I don't touch it. Have you ever had to shoot anyone?"

"Shoot anyone?" I echoed.

"Yeah, like in the movies?"

"Oh, yeah. Lots of people—but never pretty girls with braces."

She grinned and tucked her chin, hiding her teeth with her lips.

"Do you think I could take a look in the back? At the security system, I mean?"

"I can't leave the counter," she explained, still grinning while hiding her teeth, "but Gary's back there goofing off, so I guess it's okay. You can shoot him if you want to. He's always stealing slushies and soda and wasting time while I'm out here working. We're supposed to pay for whatever we eat or drink, but he never does."

"Shoot him?"

"Yeah, just like in the movies. Only don't kill him. I'm supposed to get off at three, and if you take him out, I won't be able to go. So maybe just nick him a little—give him a good scare—so he'll stop goofing off all the time."

"Just nick him?"

"Like in the movies," she grinned. "Or at least wave your gun around and scare him. Could you do that?" She laughed then, but it was sort of a creepy laugh. "Maybe that would get him off his butt so he could help me out here."

I pointed toward the short hallway behind the counter. "That way?"

She nodded, smiling that teeth-hiding grin that suddenly looked as creepy as her laugh sounded.

Hiding my raised eyebrows, I walked toward the backroom, where I found Gary sitting on his butt, drinking a blue slushy, and messing with his phone, just as the girl had described. He sat up quickly as I entered, looking startled.

"What are you doing back here? You're not allowed back here!"

I raised my hands, my badge in my left. "It's okay. I just need to check some security footage from a few years ago. Pam said it was okay."

"Pam?" he said, "Pam can't say it's okay. She's not a manager."

"Pam called Sally for me," I lied smoothly, "she okayed everything." I saw the rack with the security equipment. "This everything?"

"I guess," he grumbled. "Sally don't let us touch it."

Gary was fortyish, with thinning hair, a receding hairline, and a potbelly attached to an otherwise skinny frame and limbs.

The system was actually pretty good—nice digital quality and camera angles. Using my phone, I snapped a picture of a decal stuck to the top of the main recorder. It supplied the name of the company, its address and phone number, as well as the gas station store number.

"How far back does the company keep the video before scrubbing it?"

"I don't know," said Gary. "We don't touch it."

"Right. Sally."

"Sally," he said.

Holding my phone in front of him, I showed him Teresa and Toby's faces. "Ever seen these two?"

"They wanted for something?"

"Just questions," I assured him. "They aren't in any trouble."

He gave them another look before shaking his head no while noisily slurping his slushy through a straw.

"Okay, thanks." I turned to leave, stopped, then turned back to him. "How well do you know Pam?"

"Pam? Just here at work, mostly. Why?"

I nodded. "Just a suggestion, but you might want to spend less time back here and more time helping Pam out there."

He sat up in the chair. "What business is that of yours?"

"Easy, Gary, but have you ever seen her grin?"

"Her grin?"

"Yeah, the way she looks when she grins? Maybe while she's stocking shelves or waiting on customers—while you're *not* working?

Not helping? Have you ever noticed how she looks at you while she does that?"

Gary gave me puzzled.

"I've worked homicides where girls suddenly snap and do things you'd never expect. Bad things. Things you *wouldn't* believe. Things you *couldn't* believe. Things you *shouldn't* believe...."

Gary just sat there, staring at me, slushy in hand.

"And after," I continued, "when I'd be interviewing the girls, they all had one thing in common, and you know what that one thing was?"

Gary's eyes shifted from me to where Pam was working in the front. "The grin?" he asked timidly.

"The grin," I confirmed, nodding.

Shrugging my shoulders, I walked back out to Pam.

"I didn't hear any gunshots," she said.

"Ever hear of silencers?"

Grinning that eerie grin, she said, "Pew-pew instead of bang-bang?"

"Exactly."

Gary came out, glancing back and forth between us as if he'd come in on a secret being shared.

Maybe he had.

"Just like in the movies," she said.

After leaving the gas station, I gave the dogs a break on a long stretch of grass south of the gas pumps. Pilgrim hopped out of the vehicle and pranced from tree to tree. Max suddenly appeared twenty yards away, marking carefully, his eyes on everything. I never even saw him get out of the car.

Overhead, the sun freely shared its warmth. A cool mountain breeze played perfect contrast, carrying autumn's changing perfumes with it.

While Max and Pilgrim did their business, I did mine by calling the security camera company. After five minutes of playing the recording checklist and number-punching game, I finally reached an actual human—at least, I think she was human. These days, who can tell?

I told her I was the gas station manager, gave her the store number, accompanying machine codes, and other pertinent information, then asked how long they stored the data. After clicking and clacking for several seconds, she told me that the digital data on that system was automatically uploaded to the cloud on a five-year rotation plan. Anything recorded within those five years could be retrieved and viewed.

Five years was within my window. I only needed about a year, but going through even one year's worth of footage would take precisely that—one *year*. At least, it would have in the old days. But these days, like almost everything else, there's an *app* for that. Kenny, Mr. Universe, had equipped my laptop with an algorithm for just such a purpose.

The nice lady at the security company gave me the code to retrieve the store's data. It took about an hour to download—incredibly fast. *Thanks again, Kenny,* considering how many terabytes of electronic information we're talking about. Once complete, I inserted Teresa and Toby's pictures into the stream and let Mr. Universe's algorithm do its magic. And do it—it did.

There they both were, in the store, nearly a year ago.

And they weren't alone.

10

Billy had been sitting in his car outside Rick's office for hours. The last time he'd done surveillance was on a skinhead biker leader named Ryan Floss. On that occasion, he'd witnessed Floss murder a federal agent and plant evidence against Gil Mason, setting off a war against Billy's mafia family and a league of bikers from across the state.

This was a lot more boring.

There was a steady stream of what seemed to be ordinary people coming and going: men, women, a few teenagers—no bombs or guns or even cutting boards.

Shortly after their first meeting, Gil Mason—in a somewhat adversarial role—had hit Billy in the head with a wooden cutting board. Billy still had a scar where it hit, both on his head and on his soul. It had been a lesson to him. Looking back, he realized he should have taken better heed of the incident. If he had, he might not have been choked out by Gil's friend, Pappy—or been nearly stabbed by the man and had his shirt ruined.

These old guys were a weird lot. Full of tricks and surprises.

The last guy to go into Rick's office came back out. It had been a long visit—over an hour. The guy was white, five-nine or so, thin, wearing a gray, long-sleeved dress shirt, no tie, beige slacks, brown loafers, no socks. He stopped just outside the building, looked up at the lowering sun, blinked six times in fast succession, then, with his two index fingers, he tapped out an intricate pattern over and under his lips while counting *one-two-two-one-two-one-one-two*, six times. Then he looked back down and walked to his car.

Tree stealer?

Maybe, thought Billy—definitely a weirdo.

And at least it hadn't been as boring as just sitting here. He pulled out behind the tapper and followed him down the street and out of Denver proper toward the north and west. Traffic was heavy, so he stayed close, daydreaming of his girlfriend, Tina, as he followed on autopilot. Tina had dated Gil once or twice, but they weren't a good fit —at least, that's what she said. Billy thought there was more to it, but that was her business.

Tina was a state trooper who'd been shot during a fight. All the news agencies had dubbed it *The Incident on the Bridge* since it was pretty much a massacre. Gil had saved her, but, like the cutting board, it had left scars. It seemed like everyone associated with Gil ended up with scars. Of course, there were worse things in life than scars. Sometimes scars could be good. The cutting board lesson might just save him someday if he took it to heart.

Tina's scars might be like that too. It had been her first gunfight, the first time she'd been shot, and the first time she'd had to shoot someone else—a lot of life lessons rolled up into one scar.

Tina was the K9 trainer for the troopers, and her working dog, Viper, had recently delivered a litter of puppies. Gil's dog, Max, was the father. Billy didn't much care for Max.

The feeling was mutual.

Max had almost torn Billy's throat out on their first meeting. Billy still had the scars from that too. He would have killed Max for that, but he knew it would have put an irreparable barrier between Gil and himself. More importantly, Max had saved Irmgard's life. Irmgard was Billy's adopted daughter. Gangsters warring with Billy's uncle's mafia faction had murdered her father. They had kidnapped Billy's grandfather and hidden him in Germany. Gil, Max, and Billy had rescued him, but at a cost.

More scars.

Still, well worth it. Irmgard was worth whatever it took.

Tina had been spending a lot of time with the puppies, and Billy missed her. He'd asked her for one to give to Irmgard. Irmgard would love to have a puppy. Plus, it might lessen her obsession with Max. She still called him *Petra*—the name she'd given him when he rescued her. And besides, Billy wouldn't mind having a protector of Max's caliber with Irmgard twenty-four-seven. Billy and his family had a lot of enemies.

The tapper drove to Arvada and pulled into the garage of what looked to be an upper-middle-class house with a three-car garage. The garage door closed before the guy got out. *Probably doing his one-two-two-one shtick*, thought Billy. He parked a few doors down as he considered his next move.

The old Billy, *the mafia Billy*, would have knocked on the door, pushed his way inside, and smacked the guy around a little before searching the house for the tree, but he didn't think Gil would go for that. Gil would want him to be more ... *subtle.*

Billy decided he could be subtle. He knocked on the front door and waited patiently for the tapper to open it, which he did. Billy didn't have a PI badge yet, but he did have several stolen police badges from his criminal days. He'd brought an Arvada Police badge from his glove box and flashed it now as the tapper stood in front of him.

"Ye ... e ... ee ...es?" asked the man.

Oh great, thought Billy, a stutterer. Billy hated stutterers. He'd worked with one when he was in his late teens. The guy was good at wet work—killing, torturing, stuff like that—but *man*, conversations were murder.

"Need to talk with you about a case," said Billy, already thinking his original idea would have been better.

"Ca ... ca ... case?"

"Yeah," said Billy, pushing his way past the man and into the house. "Hit and run downtown about an hour ago. Know anything about it?" Billy scanned the room, looking for the tree.

The tapper shook his head, obviously confused. "No," he said, "noth ... nothing."

Billy walked into the kitchen, the man following. "You saying you didn't hit a yellow Tesla?"

"T ... t-t-t ... t ... Tes ... Tes ... Tesla? Where?"

"I'll ask the questions," said Billy, moving into the dining room. "You drive a white 2020 Toyota Corolla?" Billy started up the stairs toward the bedrooms.

"Ye ... ye ... ye ... ye ... y y y y y y ... ye ...."

"Yeah, I know you do," said Billy. "You live here alone?"

"Alone?"

"You got a wife, kids, significant other?"

"N ... n n n ..."

"Just shake your head," said Billy, "this'll go a lot faster. Up and down for yes, side to side for no." Billy opened each door, scanned, and moved to the next.

"Now ... now ... now ... jus ... just ... wait a min ... minute. Y ... y y y y ... you ca ... can't ... can't ... jus ... just ...."

Billy turned on the smaller man, his bulk almost as wide as the hall. "Sure I can. You got a bonsai tree?"

"A ...."

Billy held up a finger. "Nod or shake."

The tapper shook his head to the negative.

"No? Looks like this." Billy showed him the picture on his phone. "You don't got one of these? Don't lie to me. I don't like it when people lie to me."

Scared and confused, he started tapping his face. "One-two-two-one ...."

Billy gripped both wrists in one giant hand and crunched them together.

"No more of that," he said. "No tapping, no stuttering. Talk like your life depended on it." He leaned in close, watching the man's face go pale.

"You're not a police officer," he said.

"Probably not," said Billy. "But I've got a gun, so where's the tree?"

"I don't have a bonsai tree. I swear I don't. I'll buy you one—I swear I will."

Billy believed him. "Okay. This never happened, you understand? No cops, no nobody. I hear different, I'll come back, and I won't be looking for a tree. Understand?"

"Yes ... yes ..."

Billy let go of his wrists and held his finger up again. "No more of that. None of it. You're cured. You stay cured. I hear different I'll come back and doctor you some more. You want that?"

There was vigorous shaking of the head.

"No," said Billy. "Say it."

"No," said the man.

"No what?"

"No more."

"And who are you going to tell about tonight?"

"No one."

"That's good," said Billy. He moved past the man, went to his car, started it up, and drove away—no bonsai tree.

But hey, maybe he had a future as a doctor.

11

Brian Pasley pulled up behind the pickup truck, a scene he'd played a hundred times over in this small town. Shaking his head, he flipped on his red and blues. The three college boys tossed their beer cans into the open doors of the truck, acting innocent, as though they had just been standing there.

Pasley was the chief of police in Galena, Colorado. Once upon a time, he'd been an Army soldier, fighting for his country in the biggest sandbox in the world. An enemy combatant—as the Army called the man who tried to kill him—had opened up on him and a couple of his buddies with a Soviet-made Avtomat Kalashnikov gas-operated, fully automatic machine rifle, better known as the AK-47 to the civilian peoples of the earth.

The village was supposed to be friendly, but this man certainly wasn't. The three of them had just walked past the man, returning his smile and slight bow. He shot all three of them in the back. Both of Brian's friends went down. One died instantly, and the other bled out, waiting for medivac. Brian was hit twice in the upper back. His armor stopped one of the rounds while the other 7.62mm projectile tore through his protective vest, penetrating his muscles and a lung before stopping an inch from his heart.

At the last second, Brian sensed something was off and started to turn. The force of the bullets finished the movement. Instinctively, he raised and fired his rifle, pumping five shots into the torso and neck of the man who had just smiled at him before killing his friends.

Ignoring his own injuries, Brian radioed for help. He tried to save his friend by shoving clotting agent and reams of gauze into the holes, blood oozing from some and spraying from others. He kept at it until the medics and other soldiers arrived, but his friend was already dead.

Months of recovery and recuperation followed. He was given a medal, a discharge, and was flown back to the States, where he suffered horrible bouts of depression, thinking over and over of what he could have done—should have done—differently. Like recurring nightmares, the what-if game plagued him at the weirdest of times.

What if I'd seen the outline of the AK beneath his robes?

What if that smile had tipped me off?

What if I'd turned a fraction of a second sooner?

Brian tried to shake the intrusive thoughts, but they ignored his conscious efforts, striking like jagged bolts of lightning, jarring him to his core.

He self-medicated with alcohol, drugs, and women. These things helped for a while—none of them for long.

Then one day, as he relived the clotting scarlet that painted his hands and forearms as he pushed strips of once white cloth into his friend's flesh, he put the razor blade to his wrist. The tip, he thought —rusted, dirty, and disease infected—was a perfect analogy for his soul. As it slid into his inner wrist, a small stream of dark blood circled the joint of his hand and wrist like a watchband. It dripped in patters to the cracked, trash-strewn concrete of the culvert that led to the sewage tunnels beneath downtown Denver, across from the useless Veterans Administration he'd just left. Having refused his need for more drugs, they'd forced his hand—the razor his last option.

"Don't do that," came a voice as if from heaven itself. Brian was caught off guard by the sound of its profound, calm charisma.

Brian had looked up to see a well-dressed giant of a man, the sun directly behind him framing his head like a halo.

"Go away," he said, pressing the used blade deeper.

"No," said the man. "Stop now. I have a use for you."

Brian didn't know why, but he stopped.

"A what?"

"You will be my right hand," said the giant, "and together, we will remake all of creation." Stretching out his hand, the man reached down to him. "I will take away all the hurt, the pain. I will give you purpose—make sense of the madness of war you've lived."

Brian's jaw dropped. *Was this man reading his mind?*

"Yes," said the man. "I am—your mind and your soul. I see who you are. I know your purpose. I know what you've been through, but more importantly, I know what you will become. Take my hand. We have work to do, you and I."

And Brian did, just like that. He didn't know why—it was as though he couldn't stop himself. Using his arms to push himself up, he dropped the razor. As he got to his feet, he felt the dog tags dangling from the chain around his neck. He looked at them, seeing his name and SSN, but they were different somehow. Gone were the memories, the terrors, the images. Instead, he felt something he hadn't felt in so long.

Brian felt hope.

"You boys, stay right there," said Brian. "And don't act like you aren't up to no good. I saw the beer cans."

The boys were big, wearing letter jackets—football jocks. *Perfect.*

"I'm not here to bust you," said Brian. "I have a use for you."

And he did.

12

Toby finished his nighttime chores, collecting the other kids' dirty clothes and dragging the big sack to the laundry room. The mothers would do the washing, drying, and folding.

Back in the room he shared with three older boys, he cleaned his face and hands and went with them to the big hall, the sanctuary, where they all ate dinner every night. There the Gardener would give readings and issue punishments if there were any.

While in line, Toby saw River standing three places ahead, holding his tray, head down. The beating had been severe, seven stripes, until the blood ran freely. After the fourth strike, River passed out. Despite River hanging limply from the rope's end, the beating hadn't stopped. Seven stripes, the wood whistling and cracking as it cut into the boy's fragile skin. Afterward, River was sealed in the Box until the next morning. The Box sat outside the main building.

At night, in the dark—with the animals and the elements.

And who knew what else? The things in his dreams, maybe? One of the mothers had told Toby that dream monsters were real and that they haunted bad little boys. Toby was bad sometimes—he knew that —so it was probably true. He'd pushed Aspen down the other day because she called him a toad. He knew it was wrong, but it made him mad, so he just did it. She didn't tell on him, not yet anyway, but if she did...

The Box scared Toby almost more than the beatings. They'd put his mother in the Box.

His real mother.

They'd left her there, day after day, night after night, even after she stopped screaming. And when they finally did pull her out—after they'd gotten her to wake up, to drink and eat and say how sorry she was—what they did to her then, right in front of everyone, even Toby, at the Tree. *On* the Tree...

Toby still had nightmares. So did others. They'd told him. Not out loud, but in whispers and with little touches—letting him know how sad they were for him.

Everyone was afraid of the Gardener, which was good.

He said it was good.

The Gardener said fear of him was the completion of wisdom.

Toby didn't know what that meant, but he knew what fear was. He was afraid all the time. He tried not to show it, but sometimes he did—sometimes, he couldn't help it. He was afraid of the bigger kids, like Forest and Linden. They picked on all the smaller kids, and Toby was one of the smallest. Sometimes they punched him or kicked him. They liked to pinch him and pull his hair. They were careful, though. They knew better than to leave marks. They were clever that way. If the mothers caught them, they would be punished like anyone else.

Only the Gardener was allowed to order punishment. He gave some authority to the mothers for minor concerns and to certain men under the proper circumstances, but the guns, whips, rods, and knives were under his control, to be handed out when he commanded.

It wasn't just the big kids Toby feared. He was afraid of the dark, wild animals, some of the men, and, of course, *the One Tree.* The One Tree knew everything. It was the tree of knowledge. Most of all, though, Toby was afraid of the Gardener.

Toby was afraid to talk because sometimes he said the wrong

things. He didn't know he was saying the wrong things, but because he was punished, he knew he must have said something bad. Sometimes smacks or pinches, sometimes worse. Some of the mothers liked to use spoons heated in the fire to touch his bare skin. The pain and blisters were terrible, so Toby usually didn't speak at all—safer that way.

Usually.

If a mother, brother, or elder asked a direct question, not answering was even worse than saying something wrong.

Some mothers were nicer than others. Some never used the spoons. But some were very mean, with squinty eyes and frowning mouths. Like Forest and Linden, the mean ones were always looking for reasons to hurt the little ones.

Toby didn't know why they were like that. He didn't like hurting people. Even when he shoved Aspen, he hadn't meant to hurt her. He just wanted her to stop calling him a toad. It hurt his feelings—made him feel like crying—probably because he *thought* of himself as a toad. Small, skinny, weak.

Toby got his food and sat next to River at the end of a long table filled with silent boys. The girls and boys always sat at different tables. When everyone was seated, the Gardener stepped in—tall, strong, eyes of fire, with wide shoulders.

Raising his hands, he ordered, "Worship me," his voice rich and powerful.

They all spoke as one.

Hail to the One Tree
And its planter, the Gardener
The Gardener, source of all knowledge
And all power
The god of all
Creator of all
Giver of life
Taker of life

The Gardener lowered his hands.

"I accept your praise. Eat and be nourished."

Toby took the bread from his plate and dipped it under the table, passing it to River. They were not allowed to talk, not allowed to share. At first, River ignored him, but then he turned to Toby. His eyes, wide and far away, came slowly into focus. Under the table, he took the bread from Toby, gave a feeble smile, then pushed the food into his pocket. The brothers, who were not really brothers, ate their meals in fear.

Toby wished his mother had never brought him to this place. He thought of his father. It seemed like forever ago, but he remembered his father being nice. He couldn't remember ever being afraid of him, but he had been little then. Maybe he hadn't understood what it meant to be scared. His father had been killed in the war. His mother told him so. He wished his mother would take him away from this place, but she couldn't, not yet—he knew that.

She was still being punished.

13

I pulled into the town of Galena a little after seven. The place was small—very small—like town in a scary movie small.

My legs were tight and my neck stiff when I got out of the car. Rolling my shoulders, I opened the back hatch to let Max and Pilgrim out. They hopped down and ran straight for the copse of trees I'd backed up to—cop habit for a quick exit. I didn't see anyone out and about, but there were a few cars parked in front of businesses lining the street. The sun hung low in the sky, draping the town in a grayish-purple twilight.

A breeze rustled through the trees making sounds that matched the scary movie vibe. Crickets chirped. Rodents or rabbits or squirrels rummaged through the leaves and bushes completely hidden. Max was instantly out of sight, while Pilgrim stayed close, lazily marking here and there.

Shadows stretched. The high mountain smells, usually fresh and alive, suddenly felt heavy and claustrophobic. Something caught my attention—maybe Michael Myers wearing Captain Kirk's face or Jason Voorhes with his hockey mask. When I turned, it was only Max sitting by a tree. Thankfully he wasn't wearing anyone's face. Still, he was pretty much scarier than any of them—not to mention he had a higher kill count.

Somebody tapped my shoulder from behind, and I almost screamed. I didn't—it wouldn't have looked professional—but it was close. Slowly I turned.

A petite woman, maybe seventy-five, with bright eyes, standing all of five feet, and weighing in at under a hundred pounds, stood there smiling.

"I'm sorry. I didn't mean to startle you," she apologized.

I did my best Will Smith, "Startle me? No, sheesh, ha, I don't startle."

"You jumped about a foot," she smiled.

Everyone exaggerates.

"I'm Molly Doors," she said, holding out her hand. "My husband and I own the General Store right there. I saw your dogs and had to come out to see them. They're beautiful. I used to have a golden named Sally, but she died last year—cancer. So many of them die of it these days. Terrible. Do you mind if I pet them?"

My heart was slowing. I pointed to Pilgrim. "The big shepherd there, Pilgrim, is fine to pet," I said, then switched my attention to Max. "But Voorhes ...."

"Your dog's name is Voorhes?" she asked.

"I mean, Max," I corrected, "better not."

"I'm really good with animals," she bragged. "Dogs love me."

An image of Max licking wet blood from his coat after a night's foraging across my mountain came to mind. I shook my head slowly.

"Really? I mean, he looks like a pussycat."

"Did you ever see the *Pink Panther* movies?" I asked.

"Peter Sellers?"

"Those are the ones. Do you remember when Clouseau asks the clerk if his dog bites?"

"I love that one!" she said. "*Return of the Pink Panther*. The one where his boss starts to have the eye twitch."

"Right. Remember what the clerk tells him?"

"He says no, his dog doesn't bite."

"And what happens?" I asked.

"The inspector bends down to pet him, and the dog bites his hand."

"Exactly. Now, imagine me having told you that Max *does* bite and *you* thinking it's still a good idea to try it?"

Grinning, she said, "I'm picking up what you're laying down, but there's a difference."

"Difference?"

"In the movie, the inspector says *I thought you said your dog doesn't bite?* To which the clerk responds, *That's not my dog.* But *he* is your dog."

"*You* might know it," I said, "and *I* might know it. But Max, maybe not."

"Okay, I get it," she said. "I'm a dog lover, but I'm not a nut. I'll settle for—*Pilgrim,* you said?"

"The sweetheart of all sweethearts."

She called his name, and he came trotting over, limping slightly. The two made fast friends.

"He hurt?" she asked, "or just old?"

"A little of both," I said.

"Yeah, lots of old scars. Some new ones too." She looked at me accusingly. "He a rescue or something?"

"Cop dog," I said. "One of the best. Retired now."

"And the new wounds?"

"*Semi*-retired," I amended. "Like me."

"Like you? You're a police officer? Or you were?"

"Was. Now I'm a private investigator. Pilgrim and Max are my partners."

She looked from Pilgrim to Max. "Oh, I get it—good cop, bad cop —just like on TV." Turning back to me, she asked, "What does that make you?"

Holding out my hands, I joked, "Plucky comic relief."

She laughed.

"See?"

"Pretty good," she agreed. "So, are you working or touristing?"

"Working. I'm looking for a missing woman and her little boy."

Molly's expression changed immediately, and she glanced around as if expecting someone to be listening in. "In that case," she said, "we should go inside and grab some coffee. You can bring the dogs. The wind's gonna be picking up soon, and there won't be many customers this late in the day."

I nodded. "That would be nice. I could use some coffee."

We all trudged to the store, Pilgrim at her side as she stroked his head and rubbed his ears. Inside was warm, and there was no breeze. The smell of leather and wood, popcorn and coffee washed over me, both homey and commercial at the same time. The store was filled with many trinkets—souvenirs—bright and shiny, glittery and bold, sharp and round and rectangular. Slogans, mottos, and portraits, all telling Colorado's history in catchy phrases and colorful pictographs. There were knives, toys, rocks, and tiny bags of fool's gold—enough wealth on display to captivate any child's eyes. It was the type of shop you'd find in any horror flick.

"I'll toss on a new pot," said Molly. "This one's been on for a few hours."

"Please don't go to any trouble. I'm used to old brew."

"Yeah," she nodded, "you have the look. You were in the service?"

"Marines," I said, "Law enforcement after that."

"My husband was Navy," she smiled. "Sort of makes you two cousins, right?"

"Something like that," I said, grinning.

"Well, I like mine fresh, so you just look around a mite. Don't be afraid to buy some stuff. It's how we make our living."

Taking the hint, I picked out about fifty bucks worth of t-shirts and set them on the counter. Coffee streamed into the glass pot, smelling like part of the landscape. Max went to a corner, his back protected on three sides, and instantly fell asleep. Conserving energy, I figured. Who knew when he might have to kill something. Pilgrim roamed the store, sniffing everything in sight.

"Cream or sugar?" Molly asked.

"Black," I answered, "like ...."

"Your soul?" she broke in.

That stopped me cold. Molly laughed.

"I was going to say my humor."

She shook her head and set the thick porcelain mug in front of me. "Don't insult my coffee. I've heard your humor. You mentioned a missing woman and a boy?"

I handed her my phone with the pictures displayed and picked up the coffee while she studied them. She took a sip from her mug, set it back on the counter, and sniffed.

"I've seen 'em," she nodded. "But not for a few months."

"Seen them where?" I asked.

"Around town. Here, in the store." She tapped a blunt finger on the picture of Teresa. "Starflower. I think the boy's name is Bud—or Leaf—or something like that. I only seen him once or twice. Starflower used to come in pretty regular. The OTA gives them new names—usually strange ones—not that it's any business of mine."

"The OTA?" I asked.

"Yeah, the One Tree Assembly. Religious cul—er—group—I guess. They're big out this way. Own most of what you see. Not this store, but lots of others. Most of the land too. Far as you can see, anyways. Keep to themselves pretty much, but they come in for supplies and to sell stuff during peak seasons."

A religious cult?

"And, you say Teresa is part of this group?"

"If that's this girl's name. Like I said, she goes by Starflower now."

"Starflower," I said. "Is it some sort of Native American religion?"

Molly handed my phone back. "I don't know what it is. Ain't Christian, I can tell you that for sure. I may be a backslidden Baptist, but I know enough from Sunday school to know the OTA is something else—more like those Hare Krishnas and Moonies—the ones who always handed out fliers and asked for money in airports back in the seventies and eighties. The OTA doesn't dress weird like that, but they're always looking to get cash. They farm, knit, sew quilts, do wood carvings, make wreaths, knives, and swords—all kinds of things. And they sell everything. Make a pretty penny from what I see, and I got an eye for accounting."

"And when was the last time you saw her?"

"Like I said, it's been a few months. But that ain't unusual for the OTA. Sometimes one of the regulars won't show up for a year, and then all a sudden like, *bam*, there they are again. They just come and go and sometimes come back again. From what I hear, they're all over the country—maybe the world. But this is their headquarters, I guess, so most of them filter in and out sooner or later. It's kind of like their Mecca. One of them once told me they have to make a pilgrimage every so often—get their equivalent of a blessing from the Gardener, I suppose."

"The Gardener?"

Molly glanced about again, just as she'd done outside, as though she were afraid of eavesdroppers. "He's their boss, the head of their church or whatever they call it—like that Sunny Ming Moon guy. A prophet, I guess. We Baptists don't have a prophet or a leader like that. We got the Bible, some guidelines, and some conventions where they make up the guidelines—stuff like *we ain't allowed to dance*. I always hated that one. I was quite the two-stepper back in the day." Leaning in, she head-bobbed me. "I never did follow that guideline. There's plenty of dancing in the Bible." Tossing me a wink, she laughed and drank some more coffee.

I took a sip myself. "And you say the Gardener is here? In Colorado?"

"Colorado? He's here in this town practically. Their spread's about fifteen minutes to the west. He comes in a couple of times a month at least."

"Spread?" I echoed. "Like a ranch or a farm?"

Molly was about to sip from her cup, the steam rising. She stopped, set it back on the counter, and looked down.

"You remember Waco?" she asked. "Camp Davidian?"

"I do," I said.

"More like that, maybe." She looked back up at me.

"A compound?" I asked.

Molly shrugged. "My opinion, for what it's worth. Others might see it different."

"Are you saying the people there are prisoners?"

She shrugged again. "Don't know about that exactly. People seem free to come and go for the most part—always in groups, though. Never alone. Seems like there's lots of rules. Like how some Baptist tossed in the *no dancing* on account he thought it might lead to other stuff—which maybe it will. Only, like I said, *lots* of people dancing in the Good Book. Seems to me like God don't much care for people adding or taking away from what He says.

"Anyway, the OTA seems to have layers of rules around rules. So, are they prisoners? That might depend on what you mean. Sometimes people make themselves prisoners. Sometimes they let other people make them prisoners." She looked me in the eye, took a sip of coffee, and grinned mischievously. "That's why no one tells me I can't dance."

14

Billy met Tina at a coffee shop off I-25 and County Line Road. She arrived in her patrol car first and already had their drinks at the table. Although dressed in her K9 uniform, she looked loose, comfortable, and sexy—but then, when didn't she? Billy did a mental head shake. If, a year ago, anyone had told him he'd one day be dating a cop, he'd have either laughed or punched them in the mouth. Maybe both.

But here he was. And there she was.

As he reached the table, she stood and kissed him. Just a little kiss. She tried to avoid PDAs—public displays of affection—while in uniform. That was fine with him. He didn't much care for putting his personal life out in front of the public anyway. Billy had grown up in the mafia—secrecy was a way of life for him.

He took a sip of his caramel mocha Mediterranean medium roast. Tina had turned him onto it a few weeks back, and now it was one of his go-to's.

"So, what have you been up to, Mr. PI?" asked Tina, sitting back down.

Billy shook his head. "You wouldn't believe it if I told you."

"If it involves Mason, I think I would."

"You ever see the *Karate Kid* movies? The ones with, *wax on, wax off?*"

"Ralph Macchio? Of course. Kind of campy, but fun." Tina looked around them sheepishly. "But I'd take it easy on the *wax on wax off* comments. Completely different meaning for today's kids."

"Different? How?"

"I'm not going into it here but think bikini hair hygiene."

"Oh," said Billy, grinning, "got it."

"Well, that's something," Tina teased. "It would have taken Gil half an hour to finally get it."

"Old guys," said Billy, not particularly wanting to hear about a time when she was involved with his boss.

"He's not that much older," said Tina.

"You think that because you haven't seen how much makeup he cakes on to hide the wrinkles."

Tina laughed. "Someone a tiny bit jealous?"

"Should I be?"

"No, I don't play high school games like that."

"Good," said Billy.

"So, you were talking about *The Karate Kid*?"

"Right," Billy nodded, "the tree."

"Tree?"

"Yeah. Remember Mr. Miyagi? How he was always taking care of those little trees?"

"The bonsai trees? Yes."

"Well, someone stole one from Mason's shrink's office, and it's got a lot of sentimental value to the guy. I've been tasked with finding it."

Tina just looked at him.

"I know," said Billy, "sounds goofy. But the tree's sort of symbolic of the shrink's dad or something."

"Like the dog in *John Wick*?" asked Tina, excited to make the connection.

"Right," Billy agreed, "and Woody Harrelson's son in *Zombieland*."

"I loved that! So, did you find it?"

"Not yet," he shook his head, "but I got some leads. I staked out the shrink's office—watched the nut jobs that came out."

"That's not nice," said Tina.

"Call 'em like I see 'em," said Billy.

"Didn't you say he was Gil's therapist?"

"I think that sort of bolsters my case."

Tina just shook her head. "Okay, so you staked the place out. What then?"

"I picked out a guy who looked crazy enough to steal a tree and followed him to his house. Acted like I was a cop—got inside, looked around, pushed him a little. Didn't come up with anything yet, but we'll see. Besides, he was only the first guy I tried."

Stunned, Tina stared at him. "Please tell me you just made all that up."

"What?" protested Billy. "I didn't hurt him or anything."

Tina took a deep breath. "You followed an innocent man to his house—*no*—better—a possibly mentally challenged man—making it a protected class hate crime—impersonated a police officer—illegally gained entry into his house—*criminal trespass*—performed an illegal search—then threatened the protected class gentleman—turning the criminal trespass into a first-degree burglary—but—you didn't hurt him?"

Billy pursed his lips. "Sounds kind of bad when you say it like that."

"Well," said Tina, "that's pretty much how it will read on the arrest warrant."

Shaking his head, Billy laughed. "There won't be any warrant. The guy doesn't even know who I am, not to mention I made it clear, under no uncertain terms, that it would be a bad idea to get the cops involved."

"You threatened him?"

Billy looked offended. "I don't threaten, babe. When I tell someone something, it's my word."

Tina closed her eyes.

"Anyway," said Billy, "it wasn't bad like you make it sound. We were just two guys talking out an issue, man to man. I asked questions, he answered. No big deal. Done and done. Besides, Mason told me PI's got special privileges, or powers, or whatever—that we can do stuff you cops can't."

"*Some* stuff that we can't," acknowledged Tina. "Very *limited* stuff, but nothing like what you did today."

Billy shrugged and picked up his coffee. "Hey, you asked."

"I'm sorry I did," she said.

"That reminds me," said Billy, "do you care which of the puppies I take for Irmgard?"

Tina squinted at him. "How did anything I just said remind you of that?"

"I don't know, it just did. So how about it?"

"You don't seem like that much of a dog person," said Tina, "are you sure you want one?"

"No, but Irmgard does. Besides, puppies are different."

"Puppies grow into dogs," said Tina.

"Yes, I know that."

"Dogs like Max," said Tina. "He *is* their father."

"But Viper's their mom, and I like Viper. Besides, I don't think there *are* any other dogs like Max."

Tina thought back to all the assassin bikers Max had killed at her house while protecting her. How he could appear and disappear at will. How his shadow had looked and what it sounded like as she stared down that dark hallway, listening to the sounds of a man dying as Max killed him. *The fear she felt.*

"You have a point," she said. "It's a big responsibility, though."

"Irmgard will take care of most of it," said Billy. "I want it mostly for her protection. Besides, with you and Mason training it for me, it'll be an angel."

"You think Gil can train up an angel?"

Billy reached over and took her hand.

"You'll do the angel work, he'll take care of the protection for Irmgard side. You will, won't you? For me and for Irmgard?"

Tina sighed. "You knew I would before you asked."

"Yeah, I did."

AN HOUR LATER, Billy sat across and down the street from Rick's office in his car. The building was dark. Everyone except the cleaning staff had gone home hours before, and now they, too, were leaving.

Tina wouldn't like what he was doing, but that was the cop in her. He dismissed her objections, hoping she wouldn't ask him about it. He'd made a promise to himself that he wasn't going to lie to her about anything. He hoped he could keep that promise without losing her, but it was beginning to look like that might be tricky.

It took Billy about three minutes to get past the locks and security system and into Rick's office. It took a bit longer to go through the files—maybe an hour. He was simply scanning and taking pictures of the files, not really knowing what to look for since he didn't know what kind of *crazy* stole a tree or why.

When he finished, he searched the places Gil had told him to look—places where people typically hide their computer passwords. He found what he was looking for in the fifth spot, right under the desk lamp. After accessing Rick's computer, Billy clicked in a thumb drive and copied all the files. That took another ten minutes.

He was home in time to eat dinner and play a round of the board game LIFE with Irmgard. She beat him.

Which was as it should be.

15

Molly pointed me toward the rental cabins down the way. The one I chose was old, quaint, and modestly priced. It was an authentic wood cabin, which reminded me of the hours on end I played with my father's old Lincoln Logs as a child.

It took about three minutes for the water to qualify as something resembling hot, but once it did, it was steamy and lasted at least twenty minutes as I lazed under the blast. Toweling off, I brushed my teeth, shaved, redressed, and took Max and Pilgrim out into the night. The moon wasn't visible, but there were a bazillion stars bedazzling the sky. I was struck by how incredibly awesome it is that God loved us so much that He made all of this for us.

The thought made me feel a little ashamed. I was still in a bit of a scruff with my father-in-law, Nathan—the man who brought me to the Lord. We'd had a falling out after I learned he'd been preaching to Majoqui Cabrera, the MS-13 assassin who murdered my wife and baby daughter. After tracking him down, I'd tried to murder the man but failed and was fired from my job as the Cherokee County Sheriff's Office K9 Trainer. That was nearly a decade ago.

Then, a few months ago, Cabrera escaped prison and tried to kill me, along with others. I ended up tossing him off the Royal Gorge Bridge, but Nathan caught him at the last second and tried to save him. We've been at odds ever since. The whole thing makes it hard for me to talk to God since I know Nathan is actually right. I know I should reconcile with him, but I just don't have it in me yet.

But here I was, and there were the stars—the knowledge inescapable.

Thank you, Father.

Max and Pilgrim went to the trees, which looked as plentiful as the twinkling stars overhead. I lost sight of both dogs pretty quickly, but I could hear them ... well ... Pilgrim, anyway. Max was his usual ghost self, there and then gone in an instant.

The cabins were spaced reasonably far apart, my closest neighbor maybe twenty yards down and the other about thirty up. The lights from the small town shone half a mile away. I thought a little recon was in order—see if I could learn more about the OTA. And maybe someone else had spotted *Starflower* more recently than Molly.

After giving the dogs some time to rummage about, I called them back, and we drove toward the lights. The breeze was cooler, as Molly said it would be, but not too cold. Comfortable, really, *mountainy*. The town's altitude was higher than that of my hogback—less oxygen. Crisp. Winter would be blowing in before long, and up here, it let you know it was coming.

A group of cars had clustered in front of a bar called The Brew Pail. Across the street was a diner with a few small parties of two or three at the tables. Not knowing if either establishment was dog friendly, I decided Max and Pilgrim were my "service dogs." After all, they do keep me from getting anxious.

The cook behind the counter looked to be in his seventies. His eyebrows drew down when he noticed Max and Pilgrim walking in perfect stride next to me.

"Those dogs trained?"

"Absolutely. Although I sometimes wonder if I've trained them or if they've trained me," I said, smiling.

"They gonna behave?"

I commanded *sits, platz, stand, sits,* both complying instantly.

The cook's eyebrows rose. "Better than any of my ex-wives."

Which is probably why they left you, I thought, but didn't say out loud since I was hoping to get some answers from him.

"So, what's good here?" I asked.

"Burgers, fries."

My mind instantly went to early SNL with the *cheeseburger-cheese-burger-cheeseburger, no fries, chips,* skit they used to do, but the guy didn't exactly strike me as having a working sense of humor, so I let it go.

"I'll take three, please, no fries and a diet Dr Pepper."

"Pepsi," he said, "if you want diet, that's all I got."

"That'll work," I said.

Turning around to the stove, he tossed on some burgers and broke out lettuce, tomato, and onions from their rectangular containers.

"You want 'em bloody or dry?" he asked, not turning.

"Middle of the road."

"That works," he said, "since that's where I found the meat earlier this afternoon anyways."

Hey, maybe I was wrong about that sense of humor.

I laughed. He didn't.

Or was I?

"Cheese?" he asked.

"Sure," I said, thinking again about Saturday Night Live but still not mentioning it.

"I hear the OTA crowd gathers around here," I said.

He harrumphed. "Only time they show up here in crowds anymore is when there's money to clip."

"You mean they're thieves?"

"Not like that," he said. "More like tight—sticky fingers—always trying to pinch the last penny."

"And that's bad?" I asked.

"It's annoying," he said, expertly flipping the burgers. Pointing at a sign, he went on, "The prices are right there, plain as can be, easy to see. But do they care? They try to haggle every time, every one of them, *always*. It's a pain."

I looked around the small room. "Any of them here tonight?"

"Nah, it's too late for that crowd. They lockdown early—before the sun sets."

"Lockdown?" I asked. "Figure of speech?"

He set the drink in front of me. "Maybe," he shrugged. "Maybe not."

"Meaning?"

A half grin curved his lips. "You a cop?"

"Do I look like a cop?" I asked.

"You totally look like a cop," he shot back.

"Would that matter?"

"I don't talk to cops," he said.

"I'm a private cop," I explained.

"Oh, like that Mike Hammer guy? Stacy Keach, right?"

"Exactly like him," I said.

"I don't talk to private cops neither."

"What about actors?"

He shook his head. "Burgers will be up in a minute."

I put a fifty on the counter and raised my eyebrows.

"What do you want to know?" he asked.

"What can you tell me about the OTA?"

"Crazy bunch of hippy cult weirdoes."

"No," I said, "don't hold back—tell me what you really think."

He harrumphed again. "You asked."

"Yes, yes, I did. Please continue."

"They swarmed in here like a plague of locusts about ten years back. Lots of people, lots of cash. They didn't mind spending money back then. Bought up everything in sight—huge chunks of land, most of the stores and shops. For the first few years, they put pressure on those of us who wouldn't sell. They've kind of let off on that, but every once in a while, they poke us a bit."

"What do you mean by pressure?" I asked.

"Started with offers of money, then more money. Later, there were broken windows, slashed tires, a couple of small fires—nothing anyone could prove. But never happened before, so we knew."

"Fires can get serious fast," I said.

"Yeah, that's when a group of us had enough. We went to the FBI. Once they started poking around, most of it stopped."

"FBI?" I said. "Did you try starting with local law enforcement?"

"Our old police chief retired right after they moved in. He'd been a retired captain from somewhere back east. Once the OTA showed up, he mysteriously came into enough green to move to Hawaii. I hear he does a lot of sailing these days. His one officer quit, too— don't know where he went. Anyway, one of their guys ran for mayor in the next election. By then, they had us outnumbered and were able to put him in."

"They put an OTAer named Pasley in as chief of police. He's got three coppers working for him, paid mostly by the OTA. Lord knows the town ain't got that kind of money. So, we decided to jump the chain of command and go straight to the feds."

"What about the county or the state?" I asked.

"The Sheriff and his *Mounties* have their hands full with the rest of the county. And as for the state, well, let's just say they get their quota of traffic tickets, and that's about it. So, we made a group decision to go to the FBI. And, like I said, it helped. Most of the harassment stopped. But it was a little too little, a little too late. OTA owns at least three-quarters of the surrounding area."

"Sounds like an occupying force," I said.

"Yeah," said the cook, "pretty much. For a while, they were everywhere, nearly crowding us out. But once they finished the compound, that pretty much ended. Now they stay up there most of the time, except to get supplies and a few random groups selling stuff."

"Where's the compound?"

He pointed toward the door. "'Bout ten miles to the west. That's what I meant by lockdown. Come sundown, they shut the gates, and the towers light up."

"Towers?"

"Just like at prisons. Fortified with guards and lights and guns.

The FBI never made it inside. Never even tried. Guess they're a little shy after Ruby Ridge and Waco. Still, I heard they asked a bunch of questions and started looking into their finances. Whatever. The harassment stopped pretty quick then, and the feds left. I figured the push would start up again when they were gone, but it didn't. I don't know if they came to an agreement or what. But things are better. Still … creepy. I mean, who knows what goes on up there behind those fences?"

He set three cheeseburgers in front of me. I gave one to Pilgrim, who wolfed it down in a giant gulp. I don't think his teeth even touched it. I took a bite from one of the two remaining burgers.

The cook grinned at Pilgrim, then looked at Max. "What about him?"

"He's self-sufficient," I said.

"You mean he catches his own food?"

"Something like that," I admitted.

"What? Doesn't eat people food?"

I gave that one a second thought. "*Sometimes* he eats people food," I said.

The cook looked stumped, not getting the joke, and started scraping clean the stove's surface.

"What about this Gardener guy?" I asked.

"Big guy. Built like you—only taller. Very charismatic, good-looking. I think he's Hawaiian or something. Maybe that's why our old chief moved out there. Connections, you know?"

"You think it's a cult?" I asked.

"If they offer you Kool-Aid, I'd pass," he advised.

I pulled out my phone and showed him the pictures of Teresa and Toby. "Ever seen them?"

"Starflower and Leaf," he said. "She used to come in every so often—Leaf only a couple of times. Likes root beer floats. Cute kid."

"When was the last time you saw her?"

Scrunching his face in thought, he looked up at the ceiling and scratched the back of his head. "Three weeks, maybe a month?"

"That long?"

He held up his hands. "Yeah, it's been a while. Maybe she left. I hope so. Places like that don't usually end well. Better for them both if they left."

"Ever see any signs of abuse?" I asked.

"Depends on what you mean," he said. "My daddy used to beat my mom regular—every time he got a drunk on. Never left a mark where it would be visible, but there were signs—I seen them. The set of her jaw, hunched shoulders, her eyes—the way she gave a little jump at any sharp sound or word. So, no, I never seen any injuries or bruises on Starflower or Leaf, but I seen plenty of the other signs in them."

"Thanks," I said. "You more than earned the fifty."

"That don't include the food," he said, setting a receipt next to the plate.

Nodding, I tossed another fifty on the counter.

He'd been worth it.

16

Outside, the wind had gotten crisper, and it ruffled my hair. Both dogs instantly went back into the trees once I gave them leave. Three men were standing by my Escalade, their backs to me. Scanning, I walked over.

"Can I help you?" I asked.

All three zipped their pants and turned to me. They'd urinated on my driver's side door and tires.

"Get lost," said the biggest. They were all wearing letter jackets, the colors purple and brown. My guess was they were college football players. The smell of alcohol was strong.

"Glad to," I said, "soon as you move away from my car."

The big guy pointed. "You mean this car?"

Something about this situation didn't seem right. Coincidence that they'd picked my car? Not likely. A setup, then. But by who and why? Three against one, and they were all big—strong. It still wouldn't have been enough, even if those were the odds. But they weren't.

Max suddenly materialized in the dark behind them. An instant later, as if by magic, there was Pilgrim—*Max must be rubbing off on him.* Not one of them noticed. I felt a little afraid for them—but only a little.

"Who hired you?" I asked.

"You trying to get smart with me?" asked the biggest kid. His two friends moved slightly to either side, a weak attempt at a double-flanking maneuver.

"Boys, you're playing with a grownup now, and in the grownup world, you can get seriously hurt, even killed. I could beat all three of you to death without working up a sweat, and that's without touching one of the two semi-automatic pistols or the three tactical knives I carry. But I won't even need to lift a finger to destroy you if I don't want to because my two attack dogs are sitting behind you. They will shred you to pieces if I give the signal or if you move just a twitch too fast."

They all grinned like they thought I was bluffing, but then one of them looked over his shoulder and saw the wolf-like silhouettes hulking there.

"Uh, guys," he stammered.

They all turned and froze, the game no longer funny.

"Who hired you?" I asked again.

Big Kid shook his head. "You can't do nothing to us," he said. "You'd get arrested."

"I can see the headlines now," I mused, lifting my arms and spreading my hands. "Three drunk third-string college jocks eaten by wolves from the wild."

"I ain't no benchwarmer," whined the big guy.

"You ain't no genius either. Now, talk or bleed."

"Those ain't wolves," he argued, trying to work up his courage. "You said they were yours."

"Yeah, but only the four of us know that, and once you three are dead—no witnesses."

Looking scared, one of the other boys said, "Come on, Richie, this isn't what we signed up for." He looked at me. "Some guy in the bar bought us drinks and gave us a hundred apiece to scare you out of town. We wasn't going to hurt you or nothing—just make you leave. That's all."

"He still in there?" I asked.

"Naw. He took off when we went to your car."

"Shut up, Don," ordered the big kid. "I told you—he ain't gonna do nothing."

"What did he look like?" I asked Scaredy-cat.

"I don't know. Tall? Tanned, blond hair, sort of tough—older than you. He drove off in a brown open-bed Ford."

"Okay," I said. "Very slowly, no sudden moves, walk away, and don't look back."

"Just like that?" asked the big kid.

"Just like that. I'm not even going to make you clean my car."

"We took the dude's money," he said.

"Oh, so suddenly you have scruples? Beat it before I change my mind about your cleaning duties."

"Hey, Richie," said the one kid, "I think maybe we should just call it. We did our part. The guy never said we had to actually do anything to him—just scare him."

The big kid snorted. "You think he's scared?" He looked at the other kid. "I think *you're* scared."

"You see those werewolves behind us?" said the other kid.

"I ain't scared of no stupid dogs," boasted Richie.

"Well, I am," said the other kid.

"Me too," echoed the up-till-now silent third kid.

The big kid did a half-turn and pulled a four-inch buck knife from a sheath on his belt. "Dogs can die," he said, looking at Max and Pilgrim, "just like people."

The look was a feint, of course. He charged straight at me.

MAX SAT NEXT TO PILGRIM, watching everything—the boys, the surroundings, the bar, the restaurants, *the Alpha*. Why the Alpha hadn't already killed these men, he didn't understand. They were obviously preparing to strike—their postures, their tones, the adrenaline bleeding from their pores, the clenching and unclenching of their fists, the subtle shifting of their footing, the blading of their bodies. Attack was imminent.

But the Alpha continued to talk ... *allowed them* to talk.

And then the biggest pulled out a knife, turned toward Max, and charged the Alpha—started to, anyway.

Before his raised foot could touch pavement, Max hit him in the middle of his spine, lifting him from the ground as though he'd harnessed gravity itself. Max crushed him face first into the asphalt and began shredding the letter jacket, taking shirt and meat with it.

Behind him, the other two boys held their hands up, cowering and hunching down as Pilgrim slowly advanced, giant shoulders rolling like unstoppable waves, his eyes glowing like something from a horror movie under the single streetlight above the bar,

Max spit out the material while acquiring his next target, the boy's unprotected neck at the base of his skull.

∽

MAX MOVED SO FAST that all I saw was a sort of blur in the dark, and then Big Kid was gone from between the other two. I heard his face hit the street with a sick sound, like a pumpkin falling from a two-story window.

Trick or treat.

"*Aus*," I commanded, just in time to save Mr. Morality from having Max go all Predator on him, ripping his spine from skull to butt.

Max stopped, but he gave me a look I didn't like. It reminded me of the old days when I first found him in Germany fighting a bear. We didn't get along so well back then. Looking up, I saw Pilgrim about to kill the other two. I gave him the *stay* command. He stayed. The two boys were shaking from head to toe. *Couldn't blame them.*

Just then, I heard the door to the diner close, and there stood the cook, looking a little scared and a little mad, a meat cleaver in his fist.

"You okay?" he asked me, seeing Max on the boy's back, blood dripping from his canines.

"We're fine," I said. "Just playing a little catch with the boys here."

The cook pointed at Max, still standing on the unconscious football player's back.

"But-his-his-and the blood ...."

"Oh, that. Like I said before—*people food*. Max catches his own."

The cook didn't laugh, probably from the shock. I thought perhaps he'd get the joke in the morning and laugh like crazy, but in the meantime, I thought it best for him not to see anymore.

"You should probably head back in," I said, "customers."

He looked inside, then back at me. "Okay, I will. You sure you're okay?"

"We're good," I assured him. "Almost done here, thanks."

"*Foose*," I commanded, both dogs responding instantly and springing to my sides. "See?" I said to the cook.

"You want me to call the cops?"

"No, not necessary."

Nodding, he returned to the diner, the giant knife hanging limply at his side.

I turned my attention back to the players. Big Kid was unconscious, his teeth scattered across the black asphalt like candy corn from a trick-or-treater's spilled bucket.

"Either of you sober?" I asked.

The third one, who hadn't said anything, waggled a finger from his upraised left hand.

"I haven't had anything, sir," he said. "I'm only twenty."

Yeah, like that mattered.

"Take Sleepy here to your car and leave, but first, give me the three hundred bucks the guy paid you. You don't get a bonanza for trying to do something wrong—especially after screwing it up. One more thing—*this* never happened. Otherwise, all three of you go to jail for attempted first-degree assault. That's a felony. Felony means you lose your scholarships, and instead of playing football and looking pretty for the girls, you get to play *don't-drop-the-soap* in the prison shower. Do we understand each other?" They both nodded their heads.

Clapping my hands together, I said, "*Chop-chop*, let's go."

They did, and a few minutes later, I tucked the three bills into my wallet and popped the door to my Escalade. Pilgrim jumped right up, followed by Max. I stood next to him, face to face.

"What's going on in that skull?" I asked. "I thought we were over all that. When I tell you to stop, you stop—no backtalk, no *looks*. That's how this whole *master—dog* thing works."

Max didn't say anything. He didn't burp, didn't lick himself—just stared.

In the old days, it would have been spooky. Not that it shouldn't be now, I mean, at this distance, he could literally rip my face off, but it wasn't. Now I felt something else.

Disappointment.

Sadness.

I shook my head, not liking the situation but not wanting to get into it just then. Maybe he was in a mood—not that moods are allowed in the canine kingdom. Still, it was nearly Halloween, and the atmosphere could do weird things, *just like a full moon*. It's not superstition, just reality. I don't know why or how. I don't know if it has to do with gravity-induced tidal influence, the extra light, or what, but both military and police experience have provided enough evidence for me to believe it's true.

The cruise to the cabin was quiet, and once inside, I stacked wood in the fireplace and got it blazing. I stripped to my shorts and started computer searching the One Tree Assembly. An hour later and missing Sarah, I closed the laptop and called her.

"What are you doing?" I asked.

"Missing you," she said. "What are you doing?"

"The same," I said.

"Good," she said, smiling mischievously over the phone. "Anything exciting happening yet?"

"Lots of driving, checking out video surveillance, talking to the locals ... and cheeseburgers ... there was that. Everything else was boring."

"Locals, huh?" she responded. "They better not be cute locals."

Sarah was being silly, of course. She's a *ten times ten* on the beauty scale. If she were a witch, she'd have to be Elizabeth Montgomery. If she were a genie, she'd be Barbara Eden—a vampire, Yvonne De Carlo mixed with Elvira ... *both classy and sexy.*

Sarah and I go a long way back—even before my wife and daughter were murdered. She's a world-class CSI tech working for the Colorado Bureau of Investigation. We worked cases together for years and became fast friends. One night, while I was overseas training K9 for the Marines, she was raped. When I got back, the guy tried to get her again. Pilgrim and I stopped him.

"Oh sure," I said, "the cook had a five o'clock shadow and a meat cleaver. Come to think of it—he did have a cute smile. And the burgers were great."

"How much longer will you be gone?" she asked.

"Don't know yet. I think I may have a lead on Teresa and the boy, but it's been a few months since anyone has seen them. I'm hoping they're still up here."

We talked for about a half hour before saying goodnight.

I considered letting Max out to roam the wilderness, his usual routine back on my mountain, but his strange attitude and the fact he didn't actually get to kill the college kid made me decide against it.

Already snoring, Pilgrim was out cold. Max followed me to my room but stayed outside. He lay by the door, eyes not quite closed, reminding me again of our early days together.

And again, I felt sad.

17

Pappy sat at the bar, drinking his whiskey. They didn't have his namesake, *Pappy's*, but the CR was good, despite the missing purple cloth traveling bag. He'd had a difficult day speaking to the families of his fallen. And that's what they were ... *his* fallen. He took each of their deaths personally. Whenever he had leave time, he made his rounds, even long after their notifications and burials. He never failed to come to them, the mothers, fathers, wives, brothers, sisters, and sometimes even friends.

He didn't keep notes—he found that he didn't need to. The faces and conversations were burned into his heart. He'd sit with their loved ones, sometimes have a drink, dinner, or coffee, relaying stories from their shared history—what they were like *over there*, how they felt, how they acted. Their heroism. And they *were* heroes, all of them.

No matter what they'd been before, what they were like in the States. Over there, they were different. Over there, they made a difference. Lives, other than just their own, depended on them. They were responsible, loyal, dedicated. Pappy wouldn't have had them in his command if they were otherwise. Some of them needed help at first, *guidance*. But that was fine. Most of them were young, inexperienced.

Besides, it was Pappy and his NCOs' (non-commissioned officers) job to mold them, shape them, forge them into the Marines they became.

That's why Pappy made these trips—to let those who *should* respect them know why. They deserved it. His *troops* deserved it. He knew it wasn't a lot, but it was what he *could* do. And so he did. Still, it took its toll—therefore, the whiskey.

The woman at the bar was young, maybe twenty-seven, he thought—still young compared to his half-century. And tonight, after talking to the family of one of his fallen, he felt especially old. She had blonde hair down to her waist, a tight, short black dress. Black high heels. Bright blue eyes. Curvy but slim. Pretty silver necklace, matching bracelet, no wedding or engagement ring.

"What are you drinking?" she asked.

"Crown Royal," he smiled at her. "Straight, no rocks or chaser."

The bar was in downtown Denver, not far from where the old Auditorium Arena used to stand. Back in the day, the arena sat on Champa Street. It was renovated in 1948 when it was called the Denver Municipal Auditorium Arena. The municipal building was originally constructed in 1908. At the time, it was heralded as the second-largest arena in America, bested only by Madison Square Garden. It finally closed for good in 1990.

Pappy loved local history. Actually, he loved all history. The saying attributed widely to George Santayana, *Those who fail to know history are doomed to repeat it*, was always close to his lips. Conversely, so was the attendant sentiment that those who *know* history are doomed to sit by and watch as *fools* repeat it.

"Want to buy me one?" she asked.

Pappy had observed her sitting at a table with several men and women. One of the men, who looked to be her companion for the evening, was in the restroom. Pappy wasn't nosy, just sharp-eyed. It had saved him many times on the battlefield. It had also saved him in situations like this.

"You with the tall guy in the flashy gray jacket and Rolex?"

"I was, but he's being a jerk."

"What's your relationship with him?"

"Does it matter?"

"It might."

"This is our first and last date. I think I'd rather be here with you tonight."

"I'm fifty years old," said Pappy.

"I like older men. Men who know who they are. Seth doesn't. He proved that to me a couple of minutes ago. I think you ... know who you are."

"What makes you think that?" asked Pappy. Time was running short for the guy to get back from the head and see her here sitting with him.

"From the haircut, physique, and bearing, I'd guess you're military. And being fifty, during a time when our country has fought several wars for the last couple of decades, I don't think much scares you. Am I wrong?"

"No," said Pappy. "You're not wrong."

"How about that drink?"

"It might get messy," he said.

"I'm worth it," she said.

Pappy signaled the bartender, who responded immediately, and ordered her the Crown Royal. The bartender came with the bottle in hand and poured her the drink.

"That was fast," she said. "The place is packed."

"This isn't my first drink tonight," he said. "And I tip well."

She smiled, holding out a porcelain-skinned hand with long slim fingers and French-manicured nails. "I'm Holly."

"Pappy," he said.

She raised her eyebrows, and he said, "That's my callsign, my nickname. What's your last name, Holly?"

"Call sign? Like in that movie with Tom Cruise, *Top Gun,* or, what's the new one? His callsign was Maverick, right? Yes, *Maverick,* that's the movie too."

Pappy saw Seth exit the restroom. He scanned the table where he'd been sitting with Holly, noticed she was missing, then spotted her at the bar next to Pappy.

He didn't look happy.

"Yes," said Pappy. "You sure you don't mind a little mess? Your boyfriend's coming over."

She didn't even look. Instead, she picked up the whiskey, took a sip, and raised her brows again. "Smooth. Strong but smooth. And he's not my boyfriend. Still, don't make it *too* messy. Be like the drink, and I'll tell you my last name."

"Who's this?" asked Seth as he reached them.

"An old friend," she said.

"Is that right, Grandpa? You an old friend?"

"Leave," said Pappy.

"What?"

"Now."

"You don't tell me what to ...."

Pappy curled his two outer fingers over the inner ones and jabbed the reinforced spears into Seth's eyes, snapping his head back like it was on a spring. At the same time, with his other hand, he knife-handed straight up between the man's legs, striking the testicles. Neither blow was delivered with great force. It wasn't necessary. Seth crumpled in front of Pappy, who caught him close and carry-walked him back to his table, where he handed him off to his friends.

"Seth's had too much to drink. Best get him home and into an ice bath. He'll need it. I'm taking Holly home."

Sitting down next to Holly, he noticed her drink was almost gone.

"Want another?" he asked.

"No," she held her glass up in salute. "I'm ready to get out of here."

Pappy mimicked the gesture with his glass. "What are we toasting?"

"Last names," she said. "Mine's Arrison."

"Nice to meet you, Holly Arrison. I'm Kirk Sinclair."

They touched glasses, downed the whiskey, and left.

18

Max lay outside the Alpha's room, listening as he fell into a deep sleep. A few feet away, Pilgrim snored loudly.

Max did not sleep.

Max did not want to be here.

Max wanted to be with Viper and his pups.

Once again, he was questioning the Alpha's worthiness to lead. The Alpha had not reacted when the man marking their car with his urine had prepared to attack. Max had been forced to save him. And just as Max was about to kill the enemy, the Alpha stopped him and let all of the assailants escape—allowing them to pose a future risk to the safety of the pack. Maybe even to Max's own pack.

That was how Max's mind considered it—*two* packs.

The Alpha's, and *Max's*.

His animal brain struggled to overcome the complexities of the notion—nurture battling nature. The desire to submit to the kindness and companionship he had experienced with the Alpha was at odds with his drive to rise up and take command—secure the leadership, thus ensuring the wellbeing of his blood family.

But Max understood the Alpha well enough to know that he

would have to kill him in order to usurp his leadership. The Alpha would not submit.

Would Max do that?

Kill the Alpha?

There was a time when the answer would have been simple, but that was before—before so many events. Before he *loved* the Alpha.

Max could kill Viper's alpha without compunction. But *the* Alpha?

Max's mind was not designed to deliberate such human emotions and thoughts, but still, it did it in its own way. The concepts were there—the feelings and wants and needs. The drives, character traits, genetic patterns, and experiential pointers directed him to a mental conclusion. No matter how unbearable, the only possible answer was instinctually obvious.

The Alpha's weakness could not be allowed to put Viper and his offspring in danger.

Max must *become* the alpha.

~

When I woke up, Max was lying out by Pilgrim. He wasn't asleep—made me wonder if he ever really slept.

I brewed some coffee, let the dogs out to do their business, cooked up eggs and bacon stocked in the refrigerator—a nice touch—and called the dogs back inside, noting the blood on Max's chin. As always, he'd found his own breakfast. I scooped three eggs and a couple of pieces of bacon onto a paper plate for Pilgrim. We ate together while Max pretended to sleep again.

Something was going on in that spooky little brain of his. As a trainer, I knew I needed to get to the root of it, but I hoped it could wait until after I found Starflower and Leaf. This was no place to dig deep into animal psychology, especially Max's. I wanted to be closer to medical care, preferably with blood transfusion capabilities and maybe a surgeon.

A knock sounded at the front door. Looking out, I saw a police car and its accompanying officer. The vehicle sported decals declaring it belonged to the town of Galena.

Hmm, the one's the cook told me were bought by the OTA. This should be interesting.

I opened the door. The cop was tall and tanned, with blondish hair, and blue eyes, a little older than me—maybe forty—and was in good shape. He looked capable.

Curiously, he was the spitting image of the guy who hired the three guys to scare me last night.

Go figure.

"You happen to be Gil Mason?" he asked without smiling.

"I am," I answered, checking out his name tag—*B. Pasley.* "And you'd be Officer Brian Pasley?" I was guessing *Brian* from the *B* and from what the cook told me. PIs do a lot of guessing. I saw I'd hit it right by the way his brows drew down.

"I am," he said, "how'd you know that?"

"Had a drink with three college footballers last night. They mentioned you."

His tanned cheeks went a little pale, but he recovered quickly. "You had drinks with underage students?"

"Coffee," I said. "Nothing illegal about that, is there?"

"Depends," he said.

"Does it?"

"Mind if I come inside?"

I weighed my options, but the only way to get information was to talk. I held the door wide. "Please do. Want something to drink? *Coffee,* I mean."

"Sure," he said, stepping inside. He stopped abruptly on seeing the dogs sitting there like statues. He pointed at them. "They okay?"

"They've had all their shots," I said.

"Shots? Will they bite?"

"Only bad guys," I said. "They're great judges of character."

Sill pale, he looked from them to me.

"But," I said, "I can override their judgment with a command." I hand motioned to them, and they both moved to my bedroom and out of sight. "How do you want that coffee?"

"Cream, no sugar."

Yeah, he didn't look like the sugar type.

Walking past him, I entered the adjoining kitchen area, poured two cups, splashed cream into his, and popped a spoon into the cup. I gave it a few swirls before handing it to him. I indicated the couch and living room recliner.

"So, you here to welcome me to town?" I asked.

We both sat, he on the couch, I on the recliner. I took a sip, and so did he. I didn't have a gun on me, which put me at a disadvantage. Still, hot coffee in the face would be a distraction, and of course, two fur missiles were waiting to strike if it came to that.

"That, and to ask a few questions," he said. "What's your business in Galena?"

My lips twisted up in a quarter grin. "It's a tourist town."

"Off-season," he said, stone-faced.

"Well, you know my name, which means you ran my plate. I'm guessing you checked a little farther and know I'm a PI."

"And an ex-cop," he stated.

"I'm looking for a woman and her son." Leaning across, I handed him my phone with the pictures. "Teresa and Toby Ramirez. I think they go by Starflower and Leaf around here."

"Starflower. Leaf. Yeah, I know them," he said, returning my phone. "They were part of the One Tree Assembly up until a few weeks ago. They moved on."

"Moved on?" I asked. "Where to?"

"Don't know that," he said. "OTAers come and go. They're like that. Spiritual Gypsies. Come, stay for a while, move along."

"You sure they're not at the compound?"

"Compound?" he repeated, a sour expression twisting his lips. "Who called it that?"

"Lots of people. You call it something else?"

Taking another drink, he set the cup on the little wood table between us. "Compound brings up military or cultish connotations.

The OTA's nothing like that. It's an assembly, just like the name implies. Everyone's free to come or go at their leisure."

"Okay. You sure they aren't at the assembly?"

"I'm certain," he said.

"When was the last time you were there?"

"This morning. I live there."

"You live in the compound?" I asked.

"Assembly," he corrected.

"But you don't know why Starflower or Leaf left or where they went?"

"Like I said, everyone's free to come or go."

"Did they leave a forwarding address? A phone number, maybe?"

"No, nothing. One morning they were just gone."

"How do you know something bad didn't happen to them?" I asked.

"Why would I have reason to think something bad happened to them?"

"Well, you're a community, right? An assembly. A group of people deciding to live together. You must have rules, assigned chores, sleeping arraignments, work groups, days on, and days off. Schedules? Two of your members, a woman, and a small child, suddenly disappear without notice or explanation. How do you know they weren't kidnapped or murdered? Did anyone file a missing person's report? Did anyone look for them at all? You're a police officer. I'd think you'd want to make sure that they are okay."

"It's not like that. The Gardener—he's the caretaker of the Assembly—told us they left."

"Cult leaders are notorious for sexual crimes," I said. "Maybe he has them locked up in the basement."

"It's not a cult," he said. "The OTA is a religion, a belief system. The Gardener's a good man."

"Who started this belief system?" I asked.

"The Gardener did. He had a divine vision."

"A divine vision from who?"

Pasley looked up as though seeing past the ceiling and into the sky. "Aliens," he said.

"Aliens," I echoed.

Pasley shook his head. "I understand your disbelief, but everyone's acknowledging their existence these days, even the White House. The Gardener was ahead of them all."

"Aliens," I repeated. "Like Hale-Bop aliens? Purple tennis shoes? Mother Ship? Like that?"

"Like that," he said. "Only this is real."

I thought for a few seconds. "I thought this was about a tree—like from the Bible—the tree of the knowledge of good and evil."

Pasley nodded. "The Gardener planted the One Tree, as shown in the vision from the aliens. But it all came from him—from a past life. The Gardener had the aliens hold on to the knowledge until it was his time."

"His time?" I asked.

Pasley nodded sagely. "His final life."

"Reincarnation?" I asked.

"Exactly!"

"You said this is his last life? So, when he dies this time, he, what? Becomes one with the cosmic whole or something?"

"He is the cosmic whole," Pasley explained. "This time, we of the Assembly get to join him."

That sounded creepy.

"Again, like Hale-Bop?" I asked. "Jonestown?"

Pasley shook his head. "Not like that. We'll ascend."

"Like the Rapture?" I asked.

Pasley shrugged. "The Bible gets some things right."

"And exactly what books does this Gardener of yours use?"

"Books?"

"The Bible, the Koran, Book of Mormon, Watch Tower, Bruce Lee's Jeet Kune Do?"

"The Gardener uses many texts. There is truth in everything."

"Lies, too," I countered. "In the Bible, there are two trees, not one. Which tree does the Gardener promote?"

"There is only one now. The tree of knowledge destroyed the other tree."

"Yeah," I said, "that's what I thought. The wrong one."

"Well," he shrugged again, "I see that you are an unbeliever. Starflower and Leaf are gone. You have your answers, and now that you do, it's probably best you leave."

"Oh, I wasn't hired to learn they were *gone* from anywhere. I already knew they were gone from where they used to be before coming here. No, my job is to *find* them. Find them and bring them home, and that's exactly what I'm going to do. Speaking of which, I'd like to visit the compound."

"It's not a compound," he said evenly. "And I don't think that's a good idea."

"And I'd care what you think—w*hy*?"

"Because I'm the law, and I think maybe you're a troublemaker. The Assembly doesn't take kindly to troublemakers."

"Troublemakers, like someone who'd send three college kids to mess with a nosey PI? Maybe scare him a little? Rough him up a little? That type of troublemaking? I'm *going* to the compound to have a look around myself."

"We won't let you in," he said.

"Come and go as you please? That's what you said, right?"

"Assembly members, not outsiders."

I nodded, took another sip, and set my cup next to his. "Sounds like a cult to me. And, maybe, a prison for the members inside. Guard towers, curfews, armed guards, its own police force? Yeah, I'm definitely going to get a peek in your Gardener's basement. And, if I find that you've hurt Teresa or Toby, God help you." I looked him hard in the eyes, letting the mask of civility drop so he could see what was hidden deep in my soul—the rage, the hate, and the animal that still lurked in dark recesses since my wife and child were murdered.

He sat straight, his hand moving toward the gun on his right hip. He gripped the handle, his thumb unsnapping the safety strap, but suddenly stopped. He'd seen something to the side of us.

It was Max.

Chief Pasley moved his hand from the butt of the gun and held both hands up at about chest height.

"I think I'll be leaving now. You should do the same."

"And you should have learned from last night—I don't scare. See you at the compound."

This time, he didn't bother correcting me. He just stood and walked out, watching Max the entire time.

Max watched him in return.

19

Yawning hugely, Billy scanned the computer screen in front of him.

Talk about boring.

How did Mason put up with all this paperwork? All this searching? All this computer junk? Billy wanted to close it down and head to the gym for some jiu-jitsu rolling or maybe some lifting, kickboxing, maybe even heavy-bag work or boxing—anything but this.

He made himself stick to it by sheer force of will, determined to show Gil he could do the job. Thinking about Gil made him wonder where he was and if he'd yet learned anything about the woman and kid—not that he was worried about him. After all, it wasn't a dangerous job, not this one. Just find the woman and her son and bring them back. *Men* were generally the dangerous ones. Then again, Gail Davis had almost been the death of them all. And, of course, there was his Tina—she could be pretty dangerous, he thought with a smile.

Maybe he should give Gil a call.

Nah, he was being stupid. Gil could take care of himself. And if he did need help, he had Pilgrim and Max. Max could take care of all of them.

Billy realized he was just trying to find a viable excuse to procrastinate. But, like any opponent, this work wouldn't knock itself out. He rubbed his eyes, shook his head, suppressed another yawn, and focused on the computer screen.

The door opened, and in came Yolanda, Gil's spicy, fifty-something, short, Hispanic secretary, carrying two cups of coffee.

"You looked tired," she said, placing one of the cups in front of the computer as she sat across from him, "I saw you yawning. Thought you could use a pick-me-up. You work so hard—not like that *other* one."

Billy almost laughed but held it in. Gil seemed to have a strange love/hate relationship with Yolanda, and she with him. But not Billy. Billy thought she was awesome.

"I don't know what Gil pays you," said Billy. "But he needs to pay you more."

"Yes," said Yolanda, "much more. He doesn't appreciate me. But I think maybe you will set him straight."

They looked at each other, Yolanda raising a conspiratorial eyebrow. Both broke into light laughter as they sipped their coffee.

Billy gave the coffee a curious look. "What's in this?"

Yolanda grinned as she took a long deep sip and winked at him. "An old recipe from *Meh-hee-co*."

"I thought Gil said you were from *New* Mexico?"

Yolanda shrugged her shoulders and raised and lowered her eyebrows. "New, old, what's the difference? Besides, what does a *gringo* like him know?"

Billy breathed in the steam, concentrating, "I catch—cinnamon—vanilla—*brandy*? Or is it rum?"

"A keen nose," said Yolanda. "Mr. Mason would never have figured it out."

"So which is it?" asked Billy, taking a long sip.

Yolanda leaned in close. "Both!"

Billy almost spit it out. Instead, he managed to suppress his laughter and take another sip. "Well, it's delicious," he said.

"Of course," she said smugly. "It's *survived* generations. Family tradition has it that it's helped generations *to* survive."

"I'll drink to that," said Billy, holding up the mug. Yolanda clinked hers to his, and they took a quiet moment to enjoy the warm beverage.

"So, what's the deal with you and Gil?" asked Billy. "I mean, I sense some hostility."

"Mr. Mason has a good heart," she sighed. "But he's lazy. Comes in at all different times—*when* he even bothers *to* come in." She shook her head sadly, *tsk-tsk-tsking*. "I try all the time to get his gringo brain into a work mode. But Americans! What can you do with their work ethic?"

Billy said, "You do realize that New Mexico is *in* America, right?"

Yolanda waved the thought away. "Not really. That's just what Americans like to think. Believe me, New Mexico and Mexico are blood brothers—much closer to each other than to America. It's like Puerto Rico. Americans claim it, but it's just a trick to placate them—keep them in line. Subservient. Under their thumb. They try the same thing to New Mexico, but we are too hard-working, proud, resilient, self-sufficient. We are slaves to no one."

"Yeah," said Billy, "but you do understand that Puerto Rico is a territory where New Mexico is an actual state?"

Yolanda chuckled lightly. "Words. Americans play with an abundance of flowery words. They are like Sarah Gallagher, always trying to impress with her golden tongue."

"She impresses with *more* than her speech."

"Oh, yes, she enjoys showing off her other glitters." Her eyes drew into slits, and she pointed a finger. "But you watch out for her. She is bad—crafty, evil—like the witches of old who cast spells. She has Mr. Mason under one now. Don't let her snare you in her web."

Billy thought getting tangled in that particular web might be interesting, but he was with Tina, so he wouldn't take a chance on messing that up.

"No danger in that. I'm already involved."

Yolanda took another sip and sat back in her chair. "Ah, the female police officer."

"Yeah, Tina."

"It's serious then? You and—Tina?"

"I think so. Certainly is for me. I think it is for her too, but ...."

"But how can a man ever know what is truly in a woman's mind? That's what you are thinking, no?"

"Exactly! How can I really know?"

"You can't," said Yolanda. "No man can. Not now, not in the past—not ever. It is one of our secret weapons."

"One of? You mean there are others?"

"Many others," nodded Yolanda. "The golden tongue, the other glitters, makeup, our aroma, the softness of our skin, the sheen of our hair, our melody, the feel of our flesh, the look in our eyes, our minds, and so many more."

"Sounds like we poor men haven't a chance."

"No, no chance. Not when the woman is skilled. She is the master hunter. What does Mr. Mason call his dog, Max? *An apex predator.* A skilled woman is a danger to all and *in no* danger from anyone."

"Sarah seems really nice to me," said Billy.

"So does the tiger, until you get close enough to pet its head. Once there, you will be lucky to get away with only the loss of a single arm."

Billy didn't know what to say, thinking Yolanda's attitude was probably a form of envy due to Sarah's exquisite beauty.

"I see your skepticism," Yolanda noted, "but let me ask you this—before you and Police Officer Tina were a thing, didn't Tina lose Mr. Mason to the tiger?"

Yolanda had a point. After Sarah seemingly gave up on Mason, Tina started dating Gil, but in a single move, Sarah stepped back into the fight and stole Gil from Tina.

Fast, easy, and effortless—like a tiger preying on a goat. Maybe these women did have secret powers men knew nothing about.

Billy wondered—what were Tina's powers?

20

I stopped in at the souvenir shop and said hi to Molly. We shared a cup of coffee, and I told her about my meeting with Deputy Pasley.

"He's a creepy one," she warned. "Never smiles, stares straight through like he's not even seeing you. Be careful of him. He likes to hurt people. I saw him break a big guy's arm right there in the lot about a year ago. He's mean—likes to throw his power around."

"Yeah," I said, "I kind of got that vibe off him. What's the best way to get to the compound?"

She shook her head. "Don't let Pasley hear you call it that."

I took a drink. "Already did."

"How'd he take it?" she asked.

"Didn't seem to like it."

"Oh, you're a firecracker, aren't you?"

"Me? No, I just wanted to see how he'd react."

She pointed, "You be careful. I can't prove it, but I know they're dangerous. I feel it."

"Most cults are. So, best way to the compound?"

Molly shook her head as she sketched a rough map on a pad of paper.

"Firecracker," she said.

~

AFTER COFFEE, I drove into the town proper, past the diner and the bar, and saw people walking along the sidewalks and across the street. There were only a few, but they seemed happy, just regular folks enjoying the crisp mountain air and the brisk temperature. I parked a bit down from the main strip, close to a candy store and ice cream parlor.

A group of three walked towards me—a guy and two girls. Across the street stood a man eating an ice cream cone. They all ignored me —no finger-pointing while dropping their jaws and howling eerily like in *Invasion of the Body Snatchers.*

In answer to the eternal musical question, *I let the dogs out,* so they could take a break near the trees. One of the girls saw them and ran over, her companions following at a slower pace.

She was pretty—about seventeen—with brown hair, wearing jeans, a sweater, and big hoop earrings. Pilgrim met her about half-way, and she started petting him as he licked her hands and fingers. Eventually, the other two joined her.

The guy was about the same age. He also wore jeans, with a button-up shirt and several bracelets on his left wrist—no watch. The other girl was thin and tall and wore jeans with designer holes in them. Her blue hoodie bore a college logo. She had braces and a friendly smile.

"Okay to pet him?" asked the boy, pointing toward Pilgrim.

"If you can handle the slobber," I said.

Apparently, he could because he joined Hoops in petting.

Designer Holes pointed at Max.

"Oh look, another one," she cried, as though Max was a deer, elk, or maybe a bear.

"Not that one," I warned.

She had started toward him but stopped, looking sad.

"He's touchy. But Pilgrim here loves attention."

"He's so pretty though," she cooed.

"So's a rose, but they're prickly."

Pouting, she placed her hands on her hips.

I took out my phone and showed her the pictures of Starflower and Leaf.

"Have you seen these two?" I asked.

She took my phone and squinted intently at them.

"Does she go to school around here?"

"No," I said, "she was part of the OTA if you've heard of them."

That changed everything. All three stood straight.

"We gotta go," the boy backed away.

"Yeah," said Designer Holes.

"Thanks for letting us pet your dog," whispered Hoops as they turned and hurried away.

They were scared. I was about to dig deeper when an F150 with five guys stopped next to us. The college kids kept going.

I'd been in town less than an hour, and the goon squad had already arrived—*that didn't take long*. Someone was watching me.

All five got out, three of them holding baseball bats. I guessed the lot of them to be in their late twenties to mid-thirties, varying in height and weight, but all healthy, outdoor types. The baseball bats seemed pretty standard.

"Who's got the ball?" I asked the closest as he stepped forward.

Raising the bat, he said, "You're the ball."

"Is that right?" Something about the way I didn't back away, or maybe the tone in my voice, or perhaps, the stainless-steel Smith and Wesson forty-five caliber 4506 handgun I pulled out of its pancake holster beneath my shirt stopped him—stopped all of them. Pilgrim stared at them, drooling.

One of them spotted Max, sitting behind them to the side. "Hey! How did you get there?" His voice had a panicked pitch to it.

Couldn't blame him.

"Drop the bats, get back in the truck, and round your way back to home plate," I advised. "And if I see you again, I'm not going to ask questions—I'll just start tossing some balls at you fast. Like, really,

really fast. Copper-jacketed hollow-point balls that will do things to you that you *wouldn't* like—that you *shouldn't* like—that you *couldn't* like. And if there's anything left of you, Lassie and Rin Tin Tin here will clean up the remains."

They looked at me ... at the dogs ... at the gun, then dropped the bats, but before they could get back in the truck, a police car screeched onto the scene. Out stepped Officer Pasley, holding a shotgun.

"Drop the gun," he ordered.

He wasn't pointing the gun at me, and I wasn't pointing mine at him. He was wearing a vest. I wasn't. Still, at this distance—maybe fifteen yards—I figured I could put three into the ten-ring of his forehead before he knew I'd moved. Of course, in the eyes of the law, he was a duly sworn police officer, and I was just a discredited former deputy working as a civilian private investigator. These facts would mean murder charges for me and a mile-long funeral procession for him.

The quandary was I had him pegged as an OTA enforcer who'd now sent people to rough me up twice—the baseball bats were still lying on the ground, not far from the men who brought them. On the plus side, people started coming out of the shops and stores to see what was happening. Chances were he wouldn't kill me in cold blood or even let his guys come for me. And, if he did try either of those things, I still had several weapons on me—not to mention Max and Pilgrim.

I knelt slowly, the gun facing down, and gently set it on the ground, watching Pasley the entire time. I stood up, my hands open and at shoulder height, and said, "Free dogs."

Instantly Pilgrim and Max ran for the trees and disappeared. They were still there, watching, just out of sight.

Two of the men turned towards me, grins curving their lips.

"Get out of here," Pasley commanded.

They all turned to him.

"You heard me," he said. "Get."

They *got*, but they didn't seem happy about it.

Pasley set the shotgun back in his cruiser and walked over to me. "Turn around," he said. "Hands behind your back."

I did as he said and felt the cold steel of the cuffs as they clicked around my wrists.

"You're under arrest," he said.

"You'll find my concealed carry permit in my wallet, along with my PI license," I said.

"That's not the charge," he said. "I'm arresting you for harassing those men. Harassment and felony menacing with a firearm."

"Five of them?" I said, "Armed with baseball bats? I have at least four witnesses who saw the truck stop and that I was about to be attacked."

"I don't see any witnesses," he said.

"Those two girls and that guy up the street hiding behind that car," I said, head bobbing toward the ice cream parlor. "And the man who dropped his cone over there."

Pasley scanned them.

"They won't testify for you."

"You don't know that," I said.

"Yes, I do.

"Like that, is it?"

"Exactly like that," he said. "You got any other weapons on you?"

"A few," I said.

"You want to tell me?" he asked. "Or we can play TSA."

"Ankle holster on the left," I said. "Knife on my belt, along with a couple of magazines for the gun." I decided to keep the little two-inch double-sided buckle knife a secret, just in case.

Pasley removed the items, dropping them unceremoniously onto the dying grass.

"Where are the dogs?" he asked, scanning again. He couldn't see them, but I knew they were out there.

"Roaming. They'll be okay."

"We have a leash law," he said.

"Funny," I said.

He walked me to the cruiser, sat me in the back, and closed the door. After gathering all my toys, he dumped them in the trunk of his car and got behind the steering wheel. "Should have left when I told you to," he said.

"It's a free country," I said.

"Not for you. Not anymore."

At the police station, he stripped me of my belt and shoes and put me in a cell. He stood at the door, about two feet away, and punched me full force in the stomach—my hands still cuffed behind my back. I caught his movement just in time to push the air out of my diaphragm. The maneuver kept me from getting the wind kicked out of me from the blow. It's an old Karate technique called a kiai that tightens the diaphragm. You usually scream when you do it, which helps to force all the air out, but this wasn't a Karate match, and I didn't want to look silly in front of the guy with the gun.

I had to admit it was a good punch—hard and straight, the blow sounding like Rocky hitting the side of beef in the freezer with Pauly looking on. I didn't even flinch.

"What was that for?" I asked.

Pasley shook his wrist, seemingly unfazed by the lack of damage the punch had inflicted.

"The buckle knife. You didn't tell me about it. That's another charge—bringing a weapon into a detention facility."

"Forgot," I shrugged,

"You're a smart mouth," he said.

"I know you are, but what am I?"

He didn't get the Pee-wee Herman reference, but he did get mad, at least a little. Fingering his nightstick, he nodded at my belly. "You think those abs can stand up to something harder than a fist?"

"If you try, I'll kick you to death. Probably take me about fifteen seconds."

Thinking about it, Pasley pursed his lips. He walked out of the cell and closed the door.

"Turn around," he said. "Put your hands out of the bars."

I slipped the cuffs under my feet, one at a time—I didn't fancy turning my back on him just then—and stuck my arms out.

"How about my phone call?"

Still deadpan, he said, "You're a hard case, all right, I'll give you that."

He unlocked the handcuffs and brought a corded phone over from the desk. Holding the phone in one hand through the bars and the receiver in the other, I punched in the number.

Tina answered on the second ring.

"Hi Tina, it's Gil."

"What did you do now?" she asked.

21

F ollowing the police car, Max and Pilgrim ran along the tree line for as long as possible. When the car veered through town, they left the safety and seclusion of the trees and took to the streets and storefronts until they lost sight of the cruiser about a mile from where they had started.

Max instantly switched from visual searching to open-area scent detection, sweeping in big circles, scanning the currents of air that swirled and roiled. Minimal scent escaped from the car, and what did was tossed around by the vehicle's momentum and various deflections, including other cars, obstacles, conflicting air currents, and patterns. The scent molecules were broken, torn, and scattered into billions of particles, like the pixels on a monitor screen.

Even so, it didn't take long for Max to pick up the Alpha's identifiers—a tick here, a speck there, an eddy flowing for a short space before splintering beyond his capabilities.

Back to the circles.

Nose high, then low, finding a trace in the gutter where scent collected and pooled before flowing like a stream.

The game changed once again, this time from area search to

trailing—*the art of following scent that gathers along the seams and indentations of curbs, hills, buildings, tires, and trees.*

Ninety minutes later, Max and Pilgrim lay in the tall grass behind the police station.

The Alpha was inside.

He was not injured.

Not bleeding.

Not afraid.

Pilgrim fell asleep beside Max.

Max did not sleep but rested—conserving his strength for the fight he knew would be coming.

THE GARDENER WAS FINISHING his last set of bench presses. Three hundred fifty pounds, seven reps, his glistening shoulders, triceps, and chest rippling at the strain. Sweat dappled his forehead, running down his temples and into his black hair, making it look even blacker.

Grunting, he shoved the bar the final inch and dropped it into its safety hooks. Sitting, he rested for a few seconds, catching his breath, looking at the extended veins snaking through the corded muscles of his golden forearms. Kane, his traditional name, loved the feeling of power that ran through him. He truly was a god, the One Tree's representation on earth. Beautiful, wise, strong. This was not arrogance, not bragging. It was truth. His assembly proved it—as did the visions.

An idea struck, and he hurried to the laptop sitting a few feet away. His thoughts were divine. He needed to preserve and share them—inspiration and insight for his seedlings. He wrote:

Branches, supple and wise, bend with the wind, like the spirit of the One Tree, teaching those who will receive.

Next to his computer, his cell began to buzz. It was Chief Pasley.

"Yes?"

"I have him in custody."

"And?"

"He won't scare. He won't leave."

"We'll see," said the Gardener. "Wait for me."

Toweling the sweat from his face and bare chest, he looked around the room—exquisite detail everywhere. The gym alone, with its showers, sauna, and steam room, had cost over a million dollars to construct. Kane had come a long way from the poor boy who'd begged, stolen, and fought for food while growing up in the slums of the islands. But the One Tree had led him. The visions and the visitations from the Visitors had shown him the way.

He'd experienced many trials along the journey—resistance from governments, the police, the FBI. Kane had hired a team of lobbyists to handle the politicians. After that, the FBI stood down. The politicians weren't cheap, but they were worth the cost.

And now this—this man searching for Starflower and Leaf.

Irritating.

Kane considered having Pasley discreetly dispose of the man. Still, wisdom dictated that he find out what the man knew, his connections, who knew he was here, and the possible ramifications if he were to disappear. Pasley had run a check on him, learning his name and that he was a private investigator, but that meant nothing. No, Kane must question him. The One Tree would reveal Kane's next course of action.

He'd planned on spending some time with a few of his wives before working on his writings, *his Truths*, but that would have to wait. The Gardener was curious about this man.

This Gil Mason.

TINA CALLED her supervisor and told him Gil might be in some trouble in the township of Galena. Without hesitation, he gave her permission to drive up to make sure he was all right. It was a long trip, and the department would be minus a trooper out east for as long as it took, but Gil had saved her sergeant's life one dark and stormy night way back when, so he didn't bat an eye.

On the way, she had dispatch get the number of the trooper working that area, a woman named Lily Wright.

"Trooper Wright," she answered.

"Hi, Lilly, this is Trooper Tina DeWitt."

There was a pause as Trooper Wright sorted through her memory. "I think we met at the conference in Sin City back a couple of years. You have the K9?"

"That's me," said Tina, not remembering her at all. "I have a favor to ask."

"Shoot," she said.

Tina gave her what information she had and asked her to babysit until she arrived.

When Tina finished, Lilly said, "Galena is pretty weird. A lot of cult activity up there. The FBI came up a few years back—tried to shut the place down. Failed. They've got a lot of people, a lot of money. Police force is definitely shady—more like a security force for the cult. I met the guru, or whatever he is, once. Great big Hawaiian —tall and muscular. Reminded me of a politician, and I hate politicians. They've got a big group site up there that you can see from Marston Road. Looks like a military base.

"I'll go check and make sure your buddy's okay. It's been a quiet day so far, but I may have to leave if things heat up. We're short-staffed way out here—not like you city troopers."

Tina laughed. "If you only knew, sister. Be there soon as I can."

Everything Lilly had told her meshed with what Gil had said. She considered calling Billy to fill him in but decided to wait until she saw what was what—a decision she would come to regret.

I saw the Gardener walk into the small police station. There was no mistaking him. He was big, like Dwayne (the Rock) Johnson's muscular big brother big. He wore a white silk shirt with the first three buttons undone, parading a bulging chest. His pants, made of a material I couldn't identify, looked very expensive. The shoes probably cost more than my best gun ... well ... maybe my *second* best. He didn't even glance at me—just went to Pasley.

Sort of arrogant.

"Open it," he said.

"You want me to cuff him?"

For the first time, he looked at me. "No," he said. "Just open the door."

Pasley did, all cautious-like, as though he thought I might be remembering the sucker punch to my gut. *And he'd be right.*

The Gardener walked into my cell. "Wait at your desk," he told Pasley.

"You must be the Gardener. Or is it Mr. Gardener?"

"No mister, Just Gardener."

"Really? Sounds kind of ... I don't know ... kind of pretentious, don't you think? I mean, do people come up to you and say, 'Hey, Gardener?' And by the way, what is it you plant anyway? Tomatoes, corn, coconuts?" I could tell he wasn't used to ordinary mortals talking to him like this.

"You've already been told that Starflower and Leaf have left. Why are you still in my town?"

"*Your* town? Maybe I should call you *Lord* Gardener or *King* Gardener. No, wait—cult, *right*? *God* Gardener?"

He looked at me like I was a worm hardly worth considering. "You didn't answer my question. Why are you still here?"

"I don't believe they left," I said, "and I'm not leaving until I do."

"You leave when I say you leave." He looked over at Pasley. "Bring me the file."

Pasley entered my cell, handing him a manilla folder. Opening it, he shuffled through the contents.

"You've got a lot of charges here. Add to that assaulting my police chief, and you could be doing some serious time."

I didn't bother denying that last part. "Let me guess, I leave, and everything just goes away?"

"That could happen. The OTA is very forgiving."

"Yeah, about that, the *One Tree* Assembly. I'm a student of the Bible myself, and I'm wondering why you would start a cult worshiping the *wrong* tree?"

He gave me a partial grin. "I enjoy theological discussions, but not with nonbelievers unconcerned with learning the truth."

"The truth? You mean, like when Satan lied to Eve, saying, *You will not surely die. For God knows that in the day you eat of it your eyes will be opened, and you will be like God, knowing good and evil?* That truth?"

"It did make them gods. And they *didn't* die. Satan isn't who your flawed Bible says he is. He's not from here."

"Oh," I said, "He's one of your ... aliens? The ones that give you visions?"

The grin left his face.

I said, "Your ET deceived them ... or Eve, at least. He murdered them. If it weren't for God's grace, he would have murdered us all. And that tree you worship? It's sitting in Hell right now."

The Gardener shook his head slowly. "You aren't looking for the truth. So, leave or ...?"

"I *am* looking for the truth. The truth about where to find Starflower and Leaf. Tell me that, and I'll go. Otherwise, show me the compound and let me see for myself."

He turned to Pasley. "Who knows he's here?"

"Several people in town saw me arrest him, but he's obviously combative." With a shrug of the shoulders, Pasley let the rest go unsaid.

The Gardener checked his fifty-thousand-dollar watch. "I'd rather he just disappear—that way, there won't have to be an investigation. Take care of it."

Well, that escalated quickly. It was like I wasn't even there—the two of them openly talking about making me disappear.

And then they both looked at me, Pasley's hand casually reaching for the butt of his gun—made me think that maybe this was business as usual for them.

Other than his size, I didn't see a weapon on the Gardener, so I decided I'd kill Pasley first. Besides, I needed the big Hawaiian alive to tell me where Teresa and her son were.

22

Billy had had enough. He pushed away from the computer screen, rubbing his eyes. His little B&E at the psychiatrist's office had paid off, and after sifting through the data, he had compiled a list of ten crazies he thought were reasonable prospects for having stolen the tree.

He drove to the first address.

This kind of work was new to him, so he didn't yet know the ins and outs of how best to vet his suspects. Oh, sure, he'd done surveillance as a member of the Family, but that was different—find and beat up a guy for not paying what he owed, an occasional hit on a rival gang member for violating their territory, or retaliation against someone who'd insulted the organization.

This was different. He didn't want to upset Tina again by threatening anyone or beating them up, or in general by doing anything illegal. It didn't exactly work out like that, though.

As he was pulling into the apartment building of the first nut-job on his list, a street bum with ratty hair, pushing a shopping cart containing all his worldly goods, stopped right in front of him and held his hand out for money. The guy's jacket had oily splotches that had long since soaked into the material. His eyes were glazed from narcotics and years under the sun, and he jittered the way meth heads often do.

Billy rolled down his window and leaned his head out. "Move it, doper. I'm working."

"Trick or treat," said the man, a cigarette dangling from his filthy fingers. He was around thirty, stood about six feet, and maybe weighed a hundred and fifty pounds.

"Get a job, ya bum," said Billy. "But first, move!"

With his non-smoking hand, the guy reached into the back of his stained sweatpants, scrounged around for a few seconds, then came out with a wad of brown material. It took Billy a second to realize what he was holding. The man drew back his arm, preparing to throw the mass at Billy's windshield, his nasty green teeth showing through a huge grin. Billy pulled the Beretta pistol hidden on the underside of his dash and pointed the gun at the man's face. The Beretta had a silencer attached to the barrel.

The guy was high, but not so high he didn't recognize the gun. He stopped in mid-swing.

"Smell your own feet," said Billy. "And as for something good to eat ... do it."

The man looked at the waste squeezing through his fisted fingers, then back at Billy. He shook his head to the negative.

"Trick it is," said Billy as he shot off the guy's right lower earlobe.

The man touched the side of his head, smoke curling from the cigarette between his fingers. His hand came away wet and red. He dropped the cigarette, his fingers shaking. He looked at Billy.

"Eat it, and then you can beat it like I told you in the first place. Or there'll be one less bum to crap on the streets in front of decent people." For emphasis, Billy moved the barrel of the gun a few notches so that it pointed between the man's eyes.

The man did as he was told, his teeth no longer green.

"Now get out of here. And don't even think about coming back and messing with my car. It would be a really bad idea. Go—and take your house with you."

The man grabbed the shopping cart and ran as fast as he could away from Billy.

Shaking his head, Billy snapped the Beretta back in its magnetic bracket beneath the dash. He must be getting soft. Not long ago, he would have blown the guy's testicles off for such disrespect. But, because he'd remembered his promise to Tina, he'd held back. Come to think of it—he'd performed a kind of civil service. It made him feel sort of good.

After all, it might keep that creepo from squatting in front of a lady and her kids, or even a nun. And if the guy had the boldness to try and throw his crap on a man as big as Billy, what might he do to an average size person? Well, he'd think twice next time—his earlobe, or lack thereof—would help to remind him.

Billy figured he'd skip to the second name on the list in case the slight ruckus had alerted anyone in the apartments or if the bum decided to go to the cops. He didn't think that would happen though. Street people usually avoided law enforcement due to warrants, distrust, or other reasons for not wanting to be scrutinized. But, still, why take the chance?

The next place was a house in Aurora snuggled behind several trees west of Centennial Park. It looked like an upper-middle-class area, mainly two stories with a few ranch style homes scattered about. The neighborhood was big on Halloween decorations. Fake spider-webs stretched across bushes, and jack-o'-lanterns dotted every porch. A fifteen-foot skeleton brooded on the lawn next door to his target, while across the street, a bloated inflatable ghost bobbed in the breeze. Billy parked down and around the corner with just enough of a view to watch the house unobstructed.

He checked the data file he'd stolen from Rick's computer. His phone displayed the man's picture, physical characteristics, and diagnosis.

Ronald Warren, white male, six one, 210 pounds, red hair, green eyes. Somatic symptom disorder, expressed as conversion disorder. Subject displays rotating motor and sensory symptoms that lack a comparable neurological or medical explanation. Symptoms began shortly after the subject was the victim of a street robbery. Physically uninjured, the subject experienced severe mental stress with corresponding symptoms of conversion disorder following the incident.

Whatever that meant.

The file went on to state that Ronald's *rotating* physical attacks made it impossible to maintain a job and that he was currently unemployed. There was stuff about his history and his family— married, no children. His wife was an accountant at a reputable office downtown.

All of which meant that Ronald *should* be home ... *alone.*

Recalling his encounter with the stutterer, Billy decided on roughly the same tactic—*knock and talk*, as the cops call it—only this time, he'd go easier, less pushy.

Billy left his car and casually walked to Ronald Warren's home, admiring the decorations on the houses and in the yards around him. Some people went all out. He rang the doorbell, and after about fifteen seconds, Ronald answered. He wore a green short-sleeved button shirt and brown slacks. His hair was shorter and thinner than in the picture, but otherwise, he looked like a typical businessman— big, *not muscle*, loose, with a belly.

"Hi, can I help you?"

Billy flipped out the Arvada Police badge in its leather holder, then snapped it closed and put it back in his coat pocket as he spoke. "Hope so. I'm investigating a hit-and-run downtown. Cameras show your car in the area around that time. I'm not accusing you of anything. I just want to see if you might have seen or heard something useful."

"Come in, come in," said Ronald, extending his left hand for a friendly shake. "Sorry, my right hand is useless. Just went dead one day. Some kind of circulatory issue."

Billy awkwardly shook the man's hand, then stepped past the cheery host into a well-kept living room. He spotted several potted plants right off the bat but no bonsai.

"I doubt I'll be any help," said Ronald. "I don't remember seeing anything like a crash. But maybe you could use some probing questions like I see on TV. You know—to invoke a memory or get to my subconscious? I love all those CSI and mystery shows." He gestured to a lounger with his right hand. "Have a seat, please."

Billy remained standing, squinting at the man's use of his right hand.

"I thought you couldn't use that hand?"

Ronald looked at his right hand. "No, it's my left that doesn't work. My right's fine. Coffee? Tea? Something stronger? Oh! You're on duty. Right?"

"Rules are meant to be broken. What have you got?"

"Everything," said Ronald.

"Whiskey then, with ice."

Ronald's face scrunched. "Everything *but* whiskey, sorry. Oh, and no ice either—fridge's ice maker went out about a year ago. I had it fixed twice, but it keeps breaking."

"That's okay. Some brandy will be fine—forget the ice."

"Brandy," Ronald shook his head to the negative, "no, sorry. Kind of exotic, isn't it?"

"Rum?"

"Ha, talk about exotic," laughed Ronald.

"Make it vodka."

"Never understood that drink," said Ronald. "I mean—no taste, no smell, not even any color. What's the point?"

"The point is to get drunk," Billy laughed.

"I don't like losing control of my mental faculties," huffed Ronald.

"Tequila?" asked Billy, beginning to get irritated.

Ronald shook his head again. "Worms. Ugh."

"Beer?"

Clapping his hands, Ronald grinned. "Beer I have." Turning, he started for the kitchen, stopped, and turned back. "Lite okay? Calories," he said, patting his heavy belly.

"Lite beer isn't beer. You got wine?"

"Wine? Of course I've got wine. Who doesn't have wine?"

"Red?"

"Except red," said Ronald. "I'm a fish and poultry guy."

"White's fine," Billy replied, tight-lipped.

Ronald snapped his fingers. "I'll have to go to the basement to break out a new box. I finished the last one a few days ago."

"Box?" Billy held up a hand. "Never mind. I'm fine. About the accident,"

"Yes, of course—the accident," said Ronald grabbing a cane propped against a wall. He limped over to a chair, dragging his left foot like a dead weight behind him, both arms working perfectly. Sitting heavily, he sighed. "I still don't remember anything yet."

Billy sat in the lounger, deciding to change tactics.

"I see you like plants," he observed.

"I love them," Ronald boasted. "All plants. I majored in horticulture at Yale. I have a huge collection. Pretty much every plant on earth."

"You have a bonsai?"

Pursing his lips and looking toward the ceiling, Ronald thought momentarily. Finally, he said. "Doesn't sound familiar. I don't think that's a plant. Isn't it a Japanese pilot from World War II? Or maybe it's just what they would scream as they were diving to their deaths, crashing their planes into American ships."

"It's a tree. A small tree."

"Oh trees," said Ronald. "Well, that explains it. I don't know anything about trees. Just plants."

Billy hung his head.

"Are these those sneaky questions designed to elicit memories?" asked Ronald. "I remember that detective in the TV show *Psych* used to do that. Is it working?"

"Yes," said Billy, suddenly recognizing a possible way out. "Another trick is to do a quick search of the house. The movement jogs things loose sometimes."

"That's incredible," said Ronald, standing easily without the use of the cane. "Let's go find that juniper."

"Great," said Billy, standing with him.

"Could I take your arm?" asked Ronald, groping with his right. "I'm blind, remember?"

Forty minutes later, Billy made it back to his car—no bonsai. He'd started to think that if he'd had to stay in the house much longer, he might begin to contemplate suicide himself.

Or murder.

Billy wondered if Ronald might have been using some secret form of subliminal messaging on him. At odd times during the tour, he'd begun to feel a strange numbness in both legs and an arm, and his left eye went blurry for a few minutes.

This job was turning out to be more dangerous than a mafia gang hit.

23

The Gardener and Police Chief Pasley were standing in my cell, casually discussing murdering me and doing away with my body. Of course, I wasn't going to let that happen. I would kill them first.

But it did make me worry for Teresa and her child. The OTA had to be hiding something, and that something was serious enough to risk committing murder.

There was a slight hesitancy on my part, having been acquitted of murder charges and released from jail so recently. Killing a police chief and a civilian cult leader wouldn't look good. The adage *It's better to be judged by twelve than carried by six* came to mind.

And then Pasley's hand went to his gun, making everything else moot. Blading my body, I readied the skipping sidekick that would crush his ribs while jamming him into the bars.

Just then, the front door opened, and a woman trooper walked in. She saw the three of us standing in the cell, and I could tell she sensed the tension. I saw it on her face. She immediately understood that something wasn't right. Unconsciously—I think—her hand also touched her sidearm.

"Gentlemen."

Pasley looked to the Gardener, who slightly shook his head to the negative.

"Can I help you?" asked Pasley, his palm still on the butt of his holstered weapon.

"I hope so." "I'm here to speak with Gil Mason." She looked at me. "I assume that would be you?"

"That's me," I said, still watching Pasley, ready with the kick.

"What do you want with him?" asked Pasley.

Her eyes roved between the three of us as she gauged the danger in the air. With her non-gun hand, she keyed the mic on her shoulder flap. "Trooper Wright to dispatch. I'm out at Galena PD with the police chief, OTA leader Kane, and Gil Mason. I'm Code 4 for now." She looked us all over again. "We are all Code 4, correct?"

Pasley turned back to the Gardener, who, now that we were all on record as being here, made up his mind. Again, I saw the resignation on his face—nothing could happen here that would lead back to him. He gave a slow nod, but he wasn't happy about it. Police Chief Pasley removed his hand from his gun.

"Yes, Trooper, we're all fine here. But you haven't answered my question."

The trooper's eyes went to me. "The Attorney General down in Denver wants some information from Mr. Mason here. Something about a case he was involved in a little while back. The one in all the news—with the lady DA who murdered her husband. I was sent to fetch him. Is he in custody for something?"

Pasley looked to the Gardener, who looked back at me. He gave me a half smile and then shook his head.

"No," said Pasley. "He got into a little ruckus with some boys in town. I just brought him in to cool his heels."

"So, he's free to go?"

Pasley looked at me, his jaw flexing. "Yeah. Your stuff's on the desk. Go on back to Denver, where you belong. Don't come back."

A part of me was upset the trooper had stopped the confrontation. I'd just as soon get whatever needed to be done *done*—but I still needed answers, and a dead Gardener would tell no tales. Besides, there was that whole thing about how tough it would be to talk my way out of being convicted of killing another cop.

I sidled past the Gardener, not even looking at Pasley, left the cell, and picked my belt, outer shirt, and weapons off the desk.

"All ready," I said to the trooper.

She touched the brim of her drill instructor-style hat with one finger acknowledging the police chief, then gave me a once over. "Am I going to have any trouble with you?"

"No, ma'am," I said.

She opened the door. "You first."

When we got to her car, I stood by the passenger side front door while she opened the driver's side.

"No," she said. "I don't know you. Your weapons in the trunk, and you ride in the back."

"No room," I said.

"No room? What do you mean?"

I whistled. Pilgrim came trotting from the grass. Max was suddenly standing on the other side of the trooper's door. She nearly jumped when she saw him there.

"Oh, the dogs," she said.

"Yeah."

"Fine then," she said.

We each opened a back door. Pilgrim jumped in on my side after I loved him up. Max jumped in ... no loving up. We closed the rear doors and got in the front.

She held out her hand. "Lilly Wright."

"Gil Mason." We shook hands.

"What exactly was going on in there?"

"They were going to try and kill me," I said.

"What?"

"They're bad people, doing bad things." I looked her in the eyes. "You've got a real cancer here. It needs to be cut out."

"Were they—do you really think—kill you? Right there at the police station?"

"I said they were going to *try*."

She looked over my shoulder at the building. "Let's go somewhere else and talk about this."

"I could use coffee," I said.

"They were about to kill you, and you're thinking coffee?" She didn't sound at all convinced.

"I can *always* do coffee," I smiled.

~

TROOPER WRIGHT PARKED at a coffee shop in town, and we both exited.

"Let Max out, please."

"They've got a leash law," she objected. I gave her a look. "I'll pay the ticket," I opened Pilgrim's door. He jumped down and got another armful of loving. I pointed and gave him the *empty* command, and he went to the trees to do his business and sniff around.

Lilly Wright shook her head and opened Max's door. Max glided out of the cruiser, disappearing into the woods.

"Where'd he go?" she asked, looking for a vestige of him.

"Don't worry about it, Max is like that. A vampire ... turns into vapor. They'll be fine till we finish our coffee."

She didn't look convinced.

I opened the door to the shop and was instantly hit by the aroma of fresh pastries and coffee.

"Tina ask you to save me?" I asked as she walked past me.

"Yes."

"So that whole thing about the DA and their case?"

"I remembered you from the trial. You're a terrible lawyer."

"I take that as a compliment," I said.

"You should," she teased. "I meant it that way."

We both laughed.

Lilly Wright was my height, with blonde hair, blue eyes, maybe twenty-five, and athletic. She had a slight underbite that was cute and wore a simple gold wedding band. She carried a Glock 17 Gen5 with the red dot MOS (Modular Optic System). I told her I was buying and took her order while she went and found seats for us. She took artificial sweetener, no cream.

I set the two cups on the table along with matching cheese Danishes. She'd already commandeered the best chair, placing her back toward the wall, leaving me to sit with my back toward the door. I didn't like it, but her uniform trumped my unease, so I let it go ... sort of. I casually scooted my chair as far as I could to the side, giving me an angular line of sight toward the area of threat.

She noticed the maneuver but didn't say anything. Her half grin told me she approved.

"I love Danish. But that means an extra twenty minutes with the jump rope."

"Who said it was for you? I'm a growing boy."

"At your age, there's only one way to grow," she moved the treat next to her coffee. "This place has great sweets—worth the extra workout. My husband and I came here about a year ago." She tasted her drink and put in an extra pack of artificial sweetener. She shook a couple of packets toward my cup and raised her eyebrows in question.

"No thanks. I'm used to Marine Corps coffee ... so black you can never go back."

Biting into the Danish, she grinned. "I wasn't in the service, but my father was. He still talks about it."

The shop was bustling. The rise and fall of varying conversations melded like an orchestra warming up before an opera.

"So, Trooper DeWitt only gave me the basics. What's this all about?"

I gave her the *Reader's Digest* version while still revealing everything I had.

"And you really think they were going to kill you?"

Taking a sip, I set the cup down. "I've been in enough of these types of scrapes to know when a situation is turning deadly. Pasley's hand was on his gun. The Gardener basically told him to kill me."

"Basically?" she said.

"Look, the Gardener asked Pasley who else knew I was there and that I'd been arrested. When Pasley told him, he said he wanted me to disappear."

"That could mean anything. Like Pasley telling you to leave town."

"You weren't there. You didn't see their faces. Pasley was already going for his gun."

"It's hard to buy," she said.

I showed her the pictures of Teresa and Toby. "Have you ever seen them?"

"No," she said. "But I only get up here a couple of times a year. The place pretty much takes care of itself—a couple of bar fights and some tickets on the highway. Pasley runs a tight ship and hardly ever asks for cover. He's got three officers under him, and they work on rotating shifts. Not much need for us."

"Are they all OTA hires?" I asked.

She shrugged. "As far as I know, none of them are. I mean, they're hired by the town—sworn in by the mayor. I don't know that OTA has anything to do with any of that. Not that I *would* know. I work for the State of Colorado. I don't get paid to delve into municipal internal politics. And if you're saying he is, well, I'm not saying I don't believe you—just that I don't have proof. I know there are rumors—speculation. We all think it's hinky. But again, hinky isn't proof."

"I've talked to shop owners who tell me the OTA put the cops in place," I said. "They said the FBI was here."

Taking another bite of her pastry, Trooper Wright shrugged her shoulders. "Yeah, they were here—a while back, though. It looked like maybe they were going to try and take action, but then they shut it down and left. That was pretty much the end of it."

"Pretty much?" I asked.

She gave me a sneaky smile and wiped her lips with a napkin. "I got in sort of tight with their SAC, Special Agent in Charge, at the compound. Nice guy for a fed—seemed competent. Anyway, he was pretty ticked at having to pack up and leave. He hinted to me that things would've been different if he'd had it his way."

"You have his name?"

She took a sip, gave me that smile again, pulled out her phone, called up a contact, and turned the screen to me. Taking out my phone, we tapped, and I had the contact.

"Thanks," I said.

"I'm not saying it will go anywhere or even that he'll talk to you, but like I said, he seemed competent and took his job seriously. As for the townsfolk talk, could be just that—people get angry, have grudges, or just like to vent. Especially against the government. Who knows?"

The door opened, and in walked Tina in full uniform. Trooper Wright looked at her, and they head bobbed as Tina scanned the seating arraignment. Her scrunched face told me she didn't like it. She pulled a chair close to Lilly's other side and sat.

"Thanks so much for doing this. He give you any trouble?"

"He's got a story to tell, that's for sure. But he bought me coffee and a Danish."

I told Tina everything.

Tina looked at Trooper Wright with wide eyes. "Sounds like he almost got you in a gunfight."

Trooper Wright shook her head, chuckling. "No, it wasn't like that at all. Just a little tense."

Tina tilted her head, her tone pitched low like she was talking to a rookie. "If this man says they were about to kill him—they were about to kill him."

"*Try*," I said, "they were about to *try* and kill me."

Tina just shook her head, and I suddenly felt like Pasley when he kept correcting me on calling the OTA base camp a compound. *Maybe it was contagious.*

"Well ... I wasn't going to let them," I said in my defense.

Trooper Wright looked at Tina. "Is he serious?"

"Oh, he's serious. You can bet on that. I've seen him in action—up close and way too personal. You were a hair's breadth from investigating a double homicide."

"You mean, he ...," she looked at me, "you would have taken them on? You didn't have a gun."

"He wouldn't need one," Tina pointed a finger at me. "But you —*you* would have been in a world of trouble, mister."

There wasn't much to say, so I just sipped my coffee.

Trooper Lilly Wright ate the last of her Danish, sneaking glances at me from the corner of her eye while Tina finished scolding me. Looking out the window, I saw Max sitting by Tina's patrol car.

Viper was inside.

24

Max watched Viper through the window while catching everything else with his other senses. The traffic, people passing, voices, smells, the pups inside ... *his pups*.

The Alpha came out of the shop, accompanied by the two females.

"Look at that," said Trooper Wright. "Do they like each other?"

"*Like* is an understatement. I've got their pups in the back of the car."

"Oh, it's like that, is it?"

"That's how it is, all right," said Tina, going to the driver's side and opening the back door. She pulled out a carrier, and Viper jumped down, following her every movement.

Max was suddenly standing in front of her.

No one saw him move, but there he was.

"It's okay, Max," said the Alpha.

Max didn't care what the Alpha said just then. If Viper's alpha did anything to endanger his pups, he would stop her. But she calmly walked around the shop to a grassy clearing surrounded by several trees, set the carrier down, unzipped it, and let the six puppies quickly scatter about.

Max watched over them, observing everything—their small bodies, fluffy fur, the cars driving by, people walking. Viper sat to the side, eyeing Max and the pups carefully. Max went to her next, and they exchanged scent locations.

An instant later, one of the pups tried to climb a tree but fell onto his back, whimpering and crying. Simultaneously, another got a long stem he was chewing stuck in his throat and began hacking dramatically to dislodge it. Viper went to the turtled pup and nuzzled him back to his belly.

Gil's chosen puppy, Thor, bounded up to Max and bit him on the left leg, gnawing and growling while Max looked down at him, unfazed.

"Oh," exclaimed Lilly, "they are so cute!"

"Out here, they're cute," agreed Tina, "but at my house? Chewing up the couch, the loveseat, the cabinets, the coffee tables—the walls —not so cute."

"We don't call them malingators for nothing," said Gil.

"Or malinraptors," said Tina.

"Or malinranhas," said Gil.

Tina looked at him. "You just made that up."

"No, everyone knows that one."

"You're full of bologna," laughed Tina.

"No, really. It's a combination of Malinois and a piranha ...."

"I know what you're combining. But you just made it up."

"Okay, maybe," said Gil. "But it's pretty good, don't you think?"

"Accurate, anyway," said Tina.

"Malineaglefang," said Gil.

"Okay, that's enough," said Tina.

"It's from *Cobra Kai*," said Gil.

"I get that one," said Lilly. "I love *Cobra Kai*. It's so campy."

Tina shook her head. "Well, in any case, will you help me get rid of them?"

"Get rid of them?" asked Gil.

"Yeah, you know, find them good homes. Billy wants one for Irmgard, and I'll keep one to train up on the sly. You want Thor. What about the rest? I'm no breeder—I have zero experience at this puppy thing."

"Sure," Gil agreed. "No problem at all."

"They really are destroying my house," moaned Tina.

"I'm aware," said Gil. "But they *are* cute."

"Super cute," said Tina.

"Super-trooper cute," said Lilly.

Max didn't say anything, just sat there, Thor chewing at his leg.

THE GARDENER DROVE BACK to the assembly alone and in silence. He was praying—asking the One Tree for guidance. At first, he'd been upset about the trooper's interruption, but now that he'd calmed and was conversing with the *mea ao 'ē*, he saw it was for the best. If this Gil Mason had connections, his disappearance might make waves. The Gardener didn't like waves.

Besides, Mason would be out of Galena by now, back to Denver, which is what Kane wanted anyway. Still, Pasley had been foolish in letting Mason make the phone call. *What had he been thinking?—that he was a regular cop with their limitations?* Kane had stressed the point to him and knew he would never make that mistake again. If he did, he'd take his turn under the One Tree.

Kane remembered the night he'd first been visited by the alien. All that day, he'd been on the run from the police, as well as a rival gang. Everything started when he trespassed into another gang's turf. The island of Oahu is the hub of Hawaiian gang activity, and Kane had decided to prove his bravery by walking through the Waipahu streets, home to the TSK (True Samoan Kings) hood. He'd made it three-quarters of the way through and was beginning to think he was home free when two TSKs stepped out from the entrance of a graffiti-covered apartment complex. They fell in behind him, and he intuitively understood that he would not be able to complete his journey unmolested.

He stopped, turned, and faced them. Even back then, Kane was big—naturally muscular and tall. The TSKs were practically twins, tatted and shirtless, lean but firm. Without pausing, they advanced toward Kane. Kane pulled out his knife, a short machete he'd practiced with for years. As if on cue, the TSKs pulled out knives of their own—wide-bladed instruments of death they wore on sheaths at the back of their waistbands.

The teens spread apart while still coming forward. Moving swiftly, Kane swung at the closest. The attacker tried to dodge but misgauged Kane's speed. Kane's short machete cleanly sliced into the teen's forearm, just above the wrist, severing tendons and ligaments. Without a sound, the boy dropped his weapon and clutched his arm, blood pouring. Kane followed through, punching him in the face and knocking him down. Bringing the knife back into play, Kane managed to block the second attacker's blade with his own, raising a shower of sparks.

The two squared off in a slow revolving dance, slightly bent at the waist, arms wide. Kane knew he had to end this quickly. Help would come for them, but not for him. He feinted high, and when the Samoan King moved to block, Kane stepped in close, jabbing forward, plunging the tip of his blade into the boy's ribs below his sternum. The machete was designed for slashing, not straight in punctures, causing it to slant off a bone, tearing a long gash, and saving the boy's life. The King tried to slash back, but Kane kneed him in the groin, and he was out of the fight.

A swarm of teens was suddenly running from the complex. Kane had proved what he wanted to prove. He turned and ran, sweeping past high buildings, making sharp corners, jumping low fences and ditches. Kane was faster and more agile, but they had numbers—and the word was spreading. He lost them for a time, but lookouts spotted him, relayed his position, and the chase resumed. At some point, the police joined in on the search, and the game continued until nightfall.

Kane found refuge in a drainage tunnel near an apartment building. He lay as flat as possible and pulled slimy debris over his face and body, including a moldy, discarded pair of pants clumped in mud. Overhead, people ran about, shouting and talking, all looking for him. Kane knew they would find him—it was just a matter of time. There were too many of them. They would find him and kill him. The police would not be able to stop them—not here, in their hood.

It was then, when he was sure death was imminent, that the *mea ao ʻē*—the alien—visited. Kane was exhausted, wet, gasping for air, looking up at the rusted metal of the culvert when the ridged pattern began to change. And suddenly, the ridged pattern changed, turning slowly, a vortex of rotating space, stars forming and swirling, going faster and faster until in the center he saw the most beautiful light he'd ever experienced. The light grew so bright he could barely stand its intensity. It pulsed and throbbed and coalesced into a shape—the shape of the mea ao'e.

The being spoke into his mind, telling Kane he would not die tonight. It described the great things in store for him, the empire they would build together, and the power and influence it would bestow on Kane. It told Kane of the One Tree.

When the *mea ao ʻē* finished, the rain came—not the usual light Hawaiian rain that fell nearly every day, but a downpour, a cascading sheet of torrential rain that drove everyone to seek shelter, obscuring visibility to a few feet. Kane left the trap of the flooding culvert and walked unobstructed out of Waipahu and back to his own hood—his life and his mission forever changed.

No one could stop his destiny. A lone private investigator, least of all.

～

PAPPY GRINNED at Yolanda as she handed him a steaming cup of coffee. "So you like this kid?"

"Billy's a good boy. I would have been upset if you'd hurt him."

"I wouldn't hurt him," said Pappy. "Just teaching a lesson, that's all. Kids today need lessons—lessons they should have learned a lot sooner.

"But that knife," she said. "I was really scared for him."

"That little thing? Wouldn't have made it past the nerve bundle. A little stick now and then builds character."

"He has character," said Yolanda. "More than Mr. Mason. That man could learn a few things."

Pappy chuckled. "Mason's not much of a rule follower. Caused him trouble in the Marines more than once. But his heart is good. And there's no one I'd rather have by my side in a fight. Goes a little berserk sometimes, but never so crazy he loses sight of the big picture. I remember one time in the pit, a group of about fifteen hodgies ambushed us out in the hills a few miles from town. An RPG —a Rocket Propelled Grenade—took out our lead Humvee, killing four Marines inside. Gil and his dog Strider were in another Humvee right behind the one that took the grenade. He and that dog were out so fast that I didn't even see the door open.

"Another rocket hit the tail end of the vehicle, sending it over on its side. No one saw where the shots were coming from, but Strider knew. He took right off after them, Gil running full tilt behind him. I tried shouting—ordering him back, knowing he was going straight into a hornet's nest—but either he couldn't hear me or acted like he didn't. Either way, me and a bunch of the boys ran after him. By the time we got to the crest of the hill, Strider had gutted two soldiers and was tearing at a third. Gil had a bad guy stretched out in front of him and was hand-to-hand with another. The rest of the ragheads saw us, and the firefight was on, bullets flying everywhere.

"Strider finished his guy and was about to help Gil when three hodgies shot into the pup. Tore him to pieces. I saw Gil change then. I'd seen him mad before, but nothing like this. Mad wasn't what he was just then. Not angry, not crazy. It was something else. Like ... like a demon had been let loose. I'm not a big Bible-thumper like him, so I ain't saying this lightly, but what he *did*—the *way* he did it—didn't seem possible. I don't know how many he killed, not exactly, because, like I said, bullets were whizzing, but it was a lot. And it was messy ... *nasty*. Everything he touched turned into a weapon—a killing thing —first his guns, then his knives, then helmets, rocks, fists, feet ...

teeth. When the battle ended, he was covered head to boot in gore. He didn't say anything, just picked up what was left of poor Strider and carried him back to the vehicles. Gil was crying.

"Other than the first four killed by the RPG, we didn't lose anyone else—just two with minor wounds. The enemy was dead—all of them. I credit our survival to Gil and Strider. We would have been pinned down—they could have taken as long as they needed to eat away at us.

"So, you see? Even though Gil was rocked with rage or whatever it was, he didn't just go insane. I've seen men go crazy in combat. This wasn't that. He knew exactly what he was doing the entire time. What he was doing was horrible, but that's war. And he did it right—*smart, brutal, efficient*."

"That sounds like him. But he comes in late all the time. And does he tell me when he's coming back? No, hardly ever. What am I supposed to tell clients? Very frustrating."

Taking a gulp of coffee, Pappy nodded.

"Now, on *that,* we agree," said Pappy. "He can indeed be frustrating. Speaking of which, where is he?"

"Up in the mountains somewhere," said Yolanda. "He got information on the wife and son of that Marine friend of yours and went to check on it."

"Really? That was fast. Where did he go?"

"A town named Galena, but that's all he told me. See? I'm his secretary, but does he tell me anything? It's hard taking care of the office when he keeps me in the dark like this."

"Galena, huh? Maybe I'll take a little jaunt up that way."

He finished his coffee in another gulp, not at all fazed by its heat.

25

Billy parked in the same alley where he'd shot off the bum's earlobe. He looked up at his target's apartment—nice place. It wasn't the Ritz—no valet out front or uniformed door greeter—but upscale, nonetheless. His car was blocking passage, but he figured it was too late in the day for trash removal or deliveries. Private vehicles could just back up the way they'd come. He didn't figure this would take long anyway.

The air was getting chilly. A steady breeze tousled his hair when he stepped from the car. The aroma of Chinese spices and sizzling meats, rich and exotic, tempted his appetite, but a few paces closer to the building, the experience shifted to that of open dumpsters filled with rotted leftovers and waste products. Billy hurried to the back door.

Locked. Keycard access.

Looking to the left and the right, he noticed security cameras prominently mounted at several locations. It took him about twenty seconds to get the door open. He doubted the place had on-site security cops, and there would be no reason for anyone to check the feeds —he wasn't going to kill the guy after all. He just needed to ask a few questions and, if he was lucky, get the tree. Afterward, he would head home for a nice dinner with Tina and Irmgard.

That was the plan.

Once inside, he took the elevator to the eighth floor and followed the little mounted signs to Larry Gold's apartment. Before he could knock, the door opened, and there stood his target.

"Can I help you?" Larry Gold was around five-eleven, a buck eighty or so, with well-groomed sandy blond hair and super bright pale blue eyes that looked almost silver. He wore a starched white shirt, unbuttoned down one from the collar, crisp gray slacks, and brown loafers. One hand was behind his back.

Billy instantly thought, gun.

Flashing his stolen badge, Billy said, "Police. I need to ask you a few questions if you don't mind." He stashed the badge.

"That's an Arvada badge," said Larry Gold. "This is Denver." He said it quietly—not argumentatively—just a statement.

"It's about an incident that happened down in Arvada," said Billy.

"Up," said Larry.

"What's that?"

"Up," repeated Larry. "Arvada is north of here, also higher in elevation. So, technically, up."

"Yeah," said Billy, feeling the guy's weirdness like a wave of heat, "right. Mind if I come in?"

Larry looked at Billy with those silver eyes, tilted his head slightly, and said, "Not at all." He stepped aside, holding the door wider.

Billy walked into a nightmare.

TOBY CRIED INTO HIS PILLOW. Sagebrush had punched him really hard in the stomach a few minutes earlier. Sagebrush, whose old name was Cory Macon, had been making fun of Toby's mother, and Toby had pushed him for it. Sagebrush was three years older and much taller than Toby.

Toby loved his mother. He wished she'd never brought him to this terrible place, but he still loved her. He wished she was here in the room now instead of ... out there.

Toby would sneak out whenever he could to visit her. It was dangerous, and he knew she didn't want him to do it, but he had to— he missed her so much. He would talk to her—sometimes for a long time—but she never answered. She never *spoke* to him with words. She was too afraid. Afraid *for* him. But still, he could hear her, not with his ears, but in his heart. It was like praying to God back when he had done that.

His father told him that God hears all our prayers and answers them—we just can't hear His answers with our ears. Instead, we feel them in our hearts. It was like that with his mother. She didn't speak, just stared. But sometimes, he could hear her thoughts in his heart. And that was okay. She loved him, and he loved her, and that was what mattered. It made him feel less lonely.

A little less.

Sometimes he thought she was seeing him, but usually, she seemed to be staring *through* him—as though the Gardener had broken her mind in some way that Toby couldn't grasp or understand.

Thinking of his mother made him cry harder until his pillow had a big wet spot wider and longer than his cheek. The door opened, and Timber came in. He crossed the room and went to his bunk, where he began digging through a bag.

"What's wrong, Leaf?" asked Timber, glancing at him.

He hated the name *Leaf*. He hated all the made-up names. The Gardener named them all when they joined. Toby hated the Gardener. The Gardener had punished his mother, keeping them apart. And he had done bad things, nasty things, to his mother—to his mother and to Toby. That's why his mother had fought—why the Gardener had punished her. She hadn't fought because of what he had done to her—she accepted that. She fought because the Gardener wanted to do bad things to Toby. She fought, but the

Gardener did it anyway. He'd done it to Timber too. To Timber and River.

"Cory punched me," said Toby through his sniffles.

"Don't call him that," warned Timber, whose real name was Mark. "You know better. The Gardener would whip you if he heard it."

They weren't allowed to use any real names—not ever—but Toby hated the lie names. He knew Timber wouldn't tell on him. Toby liked Timber, and Timber was big enough not to be afraid of Sagebrush. Timber liked River too, although he thought River was stupid for getting into trouble all the time.

"What did you do to make him punch you?" asked Timber.

"He was making fun of my mo-mo-mother," said Toby, trying to hold back the sobs.

Timber stopped looking through the bag and sat beside Toby, putting a hand on his shoulder. "Yeah, that sounds like him. So, what did you do?"

"I pushed him."

"How hard?"

"Hard as I could," Toby looked up at him, a little smile starting at the corners of his lips.

"I'll bet you did," chuckled Timber, "you little fighter, you. Was it worth it?"

The smile got bigger, the tears beginning to dry. "It sure was!"

"Then, there you go. Stop crying and get your butt down to dinner before they list you as absent and give you a whipping."

"Why does he act like that?" asked Toby, swiping at his cheeks with the heel of a hand.

"I don't know. Maybe people treated him bad, and he doesn't know any better. You know his mom. She's pretty harsh—his dad too. Not like our mothers. Mine's nice, so's yours."

"Would you beat him up for me?" asked Toby.

"Let me see," Timber pointed at Toby's stomach.

Toby pulled up his shirt, showing Mark the knuckled red splotches on his belly.

"That ain't nothing. Not worth us getting a beating if he squeals," he leaned closer, "and that turd probably would." He leaned back, grinning. "Besides, you said it yourself—it was worth it. So, forget Sagebrush, and let's get down to the mess hall."

The bigger boy patted Toby on the shoulder and held the door for him.

26

I waited for the sun to go down, then parked a mile down the road from the compound, off the dirt road, and under some trees. No one from the road would be able to see me—not that there would *be* anyone on the road to see me anyway. I hadn't spotted a car in nearly an hour. To say we were off the beaten path would be more than an understatement.

I'd done some shopping back in town—bought a car seat, snacks, drinks, a cooler, and other assorted odds and ends. I didn't really expect to locate Teresa and Toby tonight. I was just planning a little reconnaissance to get the lay of the land. I'd return tomorrow for the Ramirez family. But one never knows ... I might get lucky. And if I did, I wanted to be able to move fast and get them out of there.

My night vision binocs spotted the guard towers. A single sentry stood in each, rifle in hand. They were far enough apart that I could drop them, one at a time, with my suppressed AR, and none of the others would know. Not that it had come to that. Not yet. But if they were willing to murder me back at the jail, just to get me out of the way, what wouldn't they do? I didn't know the whole setup, but I'd learned enough to tell me they were a very bad lot.

I'd left Tina and Lilly in town. Tina was hours out and had to get back. She had a lot of leeway due to her position and the fact that her K9, Viper, was still on light duty, but she still had responsibilities and supervisors to answer to. Lilly was about to get off duty and had offered to go with me, but I declined. She'd hamper my style. Besides, I didn't want either of them too heavily involved in case things turned dirty. Plausible deniability could mean the difference between a stern talking to and job loss or, worse, prison, maybe death. After all, we were talking about a cult, a compound, armed guard towers, possible kidnapping, and bad people in charge who weren't afraid to take good people out of the way. Permanently.

Plus, it was comforting to know the cavalry was just over the hill if I needed them ... not that I would. I had my own troops sitting in the backseat in the guise of Max and Pilgrim.

My cell vibrated. It was FBI Agent Lance Kemp, the SAC whose number Trooper Lilly Wright had given me at the coffee shop.

"Gil Mason," I answered. "Thanks for calling me back, Agent Kemp."

"And why, exactly, am I calling a private investigator from Colorado?" he asked.

"It has to do with an organization called the OTA in a mountain town called Galena."

There was a pause.

"Go ahead."

I filled him in on everything I had so far—Tina, Toby, what happened at the police station, how I'd gotten his number.

Another pause. "Okay," he said as if he'd come to a decision. "I'm impressed, and I'm not easily impressed. I'll tell you this right off—I think you're right about almost being disappeared from that police station. It wouldn't be the first time. One of our agents, a good friend named Peter Simon, was undercover at the compound. He went missing. No one has ever heard from him since. That's how I was finally able to get things started when we came out. We were looking for him. Didn't find him, though. Got pulled out before we could nail anything down."

"Why did you get shut down?" I asked.

Another pause. "Okay, look, I checked you out before making this call. I have friends in high places—Marine Corps Intelligence. You have an outstanding reputation. I also know about Majoqui Cabrera. We had our sights on him and MS-13. You did us a solid by ending that trash. Everyone says you can be trusted—that you don't tell tales out of school. Is all that true?"

"It is."

"Okay," he continued. "A group of senators shut me down—I won't name names. It doesn't matter anyway, but they have a lot of pull, meaning they're on all the right committees. I don't know who greased whose palm or what dirt somebody had on somebody else, but they went to work fast, and we were stopped with strict orders not to file the case. And that was the end of it."

"Yeah, I understand. I've been up close and personal with dirty politicians before."

"You mean Senator Marsh? That's another bullet you helped us dodge."

"Were you able to get anything on the OTA before you were shut down?"

"Lots of maybes. Things I know in my gut are true, but nothing backed by hard evidence."

"Such as?"

"The main guy, Kane, is a David Koresh, a Jim Jones, maybe worse. He's got all the women up there, the kids too. He was busted twice in his twenties for being a pedo in Hawaii. Swings both ways. Kidnapped a twelve-year-old girl first, then later a nine-year-old boy. Got away with it both times. He was a petty thief who worked his way up to robbery and eventually did some wet work for a hard-core Hawaiian gang.

"One day, he had a revelation from *aliens* about the One Tree. Said it came to him in a vision, or a *visitation*—whatever. The cult took off like a fire, and before the year was up, he had followers in seven states. Now he's everywhere."

"And your agent ... your friend?"

"Oh, I figure he's still up there, buried somewhere on the

compound grounds. One day, when Kane goes nuclear like all these nut-jobs do, eventually, I'll get back in there. I'll find him. I made a promise to his wife and kids. I mean to keep it."

"Anything you could send me that might be helpful?" A final pause. "No, nothing that could be used in court. But let me say this— be careful. This guy is bad news. I mean really bad—one of the worst I've ever seen. I'm not religious, but in my years with the Bureau, I've seen evil. And this guy is evil."

MAX WATCHED the Alpha from the back, sensing his tension. Pilgrim slept beside Max, snoring loudly. The big Shepherd had slurped some water from the spill proof bowl on their way up the mountain, then flopped down on the rubber mat before closing his eyes and drifting off. His paws twitched, and his eyes rolled under their lids as he dreamed of chasing a bad guy from his past.

Even from here, Max could see the towers. He saw the men's movements and smelled wafting tendrils of their scent brought to him along the breeze. He had them, all four of them, locked into his memory archives. The Alpha was tense, which meant they were a danger. Max could hunt them, find them, kill them. The Belgian Malinois was not afraid of them or their weapons. He detected their weaknesses. They were all afraid of something.

Max was afraid of nothing.

TOBY FINISHED his dinner and chores, then said his evening prayers and listened to and repeated the One Tree's words and laws. Timber had fallen fast asleep and was snoring lightly from the bunk across from him. Toby tried to sleep, but Sagebrush's words about his mother and the look on the bigger boy's face as he punched him kept replaying behind his eyelids. And then Toby's mother's face drifted into his thoughts. He felt tears well up, hot and thick and impossible to stop. He missed her so much. She was so pretty, so happy and nice to him—at least she had been before they came here. At first, things had been good. The Gardener and the other men and women had been so caring, so interested in them.

That was before the rules and the punishments—before the beatings and before that awful night when the Gardener had tried to take him. Toby's mother had stopped him that night, but the Gardener hit her. And then Toby bit him. The Gardener threw Toby into a wall, and his mother rushed at the big man, scratching at him with her nails. The Gardener grabbed her by the throat.

Toby sat up, pushing the thoughts away. He scrubbed at his eyes with his hands, feeling his breath catch in his chest and little hiccups burp past his lips.

If he didn't stop, Timber would wake up.

Slipping out of bed, Toby quietly put on his clothes and coat. He carefully opened his window, slid over the sill, and gently set foot on the ground below. In the distance, he saw the giant towers where guards used searchlights to scan the area. Toby wasn't worried about them. He'd been sneaking out at least twice a week and knew their pattern well. Most of the time, the lights just roamed over the fences. Toby didn't go to the fences. He didn't sneak out to escape—he had nowhere else to go.

Not that people *never* tried to escape. Some did, not many, but some. Once caught, they were brought before the One Tree and punished. Toby had watched an eleven-year-old boy get four stripes for sneaking out and stealing ice cream from the kitchen. After the beating, the boy had to spend a day and a night in the box. There was no food in the box—no food, no water, and certainly no ice cream.

And, of course, there was River. He hadn't been the same since his beating, even after the bread Toby had given him. So no, Toby did not go out to escape or steal treats—he snuck out for one thing and one thing only.

Toby snuck out to see his mother.

~

GETTING past the lights of the towers was simple for me. The guards did not appear to be trained soldiers. They stuck to set routines, arcing the searchlights slowly back and forth, probably bored with the repetitious movement, lacking the excitement they craved. Experienced soldiers usually come to a place in their career where they relish the quiet times ... times when their lives are not in immediate danger, taking what steps they can to ensure it lasts as long as possible. They know the importance of vigilance and attention to detail.

The wire snips made short work of the chain link. After Max and I slipped through, I wedged the cut portions back in on themselves. I had donned an olive-green hoodie, olive-green sweatpants, matching hiking boots, and dark green gloves. Most people think head-to-toe black is best for night work, but the truth is, black often registers on the retina with very little to no movement. The brain correlates the contrasting blackness against the greens and browns of nature, leaving a black hole, taking notice of the difference. Darker greens lend a more significant air of invisibility. I sported a fancy set of night- and thermal-vision goggles and had painted my face with a camouflage stick. Under my shirt, I wore a level-three bullet-resistant vest ... just in case.

Max and I maneuvered twenty yards down and in from the fence line, where I dropped my backpack, put Max in a *platz and guard,* and set off towards the silhouettes of the buildings I saw scattered about a hundred yards in. Max was far enough away from the fence that the lights should miss him, and if they didn't, his reddish-blond coloring blended with the dead and dying grass and scrub brush making him nearly invisible. Pilgrim rested outside the car, waiting for my call if needed.

Moving fast, I crouch-ran to a small group of trees and hid behind them. My night-vision goggles worked like a charm, and I saw my path was clear to the first building ... a shed. In front of the shed were a table and a full-sized snowcat with a flatbed cattle trailer attached. Silently I came up against its fence-facing wall. Looking back, I searched for Max. It took me several seconds to spot him—he was that still—and I even knew where to look.

I took three more short sprints playing the building-hugging game before I saw anyone ... two men, both armed with hunting rifles. They were laughing and talking as they quietly walked with the weapons slung over their shoulders. As they moved along in front of the building across from me, I saw that they had scopes but no visible night-vision gear. I had gone prone, watching and listening, as still as Max.

I was wearing a green tactical belt with a right-handed plastic green holster that held my Smith and Wesson 4506. On the left, I had a tactical flashlight, a left-handed holster with a Glock 19, and a Black Widow switchblade that, when thumbed from the side, snapped out a four-inch blade straight from the front. I carried a Tanto knife on my left ankle and a slim little G43X Glock on my right. I'd left the shotgun, with collapsible stock, in my backpack ... *in case Max needed it*. My suppressed AR hung against my chest from its three-point sling. I'd jammed the rest of the thick wide tactical belt with magazines, filled to capacity, for my guns ... running out of ammo in a fight against an army is never a good idea.

Once the two men were out of sight, I ran to another group of trees. That's when I heard it ...*muffled* ... like the wailing of a distant banshee or the haunted cries of a guilt-ridden ghost. But I don't believe in banshees or ghosts.

Tucking my AR high into my shoulder, I sighted in and advanced.

27

Pappy was off to a late start. The mother of Lance Corporal Matthew Wiggins had called, crying, asking him to please come back to answer more questions. Familiar with Gil's skills and abilities, Pappy thought nothing of altering his course to visit her. She lived in Fort Morgan, hours out of the way, but she was all alone. Her husband had died in a car crash three months earlier, and stage four lung cancer left her only half a year to live. Under Pappy's command, her son, Matt, had taken a sniper's round while trying to save a fellow Marine. Both died right there, but Matt was a true hero, sacrificing himself while attempting to save his friend. No Marine could do more.

Pappy spent several hours with Mrs. Wiggins, eliciting warm smiles as he recounted tales of Matt's pranks and the hilarious stories he told at every opportunity. After Pappy left, she'd thought up new questions she wanted to ask, so he happily returned, making the long trek to recount other acts of bravery and kindness he'd seen from her son, as well as from other soldiers on the base. Mrs. Wiggins cried a few times but, again, smiled and even laughed on occasion. Finally, she hugged Pappy tight, kissed him on the cheek, and let him go.

At last, he was back en route to Gil—a very long drive. But that was okay.

Pappy knew Gil would be fine.

~

TOBY BYPASSED the Box as he made his way into the trees away from the main buildings. The breeze was picking up, but there was no snow—not yet, anyway—although it smelled like there could be soon.

Two men walked out of the trees, heading toward the buildings. They were too far away to see him, but Toby stayed still, just in case. He knew the men, not their real names—he couldn't remember those —but the names the Gardener had given them before Toby and his mother came to live here. Both had always been nice to him. They smiled a lot, and neither had ever punished him for anything, but Toby knew they would turn him over to the Gardener if they found him out here.

When they passed out of sight, Toby navigated his way through the maze of trees, mostly pine, thick with needles and smelling fresh and clean and Christmassy. Toby missed Christmas. The Gardener did not allow Christmas celebrations.

It didn't take him long to find his mother. He had to move the dirt away so they could hold hands through the slots of her cage. It took several minutes, but once he finished, they gripped fingers through the narrow space. As always, he kept his voice low when speaking to his mother and told her about the incident with Sagebrush. She didn't respond with words, but he heard her words of comfort in his heart. He clutched her grip in his and cried as he poured out his sorrow and fears.

At first, he was quiet, but as he went on, he began stuttering and hiccupping until his words mushed into incoherent gibbering moans that became wails of grief. His mother wanted him to stay quiet—he knew she did—but he just couldn't, even though he understood the danger. He squeezed her fingers tightly, pressing his face against the wooden slats, his tears falling against their combined flesh, joining them as one. He would climb in with her if he could, but he didn't fit—he'd tried on other nights. He wasn't small enough, nor was he strong enough to break the wood. Toby knew he would have to move more dirt, but the ground was just too hard.

And so, he cried, knowing he had to stay quiet but unable to stop. "Leaf? Is that you?"

Looking up, Toby saw Riverstone and the other laughing man who had been by the buildings a few minutes before. They were both pointing rifles at him, and neither was laughing now.

"Oh man," said Riverstone, "you messed up, son. *Really* bad."

IN THE DISTANCE, I saw two men and a boy. The frightened boy was kneeling on the ground looking at the men. Tears had turned the dirt on his face to mud.

I recognized the boy as Leaf ... *Toby.*

The men I'd seen walking fire watch earlier were pointing their rifles at him. I didn't know their intentions, but I knew what I knew about the Gardener and how he planned to have me killed in a police station just a few hours ago. Could be they *weren't* about to kill Toby to get rid of the evidence that they were holding him against his will. Could be they had a perfectly innocent reason for pointing weapons at a cowering, kneeling, crying, little child.

Could be.

I shot both of them through their brainpans with my suppressed AR. They dropped like the dead weight they were. Toby watched them fall, then turned and spotted me.

"Mommy!" he cried, turning his face toward the ground.

I reached him in an instant, covered his mouth with my free hand, wrapped his chest with my other arm, and lifted him off the ground. He was holding someone's hand, but as I rose, the violence of the movement broke them apart. White fingers poked through splintered boards, and I saw a forearm covered in dirt, a portion of shoulder and face ... half-lidded eyes glazed in death.

It was Teresa.

Beneath my hand, Toby continued to scream for his dead, buried mother. Rage equaling the boy's terror and loss burned in me. I took a half step toward the buildings where I assumed the Gardener must be but stopped.

The Gardener would have to wait.

I had a job to do ... a mission. That mission was to get Toby safely to his father. Fighting an army without getting the boy hurt or killed would be difficult ... maybe impossible.

Holding him off the ground, close to my body, I turned and ran back toward Max.

But I'd be back ... *oh yes* ... and not even the *Terminator* would be able to stop me.

28

Billy opened his eyes. Swaying lightly back and forth, he was hanging upside down, his head a few feet from the marble floor. There was something shoved in his mouth and tied around his head. His wrists and elbows were secured with a thick rope behind his bare back. His knees and ankles were also expertly tied. Billy recognized skilled rope work when he saw it ... *felt* it. He'd worked with some real pros during his time with the Family and knew how much pride they took in their work. Whoever had trussed him up like this would be feeling very proud.

Billy planned on changing that—if he could get loose.

Taking stock of his situation, he saw his clothes stacked neatly on a chair.

No blindfold.

He had on his underwear—he hoped that meant no pervert stuff.

Whatever was in his mouth kept triggering his gag reflex. He tried to push against it with his tongue, but it was wedged too tightly, forcing him to retch. He stopped, afraid he might throw up and asphyxiate.

How had he gotten here?

The last things he remembered were knocking, the door opening, and ... *something* ... he couldn't quite pull what it was into focus ... and then ... *this*.

Continuing his scan of the large master bedroom, he noted the bed, a ceiling fan, two end tables, a dresser, a walk-in closet, and a door he thought must lead to a master bath. The room was plush, manly, extremely neat, and tidy. On one of the end tables sat the stolen bonsai tree.

Billy was stunned.

Just like that, he'd found it.

And if it hadn't been for the bum who tried to throw poop at him, he'd have had the culprit even sooner. Billy felt the blood accumulating in his head and wondered how long he'd been like this— trussed and hanging upside down. Getting untied was the first order of business.

He thought back to what he knew about this nut client of Gil's psychiatrist:

Larry Gold

Thirty-one years old

White male

5'11"

180

Sandy blond hair

Possible late onset of schizophrenia

Pale blue eyes—*looked almost silver in the photo.*

Everything translated to crazy whack-job stealer of midget trees with a rope fetish.

Where was he? Billy twisted his shoulders and hips, turning his body so he could scan 360.

And there he was, sitting on a folding chair directly behind him, going through the contents of Billy's wallet.

Registering the rubber apron Larry Gold was wearing brought everything back—the door opening, Billy raising the stolen badge, the apron splashed in blood, the body lying on the table in the living room, the black plastic sheets covering every inch of the room and furniture.

Billy hadn't done a lot of *wet work* for the family, but he'd seen a few things. Almost instantly, he realized what was going on. Before he could react, a cattle prod had been jammed into his underarm, discharging a lightning bolt that blanked his mind.

And now here he was.

Larry Gold finished examining Billy's wallet and then looked at him. "You're not a cop—the opposite, I think. William Carlino, nephew of Nicholas Carlino, head of the Cosa Nostra. What do you want with me?"

Billy raised his eyebrows, signaling he couldn't very well answer with the gag in his mouth.

Larry Gold nodded and pointed a finger. "Right, of course. I doubt I need to tell you this, but I'll cut something off you if you scream— not that screaming will help. The walls are quite soundproof. Do we have an understanding?"

Billy gave a single short nod. Gold slid a scalpel under the gag and sliced it off. Motioning for Billy to open wider, he grabbed the corner of one of Billy's socks he'd used as the stuffing material and pulled it free.

Flexing his jaw and trying to get some spit back into his mouth, Billy said, "My sock? That is not cool, man."

"Better than your toes," said Gold, neatly setting the stocking on the marble beside his chair.

"Yeah," said Billy, "I guess."

"So?"

Billy shook his head. "I'm not here for you—I'm here for that." He head-bobbed toward the tree.

Larry Gold followed his gaze. "Explain."

"The guy you stole it from is my uncle's shrink. He wants it back, no questions asked. It's got sentimental value."

Larry Gold sat back in the chair. Billy noticed that he'd cleaned the blood off the apron sometime between zapping him and now.

Gold shook his head. "It's mine now. He can't have it back."

"You said you know who I am—who my uncle is. Do you want to go to war with us over a tree?"

"It's too late for that," he said. "You saw what I was doing in the other room."

"Again," said Billy, "you know who we are, what we've done, what we do. You think I care about you going *Dexter* on some slob I don't know? Means nothing to me. So let me down, give me the tree, and we'll forget this ever happened."

"Right," said Gold. "And then you come back with your goons and play ... how did you put it? *Dexter* on *me*?"

"No," said Billy shaking his head. "You really think I want the other guys to know you got the best of me? Hung me upside down naked in your bedroom, and then just let me go? You think that's the reputation I want in an organization like the one my uncle runs?"

Larry Gold just stared at him.

"Dude," said Billy, "I'm a cage fighter, a chick magnet, Nick's favorite nephew—destined for big stuff in the Family. He finds out how easy you took me, that's it—I'm through. Ain't no way for me to come back. That's just how it works. So, far as I'm concerned, this never happened. You gave me the tree, we shook hands, and that's that. No hard feelings, no retaliation. It's just done, and we will never see each other again. You got my word on that. My word."

Gold seemed to be thinking it over. Of course, Billy planned to snap his neck the second he got down, but then Gold sighed, coming to a decision, and shook his head.

"Moot point," he said. "I won't give back the tree."

"Why not? It's just a plant, man. I'll buy you another one—two, three—whatever you want."

Gold's eyes slid to the tree, then back to Billy. "It's more than a tree. So much more."

Then Billy saw it in his eyes. It reminded him of what he'd seen in Gil's eyes on certain rare occasions. And for the first time since waking and finding himself in this weird predicament, he felt fear.

"It's my souvenir," said Larry Gold. "My ... trophy. I always take one from the target ... before I kill them."

29

Max watched as the men in the tower shined their spotlights around the fenced area. At one point, the light splashed directly over him, but he stayed so still that it passed by without slowing. Had the light hesitated, had the men come to investigate, Max would have killed them. But they didn't, and so they lived ... for now.

Max's thoughts turned to Viper and the pups, and a strange sensation swirled through his stomach. He wanted to see them ... make sure they were safe. He had been out hunting when the gray wolf slaughtered his brothers and sisters. Max had returned to find himself alone ... a pack of one. The urge to get up and go to them was overwhelming. Suddenly he was standing without even realizing it. The giant circle of light drifted a dozen yards ahead but did not stop.

They hadn't noticed.

Swiveling his head, Max saw Pilgrim by the car, stashed back in the trees, looking at him.

Pilgrim had noticed.

The Alpha had ordered Max to stay here.

Viper and his pups might be in danger.

Max listened for them and breathed in the scents carried on the breeze. They were too far away. If something happened, if something attacked ... *if they needed him* ... he would not be able to save them.

Turning, he ran full speed, easily slipping through the small square cut in the fence, not a hair catching on the sharp metal links, and landed in perfect stride. Pilgrim flashed by in his periphery, rising and watching as he shot past.

Pilgrim did not follow.

That was good. Pilgrim could not hope to keep up with Max, and Max would not wait for him.

Max had miles and miles to cover.

~

SEARCHING FOR MAX, I stopped at the shed. *Man, that dog could blend.* There was no trace of him, even with the night goggles. I switched to thermal imaging, knowing even Max couldn't hide his heat signature. But I was wrong ... no heat signature.

Maybe Max really was a vampire.

Appearing and disappearing like a ghost is one thing, but assuming ambient temperature? Not possible ... not for a living mammal anyway. And then it hit me. What if they'd killed Max?

Looking further, I saw Pilgrim's heat silhouette standing under the trees by the car. That put me a little at ease. If Pilgrim was still there, nothing could have happened to Max. Otherwise, Pilgrim would have broken command and gone to him.

Timing the lights, I sprinted to the fence, slid Toby through the hole, and followed almost simultaneously. Picking him up, I ran to my SUV.

No sign of Max.

~

BILLY WAS STARING into the face of madness. Larry Gold was a stone-cold psycho. Worse, a stone-cold *butchering* psycho. Billy had dealt with his share of butchering stone-cold psychos before. Sometimes it made them really good at their jobs, but usually, sooner or later, the psycho part would take over, and they'd do something beyond what even the Mafia leadership could put up with—kill the wrong guy, wife, kid, or pet, maybe be a little too free with the knife, torch, or tongs. *Whatever*. They eventually crossed the line and ended up in a desert grave or under a sports arena's cement foundation.

But having worked with psychos, he knew they could often be reasoned with—to a point, anyway.

"A trophy," said Billy. "You mean you're going to kill my uncle's therapist?"

Larry Gold's lips curved into a smile as he nodded slowly. "Yes, I am."

"Why?"

"Does it matter?" asked Gold.

"Just curious," said Billy. "My uncle seems to like him, and he doesn't like that many people. He's picky, especially with shrinks."

Larry Gold laughed at the *shrinks* reference. "Psychoanalysts like to label people. It makes them feel—*superior*. I make them feel—*less* superior."

"You mean when you're killing them."

"Yes," said Gold. "Dying slowly, painfully, is a very humbling experience. You'd be surprised how many devout atheists discover God during the process."

"Yeah," said Billy, "I've seen that myself."

"I suppose you have," said Gold.

"The guy in the other room—he a shrink too?"

"No," said Gold. "I have many interests. Mind doctors are only one of them."

"The mafia, another of them?" asked Billy.

Gold shook his head to the negative. "Not currently. But survival is always a priority."

"Yeah," said Billy, swaying slowly in a tight figure eight over the marble floor, "about that. I think we should come to some kind of arrangement."

"Arrangement," echoed Gold. "I was thinking of slitting your throat, bleeding you dry, chopping you up, and dumping you in trash cans around the city."

The blood in Billy's head was making him a bit dizzy.

"That could work," said Billy.

"Thank you," said Gold. "It always has in the past."

"That is," continued Billy, "If you don't mind getting the same treatment, only a lot worse, from my uncle."

"How's that?"

"When he finds out what you did," said Billy.

"And how's he supposed to do that?" asked Gold, smiling. "The police have been trying to discover who I am for years, but I'm too smart for them."

"Yeah, smarter than the cops. Big whoop, right? But this time, it won't be some minimally paid government worker coming for you, will it? No, this time, it'll be the smartest criminal minds on the planet, with billions of dollars and endless resources and informants behind them. And ... because it's me ... it'll be personal."

"They don't even know that you are here or why," said Gold, but Billy could see he was thinking.

"My car's chipped," said Billy. "All of our cars are. They'll know exactly where I was and for how long. As for the why? He sent me to find the tree. I did a little research, broke into Rick's office, made a list. My uncle has that list. You won't make it forty-eight hours."

Gold stared at Billy, thinking. "You know who I am," he said.

"So? A serial killer ain't nothing to me. I just want the tree."

"And you'll forget...," he waved a hand at the suspension cable holding Billy off the floor, "... all this?"

"Forgive," said Billy, "I'll forgive it. But forget? Not likely. Still, I've suffered worse. And like I said, we'll keep it between the two of us."

"How do I know you won't go to the police?" asked Gold.

"Really? The cops? We don't go to the cops for nothin'," said Billy. "Now look, the blood's going to my head, and it don't feel good. Let me down, give me the tree, and let's go our ways."

"I told you—I'm not giving you the tree."

"Yes, you are," said Billy. "That's non-negotiable. Also, pick another target. I don't think my uncle would be happy if his shrink went missing. Guys like you can always find someone else."

"You're not in much of a position to make demands," said Gold.

"Be that as it may," said Billy, "I'm getting a headache, and I hate headaches. Either cut me down or cut me up. You got sixty seconds— take it or leave it."

Gold sat there thinking, cocking his head this way and that.

Then he stood up without saying a word and pulled out the scalpel.

30

Pappy hated the civilian world. War was so much simpler. Someone needed killing—you killed them. You might have to hide the body—*not everyone agreed with Pappy's mindset*—but in wartime, that was easier too.

The loudmouths at the gas pump across from him were very irritating—not that he would kill them just for that, but they could use a good spanking. But even a spanking was forbidden in the civilian world, and he didn't have the time to cool his heels in a jail cell until things were sorted out. Pappy had an obligation to see if Gil needed help, so he ignored them.

Weird, though, how the states had become less civil than a war-torn country. The threat of instant death tended to mellow people—kept things from getting out of hand. When people feel invulnerable, they take offense at the smallest of things. In war, everyone knows the danger, and that everyone *is* a potential danger, so they tend to let the little things pass. Not everyone, of course. There were always exceptions. But exceptions were disposed to stepping over lines, and crossing too many lines got exceptions erased—bringing things back to status-quo.

Three guys and one girl were at the pump. They were all smoking, laughing, and drinking beer from bottles. None of them looked older than twenty. The girl, purple-haired and wearing a baggy red sweater, sat in the front passenger seat. She was singing to a song on the radio and flipping Pappy the bird. Her heavy eyeshadow, liner, and black lipstick made her look like a demon from the movies.

Two guys were in the backseat of the extended truck. They stared at Pappy, watching for a reaction, while the driver pumped the gas. Pappy ignored them, finished gassing, returned the nozzle, and screwed on the cap. Taking a last swig of his beer, one of the boys opened the backdoor and stepped out. Before the kid could get himself busted up, Pappy started his vehicle and pulled away. Pappy saw the kid toss the bottle at him in the rearview mirror. It didn't come close, shattering harmlessly on the asphalt.

Pappy shook his head.

The world had gone crazy while he was off fighting.

Or was he just getting old?

Maybe.

Still, Pappy knew who he was, what he was, and his course of action. The mission was always the priority, and his current mission was to get to Gil and help him to find Teresa and Toby Ramirez. The brats would have to wait another day to be spanked. Besides, they weren't his responsibility. He didn't have children of his own, and they weren't his troops, so why let their rude behavior bother him?

But wasn't that really the problem? People looking the other way, not getting involved, letting punks act like punks instead of keeping them in line? Not long ago, if a man swore in front of women and children, he would have been put in his place. Now, the women and children were just as bad. That hadn't happened by magic. No, it happened because good people were tricked into thinking they shouldn't do anything—that they should just let anyone do whatever they wanted, no matter how rude, nasty, gross, or vile.

Pappy was no saint. He didn't know much about God, or if there even was one. He wasn't like Gil. But he knew evil—he'd seen plenty of evil. He knew the only way to stop evil was to kill it, or at least pummel it down as hard as you could, so that it took a while to build back up.

No, the civilian world was anything but civil. Pappy needed to finish this as fast as possible and return to war where things made sense.

~

MAX FELT the tingle on his collar—*the Alpha.*

He stopped.

Viper, his pups.

But the Alpha.

The genetic imprinting of pack mentality compelled him. Turning, he sprinted full speed back toward the Alpha, not liking it.

Not liking it at all.

~

AFTER ACTIVATING the vibration on his collar ordering his return, I left Max's door open. I then put Toby in the car seat and strapped him in. He hadn't spoken a word since I found him crying for his mother. Of course, I was a pretty scary sight due to my size, outfit, camo paint, and guns ... not to mention I'd just killed two men in front of him, grabbed him up, and tossed him in the car.

I pulled the Kevlar panels from my duty bag and draped them over, and around him. Strapping them tight with their velcro fasteners, just in case, leaving a section open around his face so he could breathe. As I got behind the steering wheel, I glanced in the rearview mirror and saw Max sitting behind me. I hadn't heard him, hadn't felt the SUV jiggle ... he was just there ... and he didn't look happy.

"You left your post, mister," I said, and my voice was as unhappy as he looked.

Max didn't say anything.

Just as I started the car, a spotlight illuminated the trees above us. Bullets pelted the hood, the trees, and the ground all around. Spinning the Escalade, the movement slamming Max's door closed, I gunned it, tires spitting dirt and grass as we accelerated out of their range. In the mirror, I scanned Toby's face through the small opening of Kevlar. He looked blank, probably in shock. That made me mad.

They'd murdered his mother, shot at us, and caused him trauma —*who knew how much*—that could easily damage him for the rest of his life. It made me rethink having not gone for the Gardener when I had the chance. Too late now, but as I'd promised myself earlier, there would be a time.

I made it back to the road and screamed down and around the mountain, bypassing the small town and heading toward the highway.

"You okay back there, Toby?" I asked.

Nothing.

"Your dad sent me," I said. "He sent me to get you and your mother."

"My mommy's dead," said Toby, his voice sounding as dead as his mother's partially buried corpse.

"I know," I said. "I know. I'm sorry. But you're safe now. I'll take you to your father."

"My daddy's dead too. He died in the war."

"No, Toby," I said. "Your dad's alive. You're safe now."

"The Gardener won't let me leave," he said. "He won't let you leave either. He'll punish us and put us in the Box. He'll put us with Mommy."

"No," I said, "I won't let that happen."

"You can't stop it," said Toby, "no one can. He has the One Tree."

I was about to respond as I careened around a bend at sixty miles an hour when I saw a truck with a snowplow blade swerve into my lane. It was overflowing with men packing rifles and shooting at us. I tried to dodge them, but the truck swerved with and into me. Bullets punched through the windshield, spiderwebbing the glass and flashing past my face. Then, I felt a tremendous impact.

We were spinning.

I saw the truck disappear over the mountain's edge, the men

screaming. I tried to steer into the skid but realized I wouldn't make it. I pulled out my Tanto knife, saw that we were following the truck's path, reached back, slashed the seatbelt to free the car seat, saw holes in the Kevlar covering Toby, and yelled, "PILGRIM TAKE!"

The car upended ... *rolled* ... *nausea pushing through me* ... *falling-spinning-rolling* ...and then the crash ... that massive impact ... *so much worse than the first one* ... and then ... nothing.

31

The Gardener was furious. "Explain how this happened," he said to his chief of police, Brian Pasley, forcing a calmness he did not feel into his voice.

"My guess is Mason," he said. "Cut a hole through the fence, killed Stone and Root. One round each—headshots. Then somehow, he must have found Leaf and taken him. East Tower guard heard something, spotted a black Escalade, and started shooting. They radioed me right away. I sent cars to block all the exits and highways, along with a few rovers. Haven't heard anything yet, which means he's holding up somewhere. No way he got out. We'll find him come daylight."

"I want him alive," said the Gardener. "Both of them."

"That might not be the best idea," said the Chief. "Mason's dangerous. And Leaf—he's maybe seen too much."

The Gardener turned and looked at him, his eyes smoldering with fury.

"You think *Mason's* dangerous."

Lowering his gaze, Pasley held up his hands. "I didn't mean anything by it, sir. You have me in this position to give you my tactical advice. That's all I'm doing."

The Gardener cricked his neck and rolled his shoulders, bleeding off tension. "Yes, yes, all right. Still, the order stands. Both of them alive."

Pasley was about to say something else, but the Gardener stopped him with a raised finger.

"Don't worry, Brian, they won't stay that way for long. But an example must be made."

A BRANCH the thickness of my calf had punched through the windshield. It had traveled the space between the front seats, through the backseat center, and all the way into the back hatch. If I hadn't cut the car seat free, it would have torn right through Toby, Kevlar, or not. Once I woke up and freed myself, I checked to see if anyone was still in the car. The blood and fur along the edge of the passenger side rear window told me that Pilgrim had jumped. The missing car seat gave me hope that he'd been able to grab hold of Toby before he did.

Max was just gone—no blood, no fur. Typical.

I would have given Max the command to grab Toby, but we'd never worked on anything like that.

Pilgrim knew everything.

Over the years, I'd trained him on *object guard, retrieve, Palisade,* and dozens of other maneuvers I'd made up independently—maneuvers conducive to police and military work. I invented the *Grab and Take* after a hostage situation I'd been in. I'd never used it in real life until tonight.

My cellphone was intact, but there was no reception. I hoped that if I climbed high enough, I could get a signal. My main concern was that I'd sent the dogs and Toby out the windows to their deaths. Looking upward in the dark to where we'd gone over, I couldn't see the roadway. The fall had been at least seventy feet to just the tops of the trees, maybe more, and the trees stretched up another thirty or more. The mountain was primarily made up of sharp edges that jutted out, cutting off one area from another. It might take hours to traverse the rolling, rocky landscape. From up there, it might look easy, but from down on the ground, laborious and treacherous.

Something wet hit my face. Snowflakes. Just a few at first, but then the wind kicked up, brushing through my hair. It was cold. And then the snow decided to get serious. Wet, heavy flakes began pelting me. The pine trees blunted some of the assault ... some of the wind ... some of the chill ... some of the snow. But not enough. I needed to find Toby, Pilgrim, and Max.

I quickly rummaged through my destroyed car, collecting my go-bag and a few other items I thought might be useful. There were a couple of problems, though. One, I was coughing up blood. Not a lot, but still—probably a broken rib, maybe a few. I could only hope it wasn't from a punctured lung. Two, my left knee had smashed against the crushed engine compartment sometime during the carnival ride down the mountain. My entire body felt like a mushy banana.

Also, I needed to make a choice—stay here, set up camp, start a fire, wait till daylight? Or leave the car's shelter, and search for the missing three?

If I stayed, it would be easier for the dogs to find me. There would be a stronger scent pool because of all the broken vegetation and ground disturbance—not to mention the smoke from a fire. A fire would be needed to keep Toby alive as well. But if they were injured, they wouldn't be able to make it to me, and they could die from exposure to the elements. Plus, there was another problem ... the Gardener would be hunting us.

The Gardener. The thought of calling him that made me sick. *God is the Gardener.* The concept of the One Tree Assembly was an affront to the truth—a mockery of the biblical teaching of the *two trees* in the Garden of Eden. The Gardener claimed his vision was given to him by an alien—a lie that was just an updated version of saying an angel of light had visited him. Paul addressed that in 2 Corinthians, saying Satan transforms himself into an angel of light.

I thought about how the Gardener casually told Pasley to make me disappear, sealing the deal for me. Yeah, he wasn't an alien as he thought he was. No, he was of his father, the devil. I once again wished I'd sent him home to Hell when I'd had the chance—but I hadn't.

So, what was it going to be? Stay here or go looking?

If I stayed, I could set up a nice ambush and take out at least the first couple of waves. But the Gardener had a lot of resources. Besides, sitting and waiting around wasn't my strong suit—not when a little boy and my K9 brothers were in danger. Guerrilla warfare—hit and move and hit again—was more my style.

I considered the weak points of that plan: I might go in the wrong direction, the wet snow would make the terrain slippery, and the dark would hide things making the trip even more treacherous. Of course, those points worked both ways, which sort of evened the odds.

Shrugging, I made up my mind. I put on my parka, hefted my pack, and tested the wind's direction, precipitation, velocity, elevation, and swirl patterns. I decided to go down and around with it. There was a better chance Max could scent me if they had gone that way. If not, Pilgrim would easily track me once they reached the crash site.

Pulling the night-vision goggles down over my eyes, I began my descent.

PAPPY SAW the slushy snow splat against his windshield.

Great.

The rental was a front-wheel drive compact. He had wanted a Humvee or at least a Jeep, something he was used to, but this was all they had. Shrugging off the snow, he drove on, recalling the story he'd told Yolanda about Gil in the desert and the firefight. He also thought about what he *hadn't* told her—what he'd left out. He'd left it out of his official report, too—so had all the others. Not one of them ratted. The two killed in the explosion had been their friends. Plus, they owed their lives to Gil.

What Pappy had redacted from his report and what he hadn't told Yolanda was what Gil had *done* to the terrorists after they killed his dog, Strider. Mason had gone into a strange state—turned into some kind of automaton. A robot—only worse—a *monster*. He'd killed them, but that wasn't it. Most Marines had to kill in war. It was the *way*—it was his manner—as if he wasn't even there—as if he would do the same to anyone who got in his way—*the enemy*—his fellow Marines—*Pappy himself*. The memory brought chills to Pappy—and Pappy didn't chill easily.

No, not easily at all.

MAX WOKE at the first trace of snow. He'd jumped out the window at the Alpha's command ... after they'd already gone over the cliff. Seconds before that, the truck had struck them, shattering the glass and sending them into a spinning skid. Max had stretched full-out, trying to reach the ledge but missing by inches. After that, he struck rock and dirt, scrabbling for purchase on the vertical wall, feeling earth and vegetation scatter under his paws and nails. One of his rear nails had splintered, breaking at the quick and sending pain bolting up through his paw and into his leg. *Max ignored it.*

This was life and death, and death was very close.

The wall curved in toward the mountain, and Max was suddenly in free fall. Instinctively, he spun, trees rushing up at him. The first few treetops cushioned and slowed his fall, but then his chest smashed into a thicker branch, stealing his wind. After that, he was tumbling at incredible speed, crashing from branch to branch to branch, flipping his body this way and that.

Scratching with his claws and snapping with his teeth, he reached for anything to stop or at least slow his momentum.

Sparks ignited behind his eyes as his head splintered a thick branch, pine needles raking his snout and jaw. And then, Max lost consciousness.

When the snow touched his nose, he instantly came awake. Everything ached.

It meant nothing ... it was only pain.

Max took stock of his physical condition and stood. He would live ... and nothing was missing. Lifting his nose to the sky, he scented, taking in everything.

Gasoline.

Metal.

Blood ... not the Alpha's or Pilgrim's, but it was a start.

32

Tina was starting to get worried. She'd phoned Billy five times—each call being shunted to voicemail. Up until now, Billy had always answered her on the first ring. Every time. *Maybe it was just the blush of infatuation dimming.* Tina knew that every relationship had its phases. A slight cooling usually followed infatuation once the two parties became more familiar with each other. But she didn't think that was the case, not yet anyway. It certainly wasn't for her, and she didn't believe it was for Billy, either.

Which was why she was worried.

Her inner cop told her she was being stupid. She'd dealt with plenty of scared loved ones reporting their significant others, kids, even pets, as missing after only a few hours, just to have them turn up before morning—dozens, maybe hundreds.

But Billy? Billy was different.

Then again, he could be doing PI work for Gil. Perhaps he was doing something that was preventing him from answering his phone. That was probably it. Probably.

Or maybe he was working for someone else.

Tina didn't like to think that way. Billy told her he was through with the *Family* business, and she believed him. However, she'd met Billy's uncle, Nick Carlino. She knew he was difficult to refuse.

Difficult ... right.

More like impossible. Marlon Brando came to mind, sitting behind a desk in a darkened room, his cheeks stuffed with cotton, as he mumbled about an offer that couldn't be refused. Brando was impressive, but next to Nick Carlino, he was a rube, a bumpkin, out of Carlino's league. Nick was the real deal.

Had he called Billy in on a job? Was Billy in danger? Hurt maybe? Dying? Shaking her head, Tina again told herself she was being stupid. It had only been a few hours and a couple of missed calls.

Clicking the TV remote, a crime show flicked on. A uniformed police officer took a score of bullets, falling dramatically. Tina harrumphed—*so unrealistic*. And she should know. She'd taken a bullet not that long ago. *Thanks to Gil Mason.* As she quickly changed the channel, she wondered if she was being fair. It wasn't Gil's fault—not really, anyway. Not completely.

Viper, lying on the couch next to her, noticed Tina's change in mood and looked at her. The pups were in their crate, a topless cushioned box lined with absorbent pads. They were all asleep, their cute, pink little bellies rising and falling while their paws clawed the air fighting imaginary battles with their brothers and sisters.

"It's okay, sweetie," said Tina. "Mommy's just being dumb." She rubbed Viper's head and scratched behind her ears. She bent to her and kissed her snout.

It wasn't that easy to fool Viper. Despite Tina's attempt at a reassuring tone and even modulation, she sensed her alpha's unease. Tina didn't buy it either. She wanted to—tried to make herself believe it—but it didn't play. It just wasn't right.

She pulled out her phone and checked her tracking app. She felt distrustful doing it—like a jealous girlfriend checking up on a possible wayward suitor. But that wasn't it—*was it?* No, no, not at all. She wanted to make sure he was safe, and that was all. Tina knew Billy wasn't cheating on her. Of course, there had been plenty of opportunities. She'd seen the way women looked at him—*flirted* with him. He was handsome, big, muscular, strong, and charismatic. No, Tina couldn't blame other women.

But she would blame him if she had to—if there was a reason. Like him not answering her calls. Like if he was at another woman's house.

Opening the app, she saw where he was. *Downtown*. Really? At this time of night? Working, she thought. *But did she believe it?* Of course, she did. Absolutely. This was Billy. She trusted him completely.

Well, except for the Nick Carlino angle—but that was different. Wasn't it?

Trust is trust, said a suspicious part of her brain. *If he can't be trusted in one area, can he really be trusted in any?*

Tina had been cheated on in the past. She remembered the hurt, the searing pain of betrayal.

But Billy couldn't—*wouldn't.*

Standing, Tina went to the closet, took out her coat, and put it on. "I'll be back in a little while," she said to Viper, who'd jumped off the couch and walked to her. "You take care of the pups."

Tina considered bringing her off-duty weapon but remembered the pain and the seething flair of anger she'd experienced when she found out she had been betrayed on that long ago day. Would she have shot the guy if she'd had her gun? Now, as a cop, she never went anywhere without it. She considered it her duty always to be ready and thought less of other cops who didn't. *Nah, she wouldn't have shot the guy*—she was certain of that at least—almost certain anyway. *Better to leave it,* she thought.

Just this once.

PILGRIM HAD GRABBED the car seat as the Alpha commanded, his teeth crushing into and through plastic, cloth, and Kevlar. He hit the window as it exploded inward with the twisting of the frame, and the world turned upside down. He almost lost his grip, but the massive strength of his jaws proved true. The combined weight of the boy's fifty-plus pounds, the car seat, and the protective bullet-resistant material failed to rip it free.

They fell.

The wind rushed into Pilgrim's face like a cyclone. And then came the branches and pine needles. They were stabbing, tearing, crashing, grabbing, and clawing at him. His neck was wrenched to the side. Something punched into his belly. His hip smashed against a branch, flipping him, and he almost lost consciousness, but he held on, instinctually knowing that if he went out, the car seat he'd been commanded to protect would fall and be destroyed. And so, he rode out the fall, bouncing from branch to branch, crushing some and splintering others. His heavy coat, thick ribs, and solid shoulders absorbed most of the impacts as his momentum increased in a downward trajectory.

Pilgrim hit the ground hard but at an angle. He rolled as the car seat twisted and jerked at his teeth. And then he came to a stop—the world spinning and rolling as his eyes and ears fought for equilibrium. When Pilgrim finally made it to his feet, he saw the little boy unstrap himself and emerge from the car seat. It was battered and smashed, the Kevlar torn and shredded, but the boy was unharmed. He looked at Pilgrim, smiled, and hugged him around the neck. Pilgrim licked his face—a friendship forged.

33

T he snow and wind were starting to pick up, making the men grumpy, thought Randy Strait, or *Bark,* as everyone knew him. None of them wanted to be out in this kind of weather. The smart thing would be to wait until morning—they all thought so. But the Gardener thought differently, and so here they were.

Stupid.

This Mason guy was probably holed up in town. Or, even more likely, he'd made it past their blockade and was fast on his way to the cops—the real cops, like maybe state troopers. Not that he or any of the others would dare voice their opinions to the Gardener. None of them wanted a trip to the One Tree.

And then he saw it, up ahead about thirty yards, their high-powered flashlights splashing the crushed and mangled vehicle. It looked fresh, steam still seeping up from the crumpled hood. Bark couldn't believe it. He'd found Mason. Motioning to the others, he raised his rifle and advanced. The Gardener was sure to reward them for this.

As they broke through the trees, he heard moaning—low—like someone in pain. It was coming from the wreckage, but it wasn't

Mason. It was an OTA vehicle, and the people inside were OTA members. As the shock of the sight registered, Bark heard the sound of an impact and a grunt. Turning, he looked for the source, but there was nothing, just his men, the trees, and the dark. Scanning the area, he realized that one of their number, *Cedar*, was missing. He flashed his light at the surroundings but again saw nothing.

"Where's Cedar?" he asked.

Everyone looked around.

"Help," came a feeble voice from the truck, and all heads turned toward the wreckage.

They heard another impact, and there was one less of them. No grunt or cry this time—*just the thud.* Fear—*a supernatural dread*—gripped the small group in an icy fist.

"A sniper?" questioned Bark, trying to look everywhere at once. He'd done time in the army years ago. "With a silencer?"

"Maybe," said Shale, who'd done a stint in the Air Force, "except, where's the bodies?"

But it wasn't a sniper, and they were right to fear.

MAX DISPATCHED the second man as quickly as he had the first. He'd placed one of the men's scents from the compound and the towers. The others were foreign, but they were *with* the enemy, making them fair game.

Circling through the trees and the dark, he flanked the man at the very back, waiting until the others were distracted. A branch cracked in the forest, and the remaining men turned in unison, blasting their rifles into the inky blackness of the night.

The branch cracking had nothing to do with Max ... he would never be so careless.

Max struck so fast the man he took didn't know he'd been hit until he opened his eyes. He'd been catapulted away from the group and was now behind a screen of pines.

The pressure on his shoulder was excruciating. He was about to scream when suddenly the crushing force was gone, only to reveal a new terror as inch-long canines stabbed into his throat. His attempted scream came out as a gurgle. He was unconscious in seconds, dead in under a minute.

Max dropped the carcass and moved on ... setting up the next target.

∾

I FOUND MAX, but it almost killed me. I was so excited at the sight of him there in the trees that I hadn't noticed the men on the other side. When I saw them, I took a pace back to stay hidden in the dark. In doing so, I stepped on a branch, and instantly bullets splintered trees around me.

Dropping to the snow, my goggles tuned to thermal imaging, I saw Max dragging a man into the woods. Another volley of bullets whizzed over my head as I sighted in with the rifle. They were shooting blind ... I wouldn't be.

The suppressed rounds echoed under the falling snow, lending an eeriness to the otherwise beautiful atmosphere of the mountain landscape. Rising, I walked to the dead men. The heat shimmer from their blood was quickly cooling as it soaked into the thin layer of snow, destroying any notion of the beauty I harbored. A chill rippled through me.

And there was Max ... staring at me from the trees, the heat signature of blood drenching the front of his coat. I pushed the thermal goggles up onto my hood.

"Glad to see you, boy," I said.

He didn't move, just stared at me.

I shook my head. "We don't have time for this. We have to find Pilgrim and Toby ... unless you already know where they are?"

He didn't answer, just walked over to and then past me, heading for the destroyed truck and the moaning man. I followed, gun raised, covering possible traps. I needn't have bothered. Max would have alerted me if the men in the truck were in any shape to attempt an ambush ... probably by ripping their throats out.

There were three inside—two horribly mangled. I could only guess where the fourth man was. Most likely, he'd been thrown free. Pulling on my goggles, I gazed upward, gauging the distance. The trees could have been blocking my view of him. It was possible. *Probably not, though.*

The conscious man inside the truck groaned. He was a mess. Bones were sticking out of his clothes, and there was a lot of blood. He might make it if I could get him to a hospital in time.

That wasn't going to happen.

I could see, by Max's posture, he was ready to finish him. It might have been merciful, but I don't believe in mercy killing. That, and he was no danger to us. Maybe another group of his men would come along and save him ... it was possible.

"*Help*," mumbled the man.

I looked down at Max. "Find Pilgrim," I said.

Off he went.

I followed.

WHEN TINA SAW Billy's car, she drove past it, circled, and parked on the opposite side of the street. She sat there for ten minutes while the snow slowly covered her windshield. Finally, she got out, and when there was a break in the light downtown traffic, she entered the parking lot.

There were no footprints in the snow, so it had been sitting there for a while. Tina craned her neck, surveying the tall building. Moderate to high class, a doorman at the front, and a card lock in the back—no way for her to know what room he might be in.

Or was there?

She tried one of the car doors. Locked. Tried all the doors. Same. Scraping slushy snow off the driver's window with her bare hand, she peered inside, using her mini flashlight for illumination. On the dash was a piece of paper with a printed list of names and addresses. The angle prevented her from making out all but half of the bottom few.

But she'd come prepared.

Like the flashlight, she'd brought along a Slim-Jim—a thin blade of flexible metal with a rubber handle and grooved heads at the opposite end. Expertly, she slid the metal between the weather stripping and the door panel. After two shakes and pulls, the door snapped unlocked. Tina opened the door, located the address, and took note of the apartment number and resident's name.

The resident was a man—*supposedly*. For a moment, Tina considered packing it in, leaving, and waiting for Billy to call, but the memory of the betrayal pulsed somewhere in her heart. And if not betrayal, maybe Billy could use some help with whatever he was doing.

Leaving the Slim-Jim on the driver's seat, she closed the car door and went to check out the card reader.

34

Pilgrim caught their scent—they were upwind from him now. It was the Alpha and Max. He detected other odors, too—chemicals, plastics, clothing, blood, death. Pilgrim deviated from the closest trail and instead led the boy down and further into the trees. He did this because he heard men moving toward them—men closer than the Alpha. Predators hunting.

Hunting him. Him and the boy.

Pilgrim would not let them hurt the boy, but there was a problem. The men were between him and the Alpha. The men were noisy and clumsy, slipping, falling, and getting back up, their equipment jingling and jangling, making them easy to locate.

Pilgrim was injured. His muscles were battered, and he was bleeding from a score of tears, impacts, and abrasions. Blood dribbled from his scalp. Above them, a thick, rugged, twisted outcropping jutted from the mountainside. Pilgrim didn't think the boy could climb it. And in Pilgrim's deteriorated condition, he doubted he could carry the boy up the rock face. He couldn't see any other way to get to the Alpha without intersecting the men.

So, he went down into the trees, the boy following.

Too bad for the men.

He'd just re-branded them from predator—to prey.

BILLY FEARED he might have overplayed his hand. Larry Gold stood with the scalpel, staring into Billy's eyes—the image he'd seen in the living room haunting his imagination. Billy tried to think of a move that would incapacitate or at least injure the psycho, but hanging upside down with his hands tied behind him didn't give him many options. Still, he wouldn't go down without a fight. He readied himself, preparing to attempt a head butt.

"We do this," said Gold, "you'll owe me."

"How you figure?" asked Billy. "You knock me out, strip me, hang me up like a side of beef, threaten to slaughter me and give me a headache to boot. What's to owe?"

Gold grinned. "I think I like you," he said. "You've got courage. Maybe more courage than brains, but still."

"What do you want?" asked Billy, sensing he shouldn't push things any further—after all—the man was insane.

"Nothing now," said Gold. "But someday, maybe. I could get hurt or caught, or maybe I need a discreet doctor who doesn't report anything to the authorities. Something like that. Perhaps emergency money and fake IDs—passports, driver's licenses, plastic surgery."

"Yeah," said Billy. "I could see that being a possibility. We got all that. I'd agree to that."

"Would you," grinned Gold. "I'll bet you would."

"It is my life we're talking about," said Billy.

"Yes, but remember, I'm giving up something, too. The tree—and the doctor. That's not an easy thing for me."

"Yeah, yeah, I can understand that," said Billy. "Okay, deal. Now, will you get me down from here?"

Gold pulled a gun from the back of his waistband. Billy recognized it as his own.

"If you renege ... if you try anything ... to do anything to me ... I'll kill you."

"I understand," said Billy. "But, hey, when you're in the *Family,* a man's word is his bond."

"We'll see," said Gold as he moved behind Billy, placing the scalpel blade to the bindings holding Billy's wrists.

There was an instant of pressure, and Billy's hands were free. He rubbed his wrists as Gold moved to the wall where the rope was secured.

Then, there was a knock at the door.

PAPPY COULD HARDLY SEE. The snow was rushing at him with such force the windshield wipers couldn't keep up. The darkness of the night made it worse. There were so few streetlights it was as though the black asphalt was absorbing what little light there was, feeding on it like some kind of energy-draining succubus.

The car entered an unlit rock tunnel built into the side of a mountain. It was dark but devoid of snow or moisture. The momentary respite was short-lived because when he emerged, his tires went into a skid, and he almost crashed into the side of the mountain. Regaining control, he steered with white-knuckled hands. War was less stressful.

He saw a sign, half covered in snow, advertising a town with gas, lodging, and a restroom a few miles ahead. As Pappy considered stopping to get some coffee, his foot instinctually added force to the gas pedal in anticipation. The small vehicle behaved like a Formula 1 race car, lurching ahead, its front wheels hydroplaning. Pappy slammed the brakes, the ABS computer system taking control.

But the action was too late. The car went into a series of doughnuts, spinning Pappy helplessly down the highway. The car finally came to a stop in the middle of the roadway, straddling both lanes. His only saving factor was the complete absence of traffic this time of night. He sat quietly for a few seconds, gathering himself, when out of the darkness, massive lights blazed at him, accompanied by a blaring air horn.

Pappy hit the gas again, this time prepared for the hydroplane action. The car spit ice as it spun, but he steered expertly into it, avoiding the giant truck barreling past him. That settled it. Pappy would be useless to Gil if he died trying to get to him. He'd stop at the advertised town and wait until morning.

After all, there was no hurry. Gil could take care of himself.

MAX AND GIL were navigating the twisting, slippery, rocky terrain. There were so many obstacles—trees, bushes, rocks, and walls of varying heights that suddenly rose straight up—that it was tricky, even for Max. They'd had to backtrack several times, sliding their way through the ice and snow and cold.

And then Max caught something—just a wisp—blown to him on the wind. And then it scattered just as quickly as it had come.

Pilgrim.

Faint, so faint.

But it was him.

Max moved faster, the Alpha falling behind. The Alpha was injured, forcing Max to slow his pace to keep from losing him. The Alpha stumbled but got up and continued after him.

Good.

Max wanted to get to Pilgrim as quickly as possible. He wanted to leave this place and get back to Viper and his pups. He couldn't rid himself of the feeling that something was wrong. *That they needed him.*

The Alpha slipped again. Max felt the urge to grab him and drag him along—either that or just leave him. *Leave them all.* Leave them and go to his own pack.

Gunshots sounded ahead, echoing hollowly off the mountain walls and slopes. Gunshots and ... *barking.*

It was Pilgrim.

35

As I pulled myself to my feet after falling, the pain in my ribs was tremendous. The sound of gunshots followed by Pilgrim's barking gripped me with fear. He and Toby were in danger. I had to get to them, but the terrain, combined with the darkness, the snowstorm, and my injuries, made it impossible to move faster.

Max looked back at me. He was acting strange—like the Max of old after I first saved him from the dog fighting ring. It was almost as though I'd lost the ground I'd gained with him, and we were back to square one. It frustrated me, but worse than that, it made me sad. There was no time for it now ... we had to get to Pilgrim.

There was another volley of gunshots, and I heard a yelp of pain that made my skin go cold. Max was still looking at me ... judging and finding me wanting.

Coming to a decision, I nodded.

"*Go,*" I said.

He was gone before the word made it past my lips. Vanished—a ghost in the snow.

"*Save them.*"

Wiping the blood from my lips, I said a quick prayer and pushed forward through the storm.

∾

STEPPING TO THE SIDE, as all cops do, Tina knocked. It took a moment, but then a nice-looking man dressed in a shirt and slacks cracked the door. He was tall, middle-aged, had thinning sandy-blond hair, and the most brilliant blue eyes Tina had ever seen.

"Can I help you?" he asked, keeping the door nearly closed.

Tina held up her wallet badge.

"Are you Larry Gold?" she asked. She'd gotten the name from the list in Billy's car.

The man sported a lopsided smile that faded at the mention of his name. "What's this in relation to?" he asked.

Tina wasn't sure where to go from here—there was no music, no party, and no women she could see or hear. She had no idea what Billy might be up to. The thought that she might be messing up a case he was working on bothered her, but then she saw the butt of a gun tucked in the man's waistband. *Could this be mafia business?* Her anger began to build—*he'd promised.*

"Is Billy here?"

His eyebrows raised. "Billy?"

"Don't play stupid," she said. "Billy Carlino. Is he in there?" Without waiting for an answer, she pushed the door, forcing her way inside.

Larry Gold gave way, letting the door swing in, and Tina saw what was left of the butchered corpse on the table. She reached for her gun —*but it wasn't there.* She'd left it at home. The next instant, fifty thousand volts of electricity coursed into her throat and through her body. The last thing Tina saw before the world went black was the fate that awaited her splayed in the center of the room.

∾

PILGRIM STOPPED, and the little boy stopped with him. The sounds up ahead were close. Danger was close—danger for the boy. But Pilgrim was used to danger. He used to crave it when he was young. And even now, a spark ignited deep in his soul—a flaring excitement. But he had more than himself to think of.

There was the boy.

Slipping behind trees, Pilgrim circled several times and dropped into the inch-deep snow. The boy knelt beside him, petting his fur. Below them, the big dog could see the path they would have to take. He would strike the men before they knew he was there. He would injure or kill as many as possible before fading into the woods and darkness. Pilgrim was no Max—not as fast, not as fierce, and he couldn't disappear the way the smaller, lighter dog could—but he had learned some tricks from Max. And, he had tricks of his own. So, he waited.

He didn't have to wait long.

～

MAX SCRABBLED up and over a fifteen-foot wall of dirt and rock, his broken nail screaming with pain. He ignored it, as he did all things inconsequential to the mission. Pilgrim was not capable of defeating a challenging opponent. He was too old, too slow, and was hampered by ancient scars and injuries—blunted and worn down by the unstoppable march of time.

Pilgrim had been a formidable warrior once. Max could sense this in him. He had heart and drive, but that was a long time ago. What remained was a shell awaiting death.

And these men would kill him if they hadn't already. They had numbers and guns in their favor. If they killed Pilgrim ... Max would make them pay.

Traversing the sloping wall had saved Max time. He hoped it was enough.

～

BILLY HEARD TINA'S VOICE, followed by the crackle of electricity. He then heard the unmistakable thud of a body falling to the marble floor. Panic gripped him in an icy fist.

Tina.

It wasn't possible. How could she be here? A moment later, Larry Gold reemerged, dragging Tina's unconscious body by the hair. He dumped her before him.

Rage replaced the panic.

"Who is she?" asked Gold.

"A cop," said Billy, thinking as fast as he could while fighting to hide the rage.

"I know that," said Gold. "What's she doing here?"

"I don't know. Must have followed me. She's been after me for months. I took out her partner, but they couldn't pin anything on me. She's made me her pet project."

Gold nodded, bent over, and put the scalpel to her throat. "Now, you owe me twice."

THERE THEY WERE—RIGHT below Pilgrim. Recognizing the danger, the boy scrunched down tight next to the big dog, his heart racing, adrenaline surging. *Good.* Pilgrim wanted him to stay still ... hidden.

Pilgrim rose, moving down and through the trees. He wasn't a ghost like Max—silent and invisible—but the men were so clumsy and inept that they didn't hear or see him.

As a police dog, Pilgrim usually took humans straight on or found them in hiding places. This would be different. Pilgrim had watched Max hunt. Max always took the outliers first—the slow, the weak—the ones who fell behind. He then worked his way up to the fittest, who no longer had the advantage of numbers. The dark would give Pilgrim cover as he followed Max's example.

The group of four passed just feet from where Pilgrim lay silent.

And then he moved.

Jumping a few feet from his target, he struck with all hundred and twenty pounds, striking the man at the base of his skull and driving him forward into the snow face first. The man was too stunned even to attempt a scream. His rifle flew from his hands, the impact knocking him unconscious. Pilgrim tore at the man's neck for a few seconds until he realized the threat had ended.

His next target was thirty feet away. He covered the distance quickly, his arthritis barely hindering him—excitement blunting the pain. The man heard him at the last second and, turning, squared his rifle into his shoulder. Pilgrim dove under the barrel as the man fired, shoving the gun away. He caught the man high in the armpit, his massive jaws crushing in on his flesh with unbelievable pressure. Pilgrim's weight and momentum swung him back and around, driving the man to the snowy ground.

Seeing a commotion and thinking a bear had attacked their companion, the last two turned with their lights. They blasted at the animal, one with a hunting rifle, the other with a pump shotgun. They hit the ground, the trees, their friend—everything but Pilgrim. And then the creature was gone. Their comrade was left choking on blood, his side flowing, fingers twitching, and holes from their bullets punched through his parka.

Pilgrim didn't wait—*another tactic he'd learned from Max.* Cutting around and through the trees, he came up behind the men, moving straight at them. His target, the bigger of the men, sensed something at the last second. He jerked aside just as Pilgrim's teeth sliced his coat, tearing through the cloth and cutting to the bone. But it was only a glancing blow, forcing Pilgrim to slide over the man's shoulder to land five feet away, his paws slipping on the snow and toppling him to his side and face.

Both men fired, their bullets sending dirt and snow spraying like geysers. Pilgrim yelped as a searing pain burned through his chest, knocking him off his feet. Blood, hot and fast, poured down his coat. Both men sighted in on the big dog.

At five feet, they couldn't miss.

36

Having lost Max to the dark and distance almost instantly, I went as fast as possible. I prayed he'd make it to Pilgrim in time, but with this terrain, I doubted it. Fear is a good motivator, so I picked up my pace.

The shooting had ceased, but I didn't know if that was good or bad.

Memories of Pilgrim swept through my mind—the times he'd saved me, the manhunts we'd shared, the fights we'd been in. I remembered what he was like with my daughter Marla—what he put up with from her—fingers up his nose, in his ears, bows on his fur, kisses along his snout and muzzle and rounded head. Pilgrim had put up with it all, loving her as much as one being can love another. Tears stung my eyes.

I thought I was moving as fast as possible.

I was wrong.

～

MAX BOUNDED over a bush and around a craggy outcropping. Defeating the obstacles of the landscape was proving to be a slow and difficult process. The snow, although slashing ever harder, wasn't accumulating by much. In some ways, that was worse. Deeper snow would have reduced the slipperiness. As it was, each step proved treacherous, the icy undercoating threatening loss of balance or worse.

Vaulting straight up another section of rock, Viper and the pups pushed their way into his thoughts. Max didn't want to think about them. His attention had to be one hundred percent on the task ahead of him—where to hunt, scents that needed deciphering, filtered sounds, how and where to strike. Stay in place or hit and run. And once on the prey, strangulate or rend and tear. Concentration and complete dedication to the exercise were necessary and had always come automatically to him.

Until now.

He could ill afford distractions. Distractions might cost him his survival or, worse—the pack's survival. *But was this still his pack?* An Alpha who should not be alpha over him and an old once warrior, past his prime and close to death? What were they to him compared to Viper and his pups? Where did his responsibility lie? And, perhaps more importantly, what meant most to him?

His paws skidded out from beneath him as he hit a patch of ice, and he fell hard on his side, slipping over and down the side of the high hillock. Plunging fifteen feet, Max smashed even harder on his shoulder and neck, his thick muscles the only thing saving him from serious injury. Rising, he shook his head and then stopped. There was carnage everywhere—carnage and so much more.

He saw Pilgrim ... he saw the blood ... the blood, and the boy.

PANIC IS NEVER good or helpful in stressful situations ... I know this from the many firefights and other desperate situations I've experienced. But this was taking too long. Fear was fighting to take control. As a result, I pushed myself too hard, forcing a speed incompatible with the terrain and conditions. I fell, rose, pushed, slipped, and fell again, losing precious ground and taking longer to regain my position.

Not to mention the pain.

I forced myself to slow down and take stock of the situation. Using trees and branches as crutches helped. There's an old shooter's quote about drawing a holstered pistol that goes, *Slow is smooth, and smooth is fast.* I was finding the same advice worked well here. I didn't fall again—didn't have to make up wasted time. I made steady progress.

There'd been no gunshots since I heard Pilgrim's cry. No barking, no commotion. I prayed Max had found them—saved them. But I was scared, so scared.

Pushing all that aside, I climbed over a twelve-foot-high snow-covered rock outcropping. Below, I saw an image that burned into my synapses. An image I could never forget.

Pilgrim.

~

PILGRIM SAW the weapons pointed at him and felt the pain in his chest. Rising, he stood and faced them. Knowing he would die but hoping to take at least one of them with him, he would charge.

Baring his teeth, he decided on one last tactic he'd learned from Max. He would slip slightly to the side, lining the men up so only one could fire, then attack straight in, hoping to drive them into each other. Once on the ground, Pilgrim would have a chance.

Gauging the distance, he knew it wouldn't work. There was no way he could line them up before they blasted him to pieces. But it didn't matter. It was his only chance. Bunching his massive haunches, he prepared to strike as the men pulled back on the triggers.

"NO!" came from the side.

Both men turned in unison, their flashlights blazing. It was the boy, twenty feet away. Pilgrim wasted no time. He sprinted to the left, lining the men up perfectly. They turned back, trying to reacquire their target, but it was too late. Pilgrim covered the distance in a flash, smashing the closest man in the face, his enormous canines crushing in, snapping bones and teeth amidst a scream of agony.

The man flailed into his companion, Pilgrim's mass adding to the force of the impact. Landing, Pilgrim released and dove onto the fallen man who, on his hands and knees, was struggling to regain his feet, his rifle an arm's length away. Pilgrim landed on his back, shoving him straight down, arms and legs flat out. Growling like some primeval beast, Pilgrim savaged the back of the man's neck before switching to his head. Pilgrim's huge jaws stretched beyond the man's ears and crushed in. The man stiffened, convulsing in a tight spasm as his skull splintered.

Pilgrim released and turned to see the first man he'd attacked crawling to his rifle. Limping forward, feeling weak and spent, Pilgrim mounted the man's back and finished him. Afterward, Pilgrim heard an impact. Sure that more men were coming for the boy, his lips drew back in a snarl, but then he stopped.

It was Max.

37

Max forced his eyes to steady, his senses still jumbled from the fifteen-foot fall. What he saw didn't seem possible. There were bodies scattered about, torn and shredded, and only Pilgrim to account for the carnage—four men with weapons—a feat that would have challenged even Max.

Moments before, Max had thought Pilgrim useless to the pack—ineffectual—a detriment. The once mighty warrior now old and weak, nearly crippled. Max decided he would have to reevaluate Pilgrim.

A small avalanche of snow tumbled from the slope Max had just fallen from, diverting Pilgrim's attention away from him. Max didn't look—he didn't need to.

He'd already scented the Alpha.

Down below, I saw Pilgrim, the bodies, and the boy. Max was there too. I'd seen the scrabble marks in the snow where he'd fallen and the imprint where he'd landed almost directly beneath me. There were no tracks from that point to where Pilgrim stood with the bodies, which told me this could only be Pilgrim's work.

Pilgrim looked up at me. My heart filled with pride, and I smiled and waved at him. This was the Pilgrim of old—my partner in fighting crime. But then I noticed the heat image from my goggles. It showed dripping waves flowing down his chest. He staggered toward Max, regained his balance, stopped, then looked up at me again as if in apology. Dropping to his side, he lay still.

I jumped the fifteen-foot drop, landing next to where Max had been. Max was no longer there—he was running to Pilgrim. I followed suit and saw the boy running toward him too.

Max reached him first, then the boy. We all stood there, the boy crying, Max frozen like a gargoyle made of stone, staring as if evaluating Pilgrim's condition with senses that rivaled Doctor McCoy's tricorder.

Pilgrim lay there, tongue lolling lifelessly from his jaws, eyes half-lidded. I knelt, feeling for a heartbeat.

Toby screamed, *"He saved me!"*

And I felt my own heart break.

LARRY GOLD TOUCHED the blade of the scalpel to Tina's throat.

"Stop!" yelled Billy.

Gold grinned at him. "Maybe," he said, "if you stop lying and start telling me the truth. Who is she really? And why is she here?"

Billy shook his head. "She's my girlfriend. I left her in the car while I ran up here. I didn't think getting the tree was going to take long. How was I supposed to know psycho-killer was the thief? She must have thought something happened and came looking for me."

"Your girlfriend? A cop? You said the mafia didn't deal with cops."

"She's a plant," said Billy. "We do that. The *Family*—we seed the military, police, and government agencies like the FBI, DEA, and CIA with our own people. Politicians, and other helpful entities, too. They feed us information—let us know if anyone is onto or coming after us, and, if necessary, help throw them off our track. Our infiltrators bring back skills, like combat tactics, fighting—new weapons. We embed them deep—kind of like undercover cops, only better because they're ours. That's what *she* does. And she's one of our best."

Gold looked down at her and cocked his head. "I knew she wasn't a cop on duty. No gun. I checked. What cop works without a gun?"

"Undercover cops," said Billy. "They have to put it all on the line sometimes to look real."

"You had a gun," said Gold, holding Billy's up and wiggling it.

"I don't play undercover cop," said Billy. "I'm a *made man,* if you know what that means."

"I know what it means. I watch my share of mob movies. Do *made men* make a habit of chasing down stolen trees?"

"No," said Billy, "but like I said, this is special—for my uncle. And good things happen to those my uncle favors."

Gold ran the dull side of the scalpel along Tina's jaw. "Is everything you're telling me the truth?"

"Yeah," said Billy. "It's the truth. I swear."

Gold looked at him, and Billy saw what lay behind those orbs—a deadness. The slight smile was still there, and accompanied by the eyes, the effect was terrifying.

"We'll see," he said.

Gold set the gun and the scalpel next to Tina, then effortlessly scooped her body off the floor and walked out of the room. Billy had never felt more helpless.

But ... his hands were free.

∼

PAPPY SAT ON THE BED, leaned down, and unlaced his spit-shined boots. He was disappointed he'd had to stop, but *what couldn't be helped couldn't be helped* and must be accepted. The hotel seemed reasonably full—truck drivers and locals knew when to seek shelter. Pappy took a shower, the water hot, the soap sudsy, the shaving cream

—*creamy*, the razor sharp, the towels rough but absorbent. Pappy appreciated efficiency in all things, no matter how small.

He dressed in a long-sleeve, button-up shirt, jeans, and brown hiking boots before heading down to the bar. Once there, he stood at the entrance, scanning. It was always wise to perform reconnaissance before entering a possibly hostile environment—and to the wise, all environments are potentially hostile.

Pappy knew that bars were one of the best places to gather intelligence. Liquor loosens tongues, hence the saying *loose lips sink ships*. If Pappy couldn't get to Gil, maybe he could gather some intel that might help find Teresa and Toby.

Truck drivers were easy to spot, as were the working girls. Pappy had been in places like this all over the world. There were differences, of course, but some things were the same everywhere—looks, mannerisms, the tilt of the head, a sly glance, body position, the way a glass was held, a drink downed, a laugh.

Pappy took it all in, and once he was satisfied, and only then, he entered. Reconnaissance alone couldn't guarantee safety—nothing could do that short of not entering at all—but it helped reveal traps, obstacles, things to avoid. After that, it was up to him to choose the right direction, make the correct choices, and make the right moves.

And at that, Pappy reigned supreme.

38

Pilgrim rode my shoulders fireman's carry style, his body resting against the back of my neck, his front and rear legs tied at the ankles against my chest to keep him from falling. The snow was raging now, and I had to duck my head to protect my face. *I should have worn my balaclava.* The night-vision goggles shielded my eyes and helped me find my way in the dark. I'd wrapped Toby in my jacket, carrying him in my arms and keeping him safe from the wind and cold.

Max was doing what Max does, running point, as usual, nonplused by the earth's paltry elements. I had to call him back every so often because he, of course, wanted to take the shortest route ... going up walls of sheer rock. Unfortunately, I couldn't follow suit with Pilgrim and Toby onboard. It was the long road for us and couldn't be helped ... as much as I wished otherwise.

I'd managed to stop most of Pilgrim's bleeding with clotting powder and dressings from the first-aid kit in my go bag, but I'd have to do some exploring in order to get to the bullet. If he were going to survive, I couldn't do that out in the elements ... *and Pilgrim was going to survive.*

We'd been traveling for more than an hour, skirting crags and long, thick fingers of mountain that stretched hundreds of feet before flattening enough for me to cross over them. There'd been no further sign of the Gardener's men. And I'd know if there were because I would have seen the bodies ... Max would have killed them. He was in that kind of mood.

I could relate.

～

MAX SCENTED as best he could in the swirling, hard-driving wind, hoping for a whiff, a taste, a minuscule fragment of odor that could be traced back to the men in the pack that had done this to Pilgrim. Max knew there were others—many others—the men in the tower, the buildings, and the town. Max would kill them all. Max *wanted* to kill them all.

Some of his motivation was born of guilt—he understood this on the primal level that canines process information. Max had almost deserted Pilgrim. He'd *wanted* to leave him—to let him die. He'd judged him unworthy, useless, a burdensome drag on the pack—an obstacle that kept him from his other pack, from Viper, from his progeny.

The drive to leave and return to them had distracted Max. It had kept him from doing what he was capable of. Could he have made it to Pilgrim sooner had he not been distracted? The very idea stoked his rage. Max scented again. One of the men *had* to be out here.

Max needed the release.

～

BILLY STARTED TO SWAY, utilizing his hip flexors and stomach muscles. Gold had left the gun and the scalpel just inside the doorway. It was a far stretch, but Billy thought he might just make it. Back and forth he swung, fighting to keep from going off course.

At first, he had attempted to untie the ropes from around his ankles. Bending at the waist, he had reached up to the knots, his chest tight against his thighs. But the knots were unrelenting, and his weight on the rope kept everything tight, refusing to loosen even against the strength of his fingers.

After several tries, he gave up on the idea, deciding to go for the weapons instead. If he could reach them, he'd use the knife to cut the ropes and the gun to kill Gold—although he had to admit, he'd rather use his hands. Feel the life flee from Gold a little at a time as Billy crushed it from his lungs. But with Tina in danger, he couldn't take the chance. He'd shoot the psycho and be done with it.

Stretching to his limit, *he was almost there.* Just a bit more momentum, and then … *his index finger brushed the scalpel.* It scooted a smidge, and then he was swinging away. *So close.* With all the strength in his abs and quads, he rocked, pushing him toward release, and then came the sound from the other room.

PAPPY'S second contact yielded a nugget of intel. It came from a woman truck driver in her fifties. She had faded red-gray shoulder-length hair and a few wrinkles at the corners of her bright green eyes, hinting at an Irish heritage. Her name was Marge, but she wasn't large. Mason had once talked Pappy into watching the movie *Pee-wee's Big Adventure.* He recalled a scene where a ghostly female truck driver turned into a monster while giving Pee-wee a ride. *Stupid movie,* Pappy had told a disappointed Gil. *It was two hours from his life he'd never get back.* He'd rather be in a firefight, unarmed, against a swarm of Taliban soldiers than have to sit through another of those. Gil had looked at him and said, *"I know you are, but what am I?"*

Stupid, just like the movie.

Pappy bought Marge a whiskey, and, shock of shocks, they had his favorite, Pappy's, on hand. Expensive, but he thought it might prove worth it.

"Wow," said Marge. "That's good stuff. Maybe the best I've ever had."

"I told you," said Pappy.

"A man true to his word," she said. "A rare thing these days. My third husband," she paused, then looked at the ceiling, thinking, "Third? Was it my third or fourth? Anyway, he told me he'd stick with me no matter what. Then I had a bout of cancer, and what does he do? Drains the bank account, and off he goes with some nineteen-year-old hoochie. Joke was on him, though. I beat the Big C, and a few years later, seen him on the Vegas Strip with some other bimbo. I didn't say a word—just punched him in the snoot. Knocked him into one of those fountains outside a casino, then laughed my head off at him. He sat up, water and blood dripping down his face, looking like he saw a ghost. I knew what he was thinking, so I held my hands up by my ears, waggled my fingers at him, and told him I would haunt him for the rest of his life. Then you know what I did?"

"No," said Pappy, grinning, "what'd you do?"

"I yelled *BOO*, jumping at him like. He screamed and fell right back on his butt in the water. So funny. It was worth the three hundred bucks he stole from the bank account."

Laughing, Pappy slapped the bar. He motioned to the bartender. "Another round for the lady and me, and you might as well leave the bottle."

The bartender gave him a look. "You know what these babies cost?"

"This here whiskey ain't no baby, son. He's fully grown," said Pappy as he dropped a folded wad of bills next to his glass.

"Yes, sir," said the bartender. He walked over, pulled out a brand new bottle, cracked the seal, filled their glasses, then left the bottle.

Marge lifted her glass, admiring the beautiful amber liquid. "You are a true gentleman," she said, saluting.

Pappy mimicked the gesture. "And you, a lady," said Pappy. They clinked glasses and sipped.

"Marine?" asked Marge.

"Yes, ma'am," said Pappy. "What gave me away?"

"You have the look," she said. "My second husband," she paused and looked at the ceiling again. "Was it second? Anyway, whatever, he'd been a Marine for a while. Got kicked out for breaking something."

"Breaking something? What did he break to get kicked out of the Corps? I mean, we have a reputation for breaking things. It's kind of a bragging point for us. Kill and destroy—that's our job."

Downing the rest of the whisky, Marge motioned for another. "I don't know. A jet, I think. One of those ones that can go straight up. Tossed a wrench at a guy he got in a beef with, missed him, and it got sucked up in the engine or something."

Pappy looked at her with wide eyes. "A Harrier? That's a thirty-million-dollar aircraft."

"Yeah, guess it blew up real good. And the worst part was it was on one of those boats where all the planes take off to fight other boats with planes."

"An aircraft carrier?" asked an incredulous Pappy.

"Yeah, that's it. What do those cost?"

"A lot," said Pappy.

"Yeah, well anyway, I guess it blew a big hole in that too. Started a fire, which you wouldn't think was such a big deal since it's on an ocean and the ocean's water." She leaned in close like she was sharing a secret. "Turns out it is. They had to push the plane off the side of the boat to keep it from causing more damage, what with the bombs and missiles and stuff it was carrying. Also, to keep it from catching the boat on fire—which I guess it did anyway. Then they had to fight like crazy to get the fire out. Anyway, like I said, he got tossed for breaking it. Did some time in the ...," she paused again, "What do they call jail in the military?"

"The brig," said Pappy.

"That's it," she said. "He did a stretch in there. Fell for some woman guard and dumped me cold."

Pappy just shook his head, downed the rest of his drink, and grinned. "Yeah, I guess that would do it, even for a Marine."

"Yeah," said Marge, "that man wasn't much of a husband, what with the drinking and whoring and fighting, but he didn't do things halfway, gotta give him that."

Pappy raised his glass. "Here's to breaking things."

They clinked again and downed their drinks.

Marge gave Pappy the eye. "So, what is it you want from me?"

"Am I that obvious?" he asked.

"Well, it ain't so much that," she said, "but I'm pushing seventy—even though I know I don't look it—and you're at least twenty years younger. You didn't spend a hundred bucks on booze to get me into bed, so you got other motives. What are they?"

"You're a smart one, Marge," said Pappy. "And you're right. I *am* looking for information. One of my troops got blown up bad in the war, and when he got out of the hospital, he found his wife left him—took his young son with her."

"And?"

"Me and a friend are trying to find them," said Pappy.

Marge pointed at her glass, and Pappy filled it.

"Turns out she joined a cult up here in the mountains. Town's called Galena. Cult's known as the One Tree Assembly."

"I know it," she said. "Bad bunch, from what I've heard, and I've heard plenty. I don't know how much is true, but we truckers are a tight group. We keep each other up on stuff. We have a code of sorts. And the word is not to cross the OTA—steer clear of them. Don't buy nothin', don't pick them up hitching a ride, don't sleep with them—just leave 'em be. No matter how much they beg, demand, or try to talk you into something, just say no." She pointed a finger at him. "Don't be rude or rough, neither. I've heard tales of truckers that got a little *feisty* with them, only to be found later—their bodies anyway—beat to death, their trucks torched. Nothin' to lead back to the OTA except that a few bragged about their beefs before they turned up dead."

Pappy hadn't expected this.

"My advice," said Marge, "is that if this woman and her kid is with them, you forget about 'em. They made their choice. Sometimes people got to live with those choices."

"The little boy, Toby, he didn't have a choice," said Pappy.

Marge nodded, pouring herself a drink this time. S he shrugged.

"You got my advice, but being a jarhead, I suppose you'll just go up there and break something."

Pappy looked at her with cold eyes. "A lot of things," he said. "Maybe a whole boatload of things."

Marge nodded, acknowledging the look. Grinning, she held up her glass then downed it in one gulp. "I don't doubt it," she said.

39

Max seemed disappointed when we made it back to my Escalade without running into any more OTA goons. I wasn't. Pilgrim was still alive, and I planned on keeping him that way.

I gently set him on a bed of snow, went to the car, and wrenched off the driver's side door. The metal tried to put up a fight, but—like Max—I wasn't in the mood. I snapped it free, set my footing, gripped the window frame, and toppled the SUV away from the tree. It landed on its side, so I had to shove it onto its tires—what was left of them. I ripped out the center seats—I'd replaced the back ones with a rubber platform a long time ago—and cleared out the back, sweeping away the glass nuggets with gloved hands. I picked up Pilgrim and placed him inside.

Max kept guard while Toby stood silently watching. I thought it best to give him something to do to help him get through the shock he must be experiencing, so I pointed at some trees. "Get some wood. We need a fire. Look for the driest branches you can find, nothing live. Gather the dead stuff, even if it's under the snow. But don't go far, not past where I can see you. There might still be men looking for us." I pointed at Max. "Don't worry ... Max won't let anyone hurt you."

I thought he'd ask questions, maybe start crying, but he just turned and went to work. I found a dead tree and wrenched it from the ground, the roots snapping and popping like firecrackers. The action hurt my ribs, but this was for Pilgrim. I dragged it close to the car, then splintered it with punches, kicks, and sheer strength. Inside the Escalade, I used rocks I gathered to build a small circle just behind the front seats. I then formed a pyramid using the wood splinters.

Toby returned with an armful of twigs, thicker branches, and straw ... he'd obviously done this before. It wasn't a lot, he had small arms, but he'd brought me exactly what I needed. He stood just outside the car, watching as I loosely packed the straw beneath the sticks, laying some of the twigs on top and around. Cutting a section of tubing from the wiper washer assembly, I siphoned a thermos full of gas from the tank and sprinkled it lightly over the kindling. Then I lit the straw with a butane torch from my go bag, and in seconds, the fire was giving off heat. I carefully placed more wood on top until the blaze suited the cramped space.

There was no glass remaining in the windows, so smoke was not an issue. I motioned for Toby to come inside to get warm. I retrieved a tarp and some thin rope I kept folded in the emergency pocket by the rear wheel well of the car and made quick work fashioning a makeshift shelter for the SUV. I covered the missing windows and door, then tied it all down after cutting a hole above the campfire so the smoke could escape. Afterward came the hard part.

I had to get that bullet out of Pilgrim.

TINA LOOKED up and saw a man standing over her. Everything was fuzzy, foggy. Where was she? What was going on? Had she been in an accident? The man looked like a doctor, but he wasn't wearing scrubs —no stethoscope or head covering, either. Tina tried to move her arms and her legs, but nothing happened. *Was she paralyzed?* No, she had sensation, she could feel—she just couldn't raise her limbs. And

then, comprehension started to work through the fog, and she understood that she was tied down. That brought back the memory of
where she was and what she was doing here—*and what she'd seen on
the table.*

The table.

She was on a table. *That table.* Terror filled her. The shock began
to bring the rest of her senses online, and she realized she was lying
in something wet, something cold, something sticky. The image of
the body, flayed open as if on display, flashed across her mind, and
she knew what she was lying in—and what she was wearing. She'd
been stripped down to her bra and panties.

As if reading her thoughts, the man smiled down at her, the lights
above his head streaming like a halo. He reached down and touched
her chin. Reflexively, Tina jerked away, knocking and shattering a cup
of something onto the floor.

"Shhhh," he said. "It's okay. Lie still. Don't worry about my tea. I'll
fetch another—eventually. As for where you are and what's about to
happen to you, don't fret. There's nothing you can do anyway. What's
going to happen is going to happen. Fighting is useless, and it will
only make it worse for you. I'm very skilled, exact. I've mastered my
craft, and if you jerk too much, you might make a mess of things. And
don't worry—I'm not a pervert, not a rapist.

"Neither science nor medicine has an accurate title for what I am.
But, if anyone did try and catalog or categorize me, I suppose I'd be
deemed an artist or perhaps even a scientist. It's true that I don't use
traditional tools like a brush or paint or charcoal, or a chisel. I use
other mediums. I—*deconstruct*—searching for the secret of life and
death. I know it's in there, somewhere." He raised a finger and
touched it to her chest. "Inside here? Or, maybe in your brain? It's in
there somewhere, and we'll find it." He smiled wider. "Shall we find it
—together?"

∿

BILLY HEARD SOMETHING—THE sound of glass breaking and voices. Gold—*talking to Tina?* The noises diverted his concentration, making him miss his chance. Pushing the distractions from his mind, he tried again, stretching to his limit. He had it—*the scalpel*—right there in his fingers—for just an instant—then it skittered away out of reach. He gritted his teeth in frustration. He wanted to shout, to punch something, to rip Larry Gold to pieces.

The whole thing was maddening, but Billy had been learning from Gil and knew anger wouldn't help right now. He had to focus, concentrate, stay calm and cool, no matter what. And so, he held his frustration in check, forced his muscles to relax, and unclenched his teeth. Taking a deep breath, he swayed gently back and forth, eyed the scalpel, and started again.

Tina screamed from the other room, and all pretense of control vanished.

~

TOBY STROKED the dog's big head. The man was good at starting the fire, which was blazing now. The heat felt good. He hoped the dog wouldn't die. *It had saved him.* If he did die, Toby would visit him, talk to him, keep him warm—just like he had for his mother.

He missed her.

He would miss the dog too, but if he visited, they could talk. Maybe he could even pet his fur, make him feel safe, keep him from being afraid.

The man took out a flashlight and handed it to Toby. "I need you to hold this for me," he said. "Can you do that?"

Toby nodded.

"I have to take the bullet out of him," said the man. I will need to cut him—there'll be blood, maybe a lot. Pilgrim might startle, maybe try and get up. If he does, I'll take care of that. You need to keep the light where I tell you. Understand?"

Toby nodded again, feeling not so sure at all.

The man smiled at him. "You're a very brave boy, Toby."

Toby didn't feel brave. He never felt brave—just scared. And sometimes angry, but never brave.

Pointing at where blood still seeped from the dog's fur, the man said, "Right there. That's where I need the light to shine, no matter what. If my hand or body gets in the way, scoot around so it's still lit up. If my shadow, or even the shadow of my hand, blocks what I need to see, you'll have to adjust—to move—so that it doesn't. It won't be easy, but do your best, okay? It's up to us—you and me—to save him."

That made Toby even more afraid. He didn't want to do anything that might make the dog die.

"What if I can't?" asked Toby. "What if I kill him?"

The man gripped Toby's chin with two fingers and turned him until they were looking eye to eye. What Toby saw scared him.

"Don't," said the man. "You owe him." He turned Toby's chin back and pointed at the spot. "Right there."

Toby pointed the light, his chin quivering, and they got to work.

40

Not liking what he just heard from Marge, Pappy slammed back another shot. He was afraid he might have misjudged the urgency in getting to Gil. It sounded like there might be an army against him, and knowing Gil, he'd still go at them.

Turning, Pappy gazed at the storm through the big windows across the room. No way he could make it in this, not with the little compact he was driving. He looked back at Marge.

"Think you could drive me up there? I'd make it worth your while."

"In this?" said Marge. "Not hardly, honey. I ain't no ice-road trucker, and I'm hauling premium. We go into a ditch or another car? We light up the sky. Besides, I'm drunk, and that's thanks to you. Now, come morning, if it's stopped, we can negotiate what you think is worth my while. But tonight? No chance. Sorry."

"Would you let me take your truck?" asked Pappy.

Marge looked at him with a crack of a smile. "No, I wouldn't do that. I just met you, darlin'. And if *I* can't make it, you sure can't."

"I've driven tanks through almost everything," said Pappy. "Sandstorms, trees, walls, people. I think I can handle it."

"My truck ain't a tank, and I don't want it being driven like one. Besides, I think you're maybe even drunker than me."

"In the military," said Pappy, "the mission is everything, and we do whatever is necessary to complete it. Now, my friend is up there in that town, and he may be in trouble. I mean to go get him. If we were still in the Corps, I'd have one of my men get a truck or whatever I needed to get the job done, and off we'd go. And if I couldn't get the paperwork through in time, we'd just take it and square everything up when we got back."

"*If* you got back," said Marge.

"If I didn't make it back, then I wouldn't really care anyway, would I?"

"Yeah," said Marge, "but that's other people's money paid for the tank, not yours. This is mine, paid for by me. Besides, we ain't in the Marines, and you don't even know he's *in* any trouble. So how about we have a last drink, go to our respective rooms, crawl under some warm covers, and be thankful we ain't out in that blizzard? Come morning, like I said, we'll see what's what."

Pappy didn't like it, but he had to admit he *was* a little drunk. Not to mention, his experience driving in the snow, even in tanks, was from decades ago while he was stationed in Germany. Sand, the snow of the desert, is an entirely different animal. He'd probably end up going off a cliff, killing himself, and wrecking Marge's means of making a living. Marge was probably right—waiting till morning made sense. He didn't like it, but living the military life made one accustomed to accepting things one didn't like.

Gil was probably fine anyway. If he'd run into trouble, he'd have called—*if he was able to call.*

After some thought, Pappy gave Marge a half grin and nodded. "Good advice," he said. He filled both their glasses and raised his in a final salute. "To warm covers and a perfect mattress." They touched glasses and drank.

"Good night," said Pappy.

"Good night, marine."

Pappy didn't catch the look Marge gave him as he stood, proving he was drunker than even he realized.

~

MAX STOPPED. The wind and snow were blowing into him, ruffling his fur and bringing the sound to his ears,

It wasn't the men.

It was Pilgrim.

He was in pain.

Max's rage and revenge would have to wait. He launched like a torpedo, back toward camp.

~

I HELD THE SMALL, scarlet-smeared ball in front of Toby's eyes.

"Hard to believe a little thing like that could be the cause of so much blood, isn't it?"

Toby gulped, nodding.

"One hole, one pellet," I said. "Shotgun. Pilgrim's lucky that's all that hit him. It would have been all over if he'd taken the full load."

To my surprise, Toby rose to Pilgrim's defense.

"Not luck," he said, shaking his head. "The man was scared when he shot at him."

I smiled, liking his defense. "Can't say I blame him. I'd be scared too if I had all those teeth coming at me." I pushed back the hood from his jacket and rested my hand on his head. "You did good."

The procedure had been tough. Pilgrim hadn't awoken during the operation, but he'd yelped, cried, and whined several times, his paws twitching. Toby had held him as best he could with one hand while keeping the light in place.

"Will he live?"

"Pilgrim's tough as steel," I said. "You're officially in charge of making sure he does. You'll need to melt snow for him to drink, feed him bits of food, maintain the fire, keep him warm, comfort him. That's your job, got it?"

Toby petted the unconscious animal.

"It's not a job," said Toby. "Like you said, I owe him. And—I want to."

"Good," I said, "that's good."

"What do I feed him?" asked Toby.

I reached under the passenger side front seat and dragged out the water bowl that had wedged there during the crash. I handed it to him.

"This is for the water. It's metal, so go outside, scrape off the top layer of snow, scoop up a bowl full, and heat it over the fire until it melts. Don't give him too much. Start by dipping your fingers in and rubbing it along his gums and tongue. When you see he can handle that without throwing up, you can dip a torn piece of shirt into it and squeeze dribbles into his mouth. As for food, Max will take care of that."

As if on cue, I saw Max out of the corner of my eye. Somehow he'd made it under the tarp and beside me without my knowing.

Typical Max.

Toby's eyes went wide. "Is he magic?" he asked.

"Maybe," I said. "No one knows for sure."

"Why is your face like that?" Toby asked.

I'd forgotten I was wearing camo paint. Gray, black, and green ... not that concealing now that everything was white.

"Before it started snowing, it helped to keep people from seeing me," I said.

Toby looked back at Max.

"Your dog doesn't need it."

I looked at Max too.

"No, no he doesn't."

"Magic," said Toby.

Couldn't argue with that.

"When the snow stops," I said, "maybe before, I'm going to have to leave for a little while. It won't be long, but you'll have to watch after the camp."

"Where will you go?" he asked. I could see him getting nervous.

"I'm going to go kill the Gardener," I said. "Then you won't need to be afraid of him anymore."

"You can't," said Toby, his voice sounding flat. "The One Tree protects him. He'll hang you from it—*after*."

"After?"

"After what he does to you," said Toby, and I saw his chin quiver. Tears ran down his cheeks. "Like what he did to my mommy."

I picked him up and set him on my lap, the fire flickering its light around the inside of the SUV. Stray tendrils of smoke played everywhere like mischievous wisps.

"Tell me what happened to your mom," I said.

And he did. It was painful ... there was crying. I remained quiet and didn't ask questions. I hugged him and gently patted his back as he told me the horrible tale, letting him vomit out the poison he'd had to hold inside. His body shook and trembled, and he lost his breath several times. But when he was done, he seemed better ... not a lot better ... but a little.

I had him look at me. "It wasn't your fault, Toby. I know the Gardener told you it was, but that's what monsters do. They lie to you ... try to make you believe that what they did was because of you when it was only because of them. People like the Gardener are evil. They're the bad ones, not you.

"Your mother tried to protect you, and you tried to protect her. That's what's right, what's good. You have to be strong and not believe anyone who says you are to blame ... not even your own mind. Our minds sometimes try to blame us for things we didn't do. And the things bad people say make it easy for our minds to fool us. You have to fight that. You may have to fight it for a long time before you understand ... before you really believe. But if you keep fighting, you will. One day, when you're older and can understand, you will. For now, I want you to trust me when I tell you I know who this monster is and who *you* are. You helped save Pilgrim. Only someone good would do that ... because Pilgrim is good."

And then he really cried, huge raking sobs that shook him. He hugged me tight, not able to speak, only to cry and hold me with all his strength, as though he were afraid I would leave too.

Like his father left.

Like his mother left.

But I didn't leave. Not then. I stayed there, holding him in my lap until he fell asleep.

41

"Leave her alone!" Billy yelled.

There was another scream, this one more tortured than the first. Billy tightened his stomach muscles, hips and thighs, and began rocking back and forth as hard as he could. Gone was any semblance of calm or attempt at stealth—the vision of the man on the table was too real, too raw.

"IF YOU TOUCH HER ...," the warning was cut short by a guttural roar as his body slid and jerked and flew in a crude arc that threw his trajectory off target, then back on, then off, his fingers grasping and missing and grasping and missing.

And then he touched it, his nails sliding under the metal surgical device. It started to slip away, but as he reached the apogee of his forward thrust, he popped his hand and finger up and back. The scalpel catapulted, flipping end over end.

On his backward arc, Billy bobbled for an instant, clutching for the blade. Then felt it slice into the meat of his palm. The pain was instant and bright and welcomed.

As Larry Gold appeared in the doorway, he saw Billy's trajectory and instantly bent to retrieve the gun. Billy was at the end of the backswing as Gold pointed the gun at his face.

Without hesitation, Billy pulled the knife from his left palm and, in the same motion, threw it into Larry Gold's throat. Gold's eyes registered the shock, bulging with a newfound terror. Jerking the trigger, the bullet missing and shattering a lamp near the bonsai tree, he jerked the knife free and dropped it like a cross from a vampire. It bounced on the marble before coming to rest directly beneath Billy's now forward swinging body.

Gold gripped at his bleeding throat, trying to staunch the flow, as Billy scooped up the blade and bent himself in half at the waist, slicing the rope. Spinning as he fell, he landed on his feet like a giant cat, his back to Gold and the gun.

Billy expected to feel the impact of bullets, but that didn't matter to him. Saving Tina was all that mattered. Billy would not let himself die until he finished Gold. Turning, he saw the doorway was empty.

Gold was gone.

PAPPY FINISHED what little whisky they'd left in the bottle. Marge had gone to bed, and he knew he should do the same. The earlier he sacked out, the earlier he'd be sober enough to get to Gil.

But Pappy had no intention of sleeping.

Pappy left the bar, making his way through the hallway to the lobby and exiting through the hotel's front doors and into the storm. The wind was fierce, the snow like needles.

Not yet defeated by the snowmelt the staff had sprinkled on the sidewalk, ice was underfoot. Squinting, Pappy spotted the truck Marge had proudly pointed out earlier. Square-shouldered, he walked across the packed lot, his boots crunching through the snow.

He wasn't stealing the truck, just borrowing it.

Pappy hadn't told Marge he could drive *more* than a tank. He'd done a stint supervising the motor pool in Twentynine Palms, and when he took a job, he learned everything about it—*everything*. He could hitch and unhitch a big rig in his sleep and drive one through the fires of Hades or the snows of Kilimanjaro if that's what it took to save one of his troops. He hadn't told Marge because he could see right away how savvy she was. *She would have known he was up to something.*

Pappy didn't like taking advantage of her, but the mission took priority over everything—even integrity. Gripping the side handle, Pappy raised himself up on the doorstep and leaned to the side, making room to open it. As it swung past him, he had the thought that it was strange she would leave it unlocked. *She struck him as someone more security conscious than that.*

The butt of the shotgun caught him in the forehead full force, knocking him straight back. He hit the snow-covered asphalt flat out, his head snapping hard, the snow not nearly enough padding to protect him from the impact.

Marge put a booted foot on the step and looked down at the unconscious Marine.

"Just like my second husband," she said as she spat into the snow.

~

MAX STOOD watch as the boy told his story to the Alpha. He didn't understand the words, but he felt the boy's tension ... his fear, anger ... and loss. He sensed the adrenalin spikes and cortisol dumps. A thousand signals were sorted through his computer-like brain as it deciphered and cataloged what was important, prioritizing, sifting, and correlating. He became aware of the boy's pain, his confusion. The experience affected Max in a way he had never felt before. It triggered memories, thoughts, and feelings from his past ... the attack of the grey wolf, the slaughter of his pack ... his own helplessness.

Max knew he had to get back to Viper and his pack.

He silently slipped out of the car and back into the storm. The Alpha would not leave until he had destroyed the enemy. Max needed to make that happen as quickly as possible.

Disappearing into the woods, Max went hunting.

~

WHEN TOBY WAS ASLEEP, I laid him near the ring of rocks containing the fire. Pilgrim was next to him, sleeping peacefully despite the trauma he'd been through. Max had vanished while the boy told me his story. I gathered some snow in the dog bowl, brought it into our makeshift shelter, and set it on the fire. I tried my cell again ... nothing. I'd need to get to a higher elevation, maybe even above the surrounding walls of mountain. The battery was nearly dead, so I plugged it into the charger hanging from the destroyed dash, and wonder of wonders, the car's battery was still doing its thing.

The water was boiling, so I grabbed the bowl with my gloved hands and set it aside to let it cool for a few minutes. Once I was sure the temperature was right, I soaked it up with the torn cloth and dripped some into Pilgrim's mouth. Reflexively, he licked and swallowed. I repeated this twice more, then let him rest ... best not to go too fast with food or water. If his system rebelled and he started vomiting, it could prove fatal in his weakened state.

I sat there watching him. We'd been through a lot together. He was a good old boy ... the best.

My eyes started to sting and water.

Stupid smoke.

I was amazed that he'd managed to do what he'd done earlier and come out of it alive. I stroked his head and neck, and shoulder. The bandages I'd applied were still dry and clean, telling me the blood had clotted and he was in no immediate danger of bleeding out.

Stretching out beside Pilgrim and Toby, I considered what I had to do next. The task seemed impossible when taken as a whole. I needed to approach it like eating the elephant in the old African proverb ... *one bite at a time.* But for now, it would have to wait. I was beat and needed to get some rest.

A few seconds later, I was asleep. And as I slept, the storm raged.

42

Billy ran to Tina. She saw the fear on his face, the paleness, the wild eyes, the set of his jaw. He was wearing only his underwear and had a scalpel in his hand, which he used to lash through the cloth restraints. Ripping the wide strip of duct tape from her mouth, he hugged her to him. She gripped him tightly, wanting never to let go.

"Are you hurt?" he asked, pushing her back, his eyes searching for any sign of injury. "Did he cut you? Stab you?"

"No," she said, "No. He just dug his thumb into a pressure point here." She touched behind her left ear. "The mandibular nerve—that's a rough one for me. He did it twice, then slapped that tape over my mouth. I think he was trying to bait you."

"It worked," he said, "a little too well for him. I chucked a knife into his throat."

"He ran out the door," said Tina. "You need to go after him."

"Later," said Billy. "You're all that matters right now. Did he—did he do anything to you?"

Tina looked at her relative nakedness. "No," she said. She looked at his. "Did he do anything to you?"

"No," Billy grinned. "I'm still a virgin. How did you find me, and why?"

"Your phone," she said, "and because I was worried about you. You didn't answer my calls. You *always* answer my calls." She was on the verge of crying, and she *never* cried. "What's this all about?"

"The tree," said Billy.

"The what?"

"It's a long story," said Billy, seeing how close she was to losing it. He hugged her tight. "But it's okay now. Everything's okay. *You're* okay —that's all that matters. Let's get dressed and get out of here."

With Billy's help, Tina stepped off the table, then stopped, pointing to the floor.

"Wait," she said, "a blood trail."

"Okay," said Billy, seeing the droplets that led to the door. "Yeah, okay."

They dressed quickly, and because Gold still had his gun, Billy wrapped the scalpel in some gauze he found on the table and shoved it into his pocket. Bringing a knife to a gunfight was usually not a good idea, but something was better than nothing.

Tree in hand, the two of them left the apartment and went hunting for the serial killer.

SKIRTING A BIG PINE TREE, Max startled a buck that bolted into the dark. Max was hunting men, not deer, so he let it go. He still hadn't caught scent of the enemy ... they were either too far, downwind, or just not there at all. He spent the next hour circling wider and wider, always moving downwind, hoping to catch a fragment ... anything he could trace ... so he could exact some measure of justice for what they had done to Pilgrim. That, and eliminate the reason the Alpha kept them here. He needed to return to Viper and the pups to ensure their safety.

But he detected nothing. The storm had escalated alarmingly and showed no signs of abating. He knew he should head back. The heavy wet snow had soaked his coat, and even his thickly padded paws were beginning to feel the cold.

Max came across the big buck's tracks, which were quickly filling in. The Alpha, Pilgrim, and the boy would need food. Forty minutes later, Max dropped the carcass outside the car. It had been a long haul, mostly uphill and over obstacles. The animal had been a warrior, giving Max a good clout to the hip with a backward hoof strike, but Max was more than just a warrior.

Max was Max.

Slipping inside the car and out of the snow, he saw the Alpha sleeping beside the others. Could the Alpha be trusted to bring them quickly and safely out of these mountains? Max knew that Max could do it, but the Alpha? Could he? *Would* he? Without understanding why, the ancient drive to seize control of the pack edged into his mind and thoughts ... the primal drive to be the pack leader asserting itself.

He took a step closer.

"Thanks for the food," said the Alpha without opening his eyes. "Now go to sleep, Max."

Max should have known from his scent that the Alpha was awake ... from his heartbeat, respiration, sweat glands ... but he hadn't. Once again, the Alpha perplexed Max.

Spinning twice, he curled into a ball and closed his eyes.

BILLY AND TINA followed the trail down the stairs, out the rear door of the building, and into the snow. It ended near a set of fresh tire tracks that merged with dozens of others on the street.

"You have Viper in the car?" asked Billy.

"No," said Tina. "Wouldn't matter anyway. She couldn't track through all that noise."

"What?" said Billy. "I saw a documentary about dogs tracking people in cars. Doesn't their scent escape through the cracks and stuff?"

"Yeah," said Tina, "I saw that one too. The one about that poor little girl who was murdered and dumped out east? They said the dog scented out the patrol car window and tracked the other car down the freeway for dozens of miles ... days later ... after a rainstorm. *Baloney.* That same handler almost blew another murder investigation with a phony track to a murder suspect. He went to an address dispatch got from the suspect's license plate. Turns out dispatch mixed it up and sent him one block over. It wasn't his dog tracking at all. Judge reamed him out good—created a lot of bad case law for canines.

"As for finding the girl's body in the first case? It was actually a search party that found her. She was wrapped up in a canvas bag, and they called the handler to see if he could pick anything up before they disturbed the scene. Instead, he took credit for finding her. Dogs are incredible and can do amazing things with their senses, but they have limitations, just like all of us. Speaking of which, I need to call this in—get some of this blood collected for DNA evidence."

"No," said Billy.

"What?"

"No, you can't call this in. My DNA's up there. So's yours. How do we explain being here?"

"The truth," said Tina.

"I'm a gangster," said Billy.

Tina reached up and kissed him lightly on the lips. "Former gangster," she said. "Now you're a PI, and you were here on PI business. Honest business. And look, you uncovered a serial killer in the act. Almost got killed yourself. You need to start thinking of yourself as you are now. Legitimate. You're not a killer, not part of the mafia. You're a professional—one step below a cop."

"One step below?"

Tina grinned. "Maybe two."

"They'll arrest me," said Billy.

Tina kissed him again. "No, they won't. And if they do, I'll bail you out."

She took out her phone and made the call.

43

Pappy opened his eyes to the worst hangover of all time. The curtains were open to the howling blizzard outside, the gray light stabbing his eyes like twin bayonets. He tried to raise his hand to shield them and found his hands were tied together at the wrists. When he tried to move, he realized his ankles were tied as well. He was stretched out on a bed in a hotel room he didn't recognize. The bed next to him was unoccupied, empty, and made. The room smelled of lavender, and he seemed to recall Marge having a trace of that scent on her last night at the bar.

And then he remembered.

The snow.

The truck,

The shotgun.

Marge.

Wow, he must have been way more drunk than he realized—and she must not have been as drunk as he thought. Bending at the waist, he sat up. He never would have made it up the mountains in the raging storm he saw outside the window. Good thing she'd stopped him.

The door to the room opened, and Marge came in holding a

white donut shop bag and two Styrofoam cups of coffee. Pappy could smell the brew from the bed.

"You tried to steal my truck," said Marge.

"No," said Pappy, "I was just going to borrow it."

"Borrow it," she echoed.

"I'd have brought it back and paid you for the use."

"Right," said Marge. "And you think that makes it okay?"

"No," said Pappy, squinting from the obtrusive gray light that still tormented him. "But it was the mission."

"Your mission," said Marge, "not mine. I told you last night—what's mine is mine."

"I know," said Pappy. "I was drunk."

"That don't make it okay neither," said Marge.

"I know. I'm sorry."

"Not good enough," said Marge. "My ex always said sorry after beating me when he was drunk. That wasn't never good enough, neither."

Pappy laid back down, still attempting to bring his hands up to cover his eyes. "Yeah, I suppose not. But, for what it's worth, I'd have made it good if anything happened to your truck." Squinting at her, he opened one eye. "Is that second cup for me?"

"Not that you deserve it," she said, "but yes. You bought last night —I got it today." She set both cups and the bag on the nightstand between the beds. "You gonna behave?"

"Scouts honor," said Pappy.

"Forget the scouts," said Marge. "Swear on the Eagle, Globe, and Anchor."

Pappy nodded painfully, his forehead feeling about three sizes too big. "I swear on the Marine Corps emblem."

Marge pulled a pair of wire snips from her back pocket and clipped the zip ties from his ankles and wrists.

Pappy rubbed his wrists and forearms. "Okay if I sit up?"

"Hard to drink hot coffee on your back," she said, handing him a cup.

Pappy took it and swung to a sitting position. "Thanks."

Marge opened the bag. "Want an éclair? Best in the county."

Pappy gingerly sipped the coffee. "Those the ones with white cream or yellow?"

"Custard," said Marge. "Yellow."

Pappy nodded, instantly regretting the gesture. He wasn't sure if the pain was from the whiskey or the shotgun to his forehead—probably both. He held out his hand, and Marge set the beautiful pastry in his palm.

Gently, Pappy touched his forehead. "Does it look as bad as it feels?"

"Does it feel like an atomic bomb blowed up in your head?"

"That's about right," said Pappy.

"Then no. Just a little swollen with some bruising. I got ice on it pretty quick after some friends helped me drag you up here and toss you on the bed. They was making some pretty rude comments about my plans for you. Funny, but rude." She grinned. "You may have tarnished my spotless reputation."

Pappy smiled, almost nodding again but stopping himself just in time. "In that case, thanks for just giving me a love tap instead of shooting me."

"I'd have been in my rights," she said.

"Yes," said Pappy, "yes, you would."

Pappy took a bite, the chewing aggravating his headache. He was beginning to wonder if she'd broken something in there. He washed the bite down with coffee. "So, how do you know I won't try it again?"

It was Marge's turn to grin. "Not possible." She stood, walked to the window, and pointed outside. "We got three foot of snow while you slept. Roads is all closed. My truck's socked in—you couldn't get it out with dynamite. And even if you could, you wouldn't make it fifty yards. Snowplows ain't even runnin'."

Pappy made himself stand to take a look. Marge was right. In a battlefield situation, it would be time to call in an airstrike. A long run of napalm would clear those roads—of course, it would melt the asphalt too. Pappy hoped Gil was all right, but for now, patience was required.

"I'm going to take a shower in my room," Pappy said to Marge. "After that, what's there to do until the snow stops and melts?"

Marge pulled a deck of cards from a pocket. "Rummy?"

Pappy raised an eyebrow. "That'll work."

TOBY SLEPT UNTIL AFTER TEN. I'd gutted and cleaned the buck Max gifted us and had a couple of steaks cooking over the fire on a makeshift grill I'd rigged from car parts. I think it was the smell of the venison that woke him. Outside, the snow was so heavy that even Max stayed inside with us. The storm was still angry and showed no signs of slowing. Much as I hated it, we were snowed in. The Gardener would have to wait.

Toby woke up scared, his eyes wide and darting about.

"It's okay," I said to him. "You're all right. You're here with me, Max, and Pilgrim. "You're safe."

Blinking, he looked around, then gradually began to comprehend where he was and how he'd gotten here. He reached out and lay a hand on Pilgrim's side.

"Is he okay?" he asked.

"He's doing good," I said. "They don't make them any tougher than Pilgrim."

"I'm hungry," he said. "Thirsty, too."

I'd filled the canteens from my go bag with snow melt and then, after boiling them, set them in the snow to cool. I unscrewed the top from one, handed it to him, and he guzzled the cold, refreshing water. I plopped a steak on a cleaned hubcap and cut it into pieces with my knife. I handed him the meal along with another of my knives. He dug in, taking mouthfuls of water between bites. Fortunately, I always carry salt and pepper in my car and go bag, which helped disguise the meat's gaminess. We ate side by side, sharing the canteen. I'd eaten earlier but thought sharing a meal would be a good bonding opportunity.

"I'm not leaving today," I told him. "The snow's still too bad."

Toby nodded. "Good. I don't want you to die. I don't want to be alone."

"You won't be alone," I said. "Max will stay with you. And I won't die. I'll be back."

"The One Tree is god," he said. "And the One Tree protects the Gardener. You can't beat him."

"The One Tree isn't God," I said. "The Gardener lied to you—just like he lied to you about your mother's death being your fault."

"You don't know," said Toby.

"Maybe I know more than you think," I said. "Tell me about the One Tree."

"It's god," he said. "It gave us knowing—told us about fire and right and wrong. It knows everything—even what we think. It told the Gardener he was from another planet and made him in charge and says we have to love him."

"Do you love the Gardener?" I asked. "After what he did to your mother, do you love him?"

Toby was lifting a chunk of meat on the knife to his mouth but stopped halfway. He looked at me, his cheeks ruddy from the heat, his tiny face smeared with soot from the campfire and smears of Pilgrim's dried blood. A little quiver crossed his chin, and his eyes watered, but he didn't cry. I thought he was very brave for that.

"No," said Toby. "No, I can't. I hate him."

"Good," I said. "That's the right way to feel. The real God, the God of the Bible, *says* it's right. He says to love what is good and abhor what is evil. Abhor means to *hate a lot*."

I could see him thinking.

"The Bible says in Psalms 11:5 *The LORD tests the righteous, but the wicked and the one who loves violence His soul hates. And in Psalms 5:5-6 The boastful shall not stand in Your sight; You hate all workers of iniquity. You shall destroy those who speak falsehood; The LORD abhors the bloodthirsty and deceitful man.*"

He took the bite and chewed for several seconds before coming back.

"The real God?"

"You know about the Bible?" I asked.

He nodded. "From church. We went a few times when I was little. The Gardener says he's writing a new bible, though. He works on it all the time."

"Figures," I said. "Cults usually have four things in common. First, they deny that Jesus is God, either by calling Him an angel or something lower or by putting someone or something higher than Him. Second, whoever starts the cult is often visited by some form of *angel of light*—like an alien. Third, they always have a book or writings that supersede ...," I remembered I was talking to a six-year-old, "... that they *consider* more important than the Bible. And fourth, they have a living prophet who can change the rules whenever they want to."

Toby continued to eat, but I could see him thinking. "The Gardener says the One Tree came to him in a dream. You mean it isn't real?"

"Well, there *was* a tree—the tree of the knowledge of good and evil—long ago. But it's not here anymore." I could see I was confusing him.

"Do you want me to tell you the true story of the Trees?"

"Trees? You mean there was more than one?"

"Yes," I said. "There were two. God set them in the Garden of Eden, where he made Adam and Eve. One was the tree of life, and it symbolized a door. Do you know what a symbol is?"

Toby nodded. "Like the picture of the One Tree with a circle around it on the gate of the Assembly?"

"Exactly. The picture isn't the actual tree, but it gives you an idea of what the tree is supposed to be about. The first tree, the tree of life, was a symbol of the *way* to God. The *other* tree, the tree of the knowledge of good and evil, also symbolized a door. But these doors led in very different directions. One door, the tree of life, led to the Father, God. The other, the tree of the knowledge of good and evil, led away from God."

"Why would God put *that* door there?" asked Toby. "Did God want them to go away from him?"

"No," I said. "But God *wants* us to love Him so He can have a relationship with us, like your father with you. When you're little, a good father *commands* that you love him. He doesn't give you a choice because you aren't wise enough to know better. He doesn't do this because he's selfish but because he loves you more than anyone else ever could, even more than you love yourself. So, *everything* he tells you, shows you, or gives you will always be for your own good.

"He also knows that anyone who tries to get you to do something different from what he tells you is doing it for bad reasons ... things that will *hurt* you. Now that's while you are a child, while you are first learning. That's what God was doing with Adam and Eve. They were like very young children, like you. They knew a lot of things, but not enough to make the most important decision of all. So, He guarded them ... protected them ... just like your father is trying to protect you by sending me here to find you and bring you home. He wants to raise you under the protection of his love.

"But eventually, when you are old enough, you'll decide whether to continue loving your father. It's the same way with God. He wants you to choose to love Him for yourself ... without being ordered, made, or forced to do so. That's the only way to have a truly loving relationship. And that's why he made the tree of the knowledge of good and evil. It was a door for Adam and Eve to leave God if, one day, when they were old enough, they decided they didn't want to be part of that relationship."

Toby shook his head. "I don't understand."

"Would the Gardener let you leave the Assembly?" I asked.

"No, never," said Toby. "No one can ever leave."

"And do you think he loves you?" I asked.

Toby's jaw clenched. "No."

"And there's the difference," I said. "A good father controls a child until he's old enough to know better. Then he lets the adult decide to stay or go because that's how a healthy relationship works. The Gardener locks you all in and says you can never leave. That's not love ... that's sick. That's a tyrant. And God, the real God, is not sick or a tyrant."

A gust of wind blew through the tarp, scattering smoke and

sending embers swirling before dying back down. Pilgrim stirred, licking his lips but not waking. I dipped the cloth into the water and squeezed it over his mouth.

"You said Adam and Eve were too little to choose," said Toby. "Then why did God let them leave?"

"Because the angel God put there to protect and teach them betrayed God. He told them a lie. Their Father had already told them not to eat from the fruit of the tree, and they should have listened to their Father, but they didn't."

"Because of the liar?" asked Toby.

"Exactly," I said. "It was still wrong, and there were terrible consequences, but because they were so young and because the one who was supposed to protect them tricked them, God made a way to save them."

"Was it the Devil?" whispered Toby.

"Yes," I said. "It was."

"Why did God put the Devil there with them?"

"He didn't," I said. "God put one of the greatest and most powerful angels He made there with them ... to protect them ... to teach them. But the angel became envious of Adam and Eve and their relationship with God. He lied to them, hurting himself, them, and God. That lie was the first sin, opening the *door* to all sin."

"Is the Gardener the Devil?" he whispered again.

I thought about it for a second. "Yes," I said, "or at least one of his sons, and he's been trying to get you to choose the wrong door."

"The One Tree," said Toby.

"No," I said, "a false tree."

"Where did the real tree go?" asked Toby."

I thought of Ezekiel 31, where God explains that the law, symbolized by the Tree, grew until it covered the entire world. Its branches, both actual and symbolic of the law of death, spread until there was only evil everywhere. Because of the Tree, God restrained the underground waters supplying it along with the four rivers that watered all the earth, creating a worldwide drought. The pressure in the fountains of the great deep began to build, and God allowed the evil nations to enter the Garden for the first time since the fall of Adam. They cut down the tree, triggering the global flood and destroying all life except for sea creatures and the inhabitants of Noah's Ark. During the great cataclysm, God sucked the tree, along with the nations and the angels who had sought after strange flesh, straight down to Hell.

A little much to explain to a six-year-old.

Instead, I said, "God sent it to Hell, and that's where it is today. The tree the Gardener worships is a fake ... just like him. It can't hurt anyone.

I saw a shudder race through Toby.

"It does, though," he said. "It hurts so bad." His hand crept toward the top of his shoulder.

Gesturing with my chin, I gripped his arm with one hand and turned him. "Let me see." I lifted his coat and shirt, revealing a criss-cross pattern of red welts and white scars across his back.

What I felt at that moment can't be described. I looked out at the blizzard through a small rip in the tarp. This snow needed to stop.

There was killing to be done.

44

After an entire night, morning, and afternoon of interviews with Denver PD, Billy and Tina drove to Rick's office together. Although the snow was light, radio broadcasts were warning that the mountains were getting hammered. It was almost five in the afternoon, and they were exhausted, but Billy wanted to get this stupid tree off his hands. He had considered waiting until the next day, but after confirming, via phone, that Rick was still at his office, he decided to get it over with.

They parked across the street and sloshed their way to his building. The cold, intensified by a brisk wind, penetrated their coats, hats, and gloves. Billy wondered what kind of luck the cops would have finding Larry Gold in these freezing temperatures. One thing was for sure—he would have to work fast. He planned on finding Gold first, and he would enlist all of the Family's resources to get the job done.

Gold had hurt Tina—stripped her nearly naked—and he knew who they both were. There was no way Billy could leave a threat like that out there to haunt them. He was painfully aware of Gil's family story and would take no chance on a repeat. If, by some chance, the cops did get to Gold first, Billy would have him killed in jail. Either way, Larry Gold was a dead man—he just didn't know it yet.

Rick met them at the outer office door, his two interns standing in the background. Billy saw they all had their coats on and briefcases in hand. "Going somewhere?" he asked.

Rick greeted Tina with a smile, then turned back to Billy. "Taking off early due to the snow. I already let my secretary go, but since you said it was important, I decided to wait for you. Those two were taking notes on my last appointment of the day and wanted another chance to evaluate you, so they stayed too. Is this about my tree?"

Billy reached into the bag he held and produced the juniper, holding it out for Rick.

"No," said Rick, marveling as he took it. "It is—*it is*. This mark right here happened years ago. You found it! How?"

"It's quite a story, actually. It was taken by one of your clients, just like you thought," said Billy.

Rick held up the tree, rooted in its pot, showing it off to the two interns as he walked back into his office, Tina and Billy following.

"I knew it," said Rick. "Who was it?"

Billy saw the feet behind the door a second before something crashed into the side of his head, lights, spangles, and flashes exploding as he was knocked unconscious. Tina reached for the gun she still didn't have on her but stopped when the big-bored pistol pointed at her face.

"That would be me, Doctor," said Larry Gold with a raspy voice, sporting a thick white bandage on his throat, held in place with medical tape.

Rick's last patient of the day.

~

THE SNOW HADN'T STOPPED, but it had slackened, so I decided it would have to do. It was getting dark, and I needed to get Pilgrim to a hospital. Waiting longer was becoming less of an option. I cooked up another steak for Toby, deciding I'd eat later. If I were to get shot in the stomach, an empty gut was less likely to be fatal—less junk to bleed into my system.

I gave Pilgrim more water, stroked him, and looked at Toby.

"This will be scary for you," I said, "but I have to leave. Max will look out for you. *You* look out for Pilgrim. Deal?"

"What will I do if he kills you?" asked Toby, and I could see he was near crying again.

"Right there," I said, ignoring his question and pointing just outside the door, "I packed meat for you. It's buried under the snow, but not deep. I also stacked up plenty of wood. Don't put too much on at once ... you don't want to burn the car up, okay?"

"I don't want you to."

"I know," I said. "I don't blame you for being scared, but the Gardener won't let us out of these mountains if I don't do this. He owns the police up here. He's got spies everywhere. As long as he's in charge, he can block the roads, choke off all our exits, and send out search parties until he finally takes us out. But once I cut the root, the rest of the tree will die."

"You can't kill him," said Toby, a fat tear rolling down his grimy cheek.

My lips twitched just a fraction. "Yes, I can. And I will. You'll see when I get back. And then you'll never doubt again. Okay?"

Another tear streaked toward his quivering chin, and my heart nearly broke. This situation was way above his years, but that couldn't be helped, only prolonged. The longer I waited, the more the Gardener's odds of capturing us improved.

"You're a good boy, Toby. Your father will be very proud when I tell him how brave you've been. Take care of Pilgrim."

I'd already packed my go-bag with the items I would need. Most of the camo paint had washed off my face, but I didn't reapply it because neither my clothes nor the paint would help in the snow. I wished I'd brought white snow gear just in case, but I hadn't. It was okay, though ... the attack I had planned wasn't of the hidden or camouflaged variety ... nor was it a hit-and-run or come-from-behind assault.

I thought of the scars on Toby's back, Pilgrim's unconsciousness and nearness to death ... Toby's clutching his dead and buried mother's fingers.

No, this would not be a game of hide and seek. It was going to be a completely different kind of game.

～

TRYING to find a way up the mountain, Pappy had called every snow equipment shop, maintenance shed, and rental place he could locate. Nothing had panned out.

Marge had been good company—they'd played Rummy, Spades, Crazy Eights, and now were well into a marathon game of poker. Marge was up about seventy bucks, and Pappy hadn't let her win a single game, even though he figured he owed her for the truck incident. She definitely knew her way around a deck of cards.

He'd called Gil several times with no answer, and although he was getting more worried by the moment, there was nothing he could do. The snowfall had slowed, but the plows still hadn't reached them, and Marge's truck wouldn't make it out of the parking lot, let alone up the winding switchbacks of the mountain roads. There was nothing to do but wait.

Pappy laid out his three-of-a-kind, beating Marge's two pair, and scooped up the meager pot.

"That was fun," said Marge. "But I think it's about time to head down to the bar. What do you think?"

Pappy looked out the window. "You sure a driver as good as you couldn't make it up there?"

Marge grunted. "Any driver as good as me knows better than to try, honey."

"How much would it take for you to give it a go?"

"Ain't happenin'. Don't even think about it. My rig's worth more than you got, and my life's worth at least twice that. So, no. And let that be the end of it, or we part company right here, and you won't have no way to get to him even after the plows clear a path. It's still gonna be nasty in spots, and that puny compact of yours ain't gonna cut it."

Holding up a hand, Pappy admitted defeat. "Okay, drinks are on me."

"Yes, they are," said Marge. "And that stuff you got last night will do just fine. But no gettin' drunk tonight. You try and steal my truck a second time, and you'll get the front end of that scattergun. You copy?"

"Roger that," said Pappy, rubbing the bruise on his forehead.

MAX WATCHED as the Alpha disappeared into the night. He kept track of him with his other senses for nearly an hour, but eventually, all sound from him blended into the cacophony of the storm. After that, even the vagaries of his scent, coupled with ground disturbance, fragmented beyond his ability to discern.

Max did not like that the Alpha left without him. He knew from the Alpha's scent ... bearing ... mannerisms ... and chemical makeup that he was about to go to war. The Alpha would need him.

But the Alpha had ordered him to stand guard.

To guard Pilgrim.

To guard the boy.

The old conflict raged hotter inside his mind ... his drives pushing him to disobey. He wanted to follow the Alpha, protect him, and end this so he could return to Viper.

But Pilgrim needed protection, too, as did the boy. They were both helpless. And if more hunters came, there was only Max to save them. A vision of Pilgrim, surrounded by blood-soaked snow and bodies came to him ... his old pack member was still a warrior after all.

Max walked the perimeter, marking as he went. Max would protect the pack.

45

I made it to the edge of the tree line, close to where I'd parked not long ago. The trip had been rugged, slippery, and steep, made worse by my injured ribs and slight limp ... but at least I wasn't coughing up blood. From here, I could see the guard towers, the two closest anyway. Snow slashed in front of me at an angle, interfering with visibility.

Assuming a kneeling stance, I switched my scope from night vision to thermal. Heat was what I was looking for, and heat I found. The guard in the tower was smoking a cigarette, its tip glowing brighter than his body temp. I shot him through the heart, initiating the process that would eventually bring his body to ambient temperature, making him one with the storm. The suppressor on my AR blunted the sound to a low cough, drowned entirely by the elements. I sighted in on the second tower.

I would have gone for headshots ... reducing the chances of screams alerting the others ... but the wind and snow made for less-than-optimum shooting conditions, even at this range. Besides, the chaos of the storm smothered most sounds. So, center mass it was.

This guy wasn't smoking. He was scanning the grounds with a pair of field binoculars. In this mess, they had to be thermal, like mine ... otherwise ... he wouldn't be able to see a thing. He scanned past me, stopped abruptly, then zipped back my way. This guy was sharp.

My bullet exploded his heart.

I did a quick scan and ran closer to the compound, chancing the open expanse. About halfway to the gate, I stopped, knelt, sighted in on the third tower, dropped the guard, then sighted in on the fourth. Target acquisition wasn't great, so I moved to the right and up about ten yards.

Good.

The slight recoil butted my shoulder, and the man went down. Running through the snow, I found where I'd cut the fence. It hadn't been repaired, which meant they either hadn't found it or they were getting sloppy. I edged through and continued to the shed where I'd seen the snowcat, near where Toby's mother was buried. Three men were bustling about, carrying snow shovels and wearing parkas, hats, and gloves. I saw rifles standing against the shed next to them. One of the men saw me, tilted his head like a curious dog, then dropped his shovel and grabbed for a gun.

Shooting from the hip, I put three rounds into his torso. I quickly shifted and put two more into the next closest man's body. The third guy held his hands up, shaking and begging, "Please, don't shoot. I'm unarmed. Please ... please."

I walked up to him and smacked him in the head with the butt of the AR, knocking him down but not out. I zip-tied him, threw some tape across his mouth, and dragged him into the shed. A single light-bulb hanging from a beam gave the shed a weak yellow glow. Leaving the two dead men where they lay in the snow, I smacked the dazed man fully awake. He looked at me with wide, frightened eyes.

"I'm going to ask you a question," I said. "You're going to tell me the truth. If you lie, I'll know, and I'll kill you. If you scream or yell or do anything but answer the question, I'll kill you. Understand?"

He nodded, sweating, despite the cold.

I ripped off the tape. "Where's the Gardener?"

"He's in the sanctuary," said the man, "with everyone else. It's dinner. Everyone meets for dinner except work crews and the guys out searching for you."

"How many total?"

"Sixty—maybe seventy, in the sanctuary. Another thirty searching and working outside the camp."

"How many kids, women?"

"More than half," he said.

"Half of the sixty or half of the ninety?"

"Maybe forty women and kids," he said.

That left thirty or more fighting men. I did the calculations, nodding to myself.

I had more than enough ammo.

~

BACKING SLOWLY, Tina raised her hands to shoulder level.

"That's far enough," said Gold.

"Larry," said Rick, stunned, "what's going on here?"

Gold shrugged. "I'm sorry, Doctor, but I'm the one who stole your tree."

"My tree? But why? And what does that have to do with this? I mean, it's not worth it. Go ahead and keep it, just don't hurt anyone."

"To answer your questions," said Gold calmly, "yes, *your* tree. As to why? It's a trophy. What does it have to do with this? These two found out it was me who took it. And yes, this *is* all worth it because I take my trophies very seriously."

Uncomprehending, Rick looked to Tina for clarity.

"He's a serial killer," said Tina. "Fancies himself a Dexter or maybe a Hannibal Lecter. He was going to kill you, so he took the tree as his trophy. Billy found him, but he got away from us."

"In a nutshell," nodded Gold. "Except for the part about how I *was* going to kill you. Turns out I *am* going to kill you. *All* of you."

The two interns shrank back as he smiled at them.

"There's no reason to kill them," said Tina. "The police already know who you are. They have your fingerprints, your DNA, and by now, your picture from security cameras inside the apartment building. Killing them won't help you."

Gold pursed his lips. "Okay, I'll make a deal. Everyone agree to behave—do exactly as I tell you—and I'll let them live. Maybe even you and your big boyfriend here too. The doctor is my prize. The rest of you are incidental. After all, I'm an artist, not a psycho. I don't enjoy killing for killing's sake." Holding out his free hand, he looked at Rick. "The tree."

Rick handed it to him, and Gold set it on an end table.

"Do we have a deal?"

THE FIRST SNOWPLOWS made it through at five twenty, clearing the roads and making a path up and around the mountain. The night before, Marge had consumed exactly two shots of whiskey, Pappy, one. They were sitting in Marge's truck. Pappy had already unhitched the giant gas trailer. Half an hour earlier, a female state trooper riding a snowmobile had alerted them of the coming snowplows. After delivering the news, she headed toward Galena. Pappy would have tried to hitch a ride, but the coming plows would make that unnecessary. Instead, he waited with Marge and, right on schedule, the big shovels plowed straight on through, clearing the way.

Marge drove, changing gears like the pro she was. There were still slick spots scattered haphazardly along the way, causing the big rig to slide dangerously close to hundred-foot drop-offs, giving Pappy a closer view of eternity than he cared for.

After another close call, he nervously glanced at her. She looked back, grinning like a maniac in the face of danger, her face illuminated by the dash's lights, her gray hair flaring like a halo. Suddenly she did remind him of Large Marge from *Pee-wee's Big Adventure*. In that instant, Pappy wouldn't have been surprised if her eyeballs shot out of their sockets, her tongue flicking like a snake. But all she did was grin, and up the mountain they went.

STATE TROOPER LILLY WRIGHT was about twenty minutes ahead of the plows, cruising along the highway on her treaded snow machine. It wasn't the first time she'd cruised the mountains this way, but it was the first time this year. Her visit ahead of the road clearing crew had a dual purpose—the first was to ensure no boulders or trees had fallen that would impede the plows, and the second was to check on Gil Mason. Lilly had promised Tina she'd keep an eye out for him, so here she was.

Not that she was worried.

Not really.

After all, what kind of trouble could he get into in this weather? Lilly figured he was sheltering safely in place until the snow stopped, like everybody else.

Well, almost everybody.

A gust of wind slashed through her thick parka, making her shiver. *She* didn't count, of course. She was doing her job, and it was a job she was happy to perform. Cops lived the old postmen's creed more than they ever had—*Neither rain, nor snow, nor sleet, nor hail shall keep the postmen from their appointed rounds.* Well, here she was, a state trooper, and not a postman in sight. The thought made her grin, which proved to be a bad move—the freezing air hurt her teeth. Closing her lips, she gunned the throttle.

Mason better appreciate this.

46

The Gardener held up his hands, quieting everyone in the sanctuary. "Someone has been bad," he said. Tension filled the room. "The One Tree has spoken to me. There will be punishment tonight."

Brian Pasley, the Gardener's chief of police, stood next to him. "River, Timber, come to the One Tree."

The boys looked at each other briefly, then stood and did as commanded. River's legs wavered as he stopped before the Gardener and Pasley. The Gardener gripped both boys by a shoulder and looked down at them.

"These boys," he said to the Assembly, "knew that Leaf was sneaking out at night—that he was visiting his mother. The One Tree has told me this. Because of them, Leaf is dead. They will now tell me what they know of the man who killed him." He looked at them—into them. River shrank from the gaze, while Timber stared back, not defiant, just accepting."

"I don't know anything about him," said Timber.

River shook his head, quivering.

The Gardener nodded. "We shall see."

He twitched a finger toward Pasley, and four men came forward from the Assembly. They stood the boys beneath two thick, gnarled branches jutting from opposite sides of the tree about nine feet above the ground. The boys' shirts were removed and tossed to the floor, their wrists secured to ropes hanging from the branches, their backs turned toward the congregation. The men backed away as the Gardener approached the table where the rods were neatly aligned. He carefully examined them, taking his time to select the right one.

"The first to tell me the truth shall live," said the Gardener. "The other shall be banished from the One Tree forever."

Some in the Assembly winced at the sight of the scars emblazoned across the boys' backs. Those on Timber were well healed, but River's were fresh and raw.

The Gardener flexed the chosen rod between his giant hands, then pulled back his arm.

∼

NOBODY SAW me enter through the side door ... their attention focused on the two boys being bound to the tree at the front of the Assembly. I counted maybe fifteen armed men. Fifteen was a lot, but they'd have to be careful if they were to hit only me. I had free range to shoot any or all of them. At least ten other men were scattered among the women and children, but they didn't seem to be carrying.

I'd run up against four others as I entered the hall. Guards ... but not good ones. They were all dead. A lot of the men in this room were about to join them.

I'd heard the Gardener's proclamation. It sounded like the threat he'd made about having me killed at the jail. He was going to kill one or both of these twelve-year-old boys. I wondered how many others he'd murdered. I wasn't sure I'd ever learn the answer to that, but of one thing I was sure ... he would murder no more.

Ever.

As he pulled back his arm to deliver the first blow, I stepped forward, making myself seen. "I'm right here, coward."

As the Gardener turned, a sudden look of shock, confusion, and fear crossed his face as he saw me holding the AR. I'd taken the time to remove the suppressor ... it was time for some noise.

Going for his pistol, Brian Pasley stepped forward to defend the Gardener. He never made it. I put two rounds into his chest, one in his pelvic girdle, and a fourth in his forehead, just in case he wore a vest ... not that a vest would stop the .223s, but why take chances? And besides, I was going for effect. I could have shot the Gardener right out, but, like I said, I was making a statement ... a declaration. The children needed to see he was no God, no prophet—just an evil man who was about to pay for his deeds.

The fate of the adults would depend on what they chose to do. I had little sympathy for them, men or women. They might be victims of a sort, but *they* signed on for this place—their children hadn't.

The sanctuary erupted, women screaming, men raising guns. The two men who had tied the boys to the tree looked at me, stunned, their rifles dangling on slings.

"Drop the guns or die," I said, my eyes scanning the other men in the crowd. "That goes for everyone in this hall."

The Gardener gathered himself and took a step forward—*I'll give him credit for that.*

"Don't do it," he said. "He can't kill all of you."

"Yes, I can," I said. "But I won't need to." I swiveled the AR to the Gardener's face. "I'll kill you first, and when they see you're a false god, they'll run."

"You won't shoot me," he said. "You want to take me to the police. Besides, the One Tree will protect me. You can't kill me."

"You have me all wrong," I said. "I never planned on taking you to the police, and I *am* going to kill you. You aren't a god, and your phony tree can't protect anyone. I'm going to prove that to everyone here."

One of the two men gripped his rifle, so I put a bullet into his stomach. The brief distraction gave the Gardener his opportunity. He grabbed the boy closest to him, produced a short machete from somewhere I didn't see, cut the rope holding the boy to the branch, and ran at me, using the child as a shield.

The second man drew his weapon to his shoulder, dividing my attention and making it impossible to take out the Gardener's legs. I blasted the man away, and then the Gardener impacted me with the boy's body. I gave with the contact, trying to protect the child from being crushed, and the three of us went to the floor.

Chaos erupted in the sanctuary.

~

TINA DIDN'T BELIEVE Larry Gold. She was sure he was going to kill them all—not that it mattered. She wouldn't let him kill the psychiatrist, no matter what he promised or planned. The question was, how to stop him. For the third time, she berated herself for having left her gun at home, then pushed the thought away. Wasting time on regrets was useless—she needed to focus on what to do and nothing else.

Gold had the gun. He was a whack job, but he probably wasn't an expert shot or efficient at hand-to-hand combat. If she could get the gun barrel out of line with her body, she would attempt to take him down. He was big, but not like *Billy big*—more like farm boy big.

Sidestep—kick to the testicles—a jab to the throat or eyes—grab the gun—twist in—snap his trigger finger—jerk back—gun now in her hand.

Sounded good.

She'd practiced the move hundreds of times in defensive tactics classes and was successful *most* of the time. Of course, that was always against a fellow cop or instructor with a fake gun. And even then, she'd missed maybe one out of five—not bad odds—*unless* you were in a real-life situation. Suddenly the nerves set in. A single miss might mean a bullet to the heart or face.

Almost as though he were reading her mind, Gold smiled at her, leaned back out of range, and pointed the gun at her chest—*bigger target than her forehead.*

"Take your handcuffs—I know you have two sets—and restrain Tom and Jerry here behind their backs. If you try anything, I'll just start shooting everyone."

Tina took out her first set, cuffed the closest intern, and followed with the second. She turned to Gold and raised her eyebrows, implying—*and?*

"Sit them down behind the desk," he said.

"Larry," said Rick.

"Not now, Doctor. Couch talk is over." Gold removed a handful of zip-ties from his inside jacket pocket. "First, your boyfriend," said Gold, chinning toward Billy's body.

Tina looked down at him. "There's no way I can turn him onto his stomach by myself," she said.

"That's fine," said Gold. "You can tie him in front. But do his ankles too."

Tina left as much slack as she thought she could get away with, but when she started to look up from her kneeling position Gold kicked her in the forehead, snapping her neck back and knocking her out.

He looked at Rick and grinned.

"Lay on the couch. It's my turn to play doctor."

PILGRIM AWOKE FULLY ALERT and in pain. The boy slept beside him, his hand resting on Pilgrim's shoulder. Max lay close, looking him in the eyes as though he had been waiting for him to return. A bowl of water sat next to him. Feeling weak and nauseous, he lapped up a little, and when he saw he could hold it down, he decided to drink a bit more. Afterward, he rested his tired head on his paws.

Max padded over and nuzzled Pilgrim's nose and muzzle. He then slipped under the tarp and into the night snow. Pilgrim stayed awake guarding the boy.

Max went to find the Alpha.

THE GARDENER WAS surprised when Gil Mason absorbed the impact, allowing the three of them to hit the floor almost simultaneously.

He'd expected the child to be crushed between them, hurting him, maybe even breaking the boy's bones, giving Mason pause, and affecting him psychologically. Instead, they were all sprawling.

No matter.

The Gardener knew he could not lose. He was a god. Mason was only a man—an irritant to be removed. The killing of Pasley, although disturbing, offered an opportunity. When finished with Mason, he'd bring Pasley back to life. The miracle would cast out all doubt, cementing him as the deity he was in the minds and hearts of his followers. Word would spread to all branches of the OTA, reaching the individual members wherever they were, spreading his influence just as the biblical tree of the knowledge of good and evil had spread its branches over all the earth. His numbers would grow, and with them, his power.

Rolling smoothly, the Gardener gained his feet. All that was left was to kill Gil Mason.

He would crush the life from him.

47

Larry Gold secured Rick to the couch, an armless black leather chaise with an adjustable headrest. After gagging both interns, he'd stripped the doctor to his underwear. On the small coffee table next to the couch, Gold unrolled the leather apron he'd brought, revealing a set of shiny metal tools—pliers, forceps, a bone saw, a set of scalpels. All that was missing was the scalpel he'd pulled from his throat and dropped on the floor back at his apartment.

"Larry," said Rick, assuming a calm, therapeutic voice, "why are you doing this? I've done nothing but try and help you."

"That's just it, Rick—I don't need help. I never did. I came here and took you on as my doctor strictly to ascertain whether you were worthy of joining my collection." He pointed a finger at him, winked, and smiled. "And you are. You should take pride in that. I choose only the best."

"The best of what?" asked Rick, growing more nervous as Larry continued to lay out his instruments like a surgeon preparing for surgery.

Gold stopped, thought for a second, and turned back to him. "Anything, everything. The best cop, the best prostitute, trash man, rocket scientist, boxer, dancer, hoarder, philanthropist, rich man, poor man, beggar man, thief. I always choose those who are of excellent repute among their peers." He pointed at Rick again.

"Like you—with praise heaped upon you by experts in your field. And not just those who like you. Oh no! The greatest compliments come from those who despise you, those who are jealous, envious— those who want to *be* you but lack the talent, work ethic, and drive. Considering what I do, I'm obviously not religious, but I've always found it inspiring how the greatest proof of Jesus Christ comes not from what those who followed him thought about him but rather from what his enemies thought.

"For instance, they never denied his miracles and claims, never refuted his statements. No, they admitted to those freely. What they did do was scheme to shut him up—do away with him. To make him stop. And that, I contend, is the greatest form of praise.

"Several doctors in your field are like that with you. They don't deny your success. They don't dismiss your methods or technique. No, they try to dismiss *you* by saying you are a glory seeker— publishing everywhere, speaking in places no one will ever ask them to. They wear their envy on their sleeves, their eyes green with jealousy, proving your value more than a thousand awards ever could." He stopped to clear his throat, holding the large white bandage tight against his neck, wincing at the pain.

"And this one," he said, indicating Billy lying unconscious on his back, "not the best at anything. Just a thug. A nothing—important to some simply because of his Family connections—riding the coattails of his betters. His uncle, on the other hand—I might consider him, but that's for later. This one, though? Unworthy as he is, he hurt me. Almost killed me." Gold looked back to Rick.

"So, I'm afraid I did lie about not killing everyone. But in fairness, I'll make everyone else's death quick and relatively painless. Everyone but yours, of course. Oh, and his. Yours will be out of respect—I need to see what makes you what you are. I must dig deep to learn that. But his? His pain will be purely for my pleasure."

"Please, let them go. After you finish with me ... and him," Rick said reluctantly, "just let the others go. I'll give you whatever you want."

"Noble," said Gold. "I'd expect no less from you. But it doesn't work like that. You can't give me what I need from you. No one can. I have to take it. It can't be a gift. Like the trophy—it has to be earned."

"You mean stolen," said Rick.

"Potato—pa-tah-toe. I contend a genius art thief who steals a Rembrandt from a heavily guarded museum through careful planning and execution has certainly earned his reward." Gold stepped over to the couch and stood above Rick, a curved needle and thread resting between his fingers.

"I'll start by stitching your eyelids open so you can watch the rest of the procedures and so that I can see what's going on in your soul. That's where the truth lies, after all—at the center of your being, somewhere between soul and spirit. I advise that you be careful not to move. It would be most unpleasant to deal with a punctured eyeball on top of everything else. And trust me—there *will* be much more to deal with."

Rick tried to be strong. He thought of Gil Mason and all he'd dealt with—deep physical, mental, and spiritual wounds. Rick wanted to be strong like that. Strong like he knew Gil Mason would be. But Rick was only Rick, and as Larry Gold bent over him, piercing his living flesh with the metal point of the needle, he learned that he was not that strong—not that strong at all.

I ROLLED, cradling the boy in my arms as we tumbled. Men were rushing toward us, weapons drawn, aiming at me. I was afraid they would hit the boy, so I threw him as far from their line of fire as possible. I continued my roll and came up with my rifle at the ready, pointing at the Gardener.

"Stop!" he screamed. "Everyone, stop!"

I would have taken him out then and there, but since I counted maybe twelve guns pointed at me, I decided to wait and see what he had to say.

"Drop your weapons," said the Gardener. "Drop them, and I will prove to you and everyone here the true power of the One Tree. A test of strength and will and just who really is the true god of the universe. No guns, no knives. Just you and me, Mason, and the tools we were born with."

"Deal," I said, without hesitation, as I unslung my rifle and set it next to my feet. There was a strong possibility he would order his men to kill me now that I wasn't aiming my rifle at him, but I didn't think he would. His rep was on the line, and false gods really have nothing without their reputations. Besides, he was cocky, overconfident. He was a big, strong man who'd survived by being bigger and stronger than others. He was a bully who thought he could take me.

"Cut the other boy down first," I said. I stripped off my vest and set aside all my weapons, including my buckle knife.

The Gardener waved a hand toward the boy, giving me permission to approach.

I'd dropped my knives, so it took me a few seconds to untie the knots. "What's your name, son?" I asked as I slipped the rope from around his wrists.

"Timber," said the boy, rubbing his chaffed skin.

"You know Toby?"

A frightened look flashed across his face as he nodded and glanced toward the Gardener.

"He's not dead," I said. I tied the rope that had held him into a crude slipknot, still draped over the branch. "And as soon as I kill this," I chinned toward the Gardener, "I'm going to get the rest of you kids out of here. Okay?" He nodded again, looking pale and shaken, but I thought he understood. "Good, be ready."

I turned to the Gardener. "The Bible says, *Cursed is everyone who hangs on a tree* ... a foreshadowing of Christ taking our place on the Cross. But it worked for Judas, and it'll work for you, too. I'm going to hang you from this tree, then burn it, you, and this building to the ground."

The Gardener grinned, and I saw the madness in his eyes. I felt certain he'd frightened many with that look.

It didn't scare me though.

I'm not afraid of crazy.

~

THE SCREAMING BROUGHT BILLY AROUND. He opened his eyes, but only a little. Just enough to see what was what. His hands were zip-tied, and so were his feet. Not so long ago, he'd been in nearly this same position back at Larry Gold's butchery. But this time, he wasn't hanging upside down, and his hands were in front instead of behind his back.

The hands would be no trouble—he could snap the ties with ease. The ankles, though, posed a bigger problem.

No leverage.

And then he remembered the scalpel wrapped in gauze inside his pocket.

~

MASON HAD PLAYED PERFECTLY into the Gardener's plan. He would kill him, then raise Pasley from the dead. He considered striking Mason with lightning—what a show that would be—but no. Mason had insulted him, taunted him, threatened him. The Gardener wanted to crush the life out of him with his own hands.

Glancing at the One Tree, he remembered going to the forest to find it. The visions had led him—the visions he had entrusted to the aliens in his past life. Its removal and replanting had cost a fortune, but here it stood, a receptacle for all the knowledge and power he'd invested in it for safekeeping.

And now was the time.

The Gardener—*Kane*—the Hawaiian god of wild foods and plants, the highest of the four major Hawaiian gods, chief of the Hawaiian trinity, raised his hands and called on the One Tree. Its strength and knowledge rushed into him, its power glowing from him in an encompassing halo of light.

Nothing could stop him or stand before him now.

Kane had never felt such power.

THE GARDENER CHARGED as he had before, his long arms sweeping out, looking to scoop me in a giant bearhug so he could crush the life from me, but this time, he didn't have a little boy to shield him. I jumped up and forward, snapping my knee hard into his chin and coming down with an elbow on the top of his head, a move I'd learned from watching legendary Tai martial artist and actor Tony Jaa. The double crack sounded like twin explosions in the sanctuary.

He crumpled, his knees sagging, but to his credit, he didn't go down. Spinning, I caught him on the temple with a back fist and buckled his ankle with a sidekick, the bone splintering with a crack. He screamed in pain with that one.

Pansy.

I stopped the scream with a punch to the throat, then wrapped around him with some fancy footwork, hooking the first two fingers of my right hand into his nostrils from over and behind his head, jerking him back and over, the cradle of the back of his neck wedge over my right shoulder. I dragged him, his feet shuffling backwards to keep from falling as I brought him to the rope that hung from the branch. Looping it around his neck, I untied the other end as he dropped to his knees, blood pouring from his nose and mouth. Pulling, I hauled his giant frame up, the makeshift noose tightening, until he stood high ... then higher to his tippy toes ... and higher still ... his feet kicking in the air.

There was a look in his bulging eyes, as if they wanted ... *needed* ... to tell me something.

Too bad. I wasn't in a listening mood and didn't care what he had to say.

One expensive shoe dropped off, leaving his socked foot to twitch and fight for a purchase that wasn't there.

They could have shot me—I wasn't armed. I stood out in the open, an easy target, but I had just defeated their god. They were scared, lost. Or perhaps they were waiting to see if, by some miracle, the tree would save him, justifying everything they'd given up to follow him.

Instead, they watched him twitch and jerk and gag ... and die.

BILLY SAT STRAIGHT UP, simultaneously jerking his elbows back to the sides of his body. The zip tie snapped like simple twine. An instant later, the gauze-wrapped scalpel was out of his pocket, cutting the plastic holding his ankles as easily as it had earlier sliced through the flesh of his palm.

Larry Gold turned just as the needle pierced Rick's right eyelid. Billy grabbed the porcelain potted bonsai tree from the table and ran, hitting Gold in the face with it so hard it crushed his cheek, nose, and orbital socket. Gold dropped to the carpeted floor, where he lay unconscious. Pouncing, Billy landed on top of him, the scalpel going to his throat.

"No!" yelled Rick from the couch. "Please, Billy, don't kill him. He's sick. He needs help. Please."

Billy almost finished it—knew that he *should* finish it, that it was foolish not to. Just then, Tina sat up, pressing a hand to her bruised and scuffed forehead.

"He's right, Billy. Don't kill him. Do it the right way. Let the law handle it."

The scalpel's edge had broken the skin just above the white bandage, creating a line of blood that ran down, soaking the patch.

"Please," said Tina, "for me, please."

Gritting his teeth, Billy threw the scalpel across the room, where it bounced off the wall and landed anticlimactically next to the curtain near the interns.

"I think you're both wrong," said Billy. "Gil wouldn't have stopped —not even for you."

"No," said Tina, "he wouldn't have. And that's why I'm with you and not him."

The two of them met in the center of the room wrapping their arms around each other. She kissed him.

"I love you," she said.

"I love you too," said Billy.

She smiled at him, nudging her chin toward the scalpel. "I know."

I RETRIEVED MY WEAPONS, put them back on, and strapped my vest in place. I took my time, giving the shooters in the room plenty of opportunity to retaliate. None of them attempted anything. I walked to the fireplace, used the poker to haul out a good-sized hunk of burning wood, and set it at the base of the tree. Then I went to Timber, the shirtless boy I'd released from the rope.

"Take all the children out that door. There is a snowcat parked next to the building across from here. It has an extended cattle trailer hitched to it. Get them all inside. Go now."

Murmurs began to circulate among the people in the sanctuary.

"The children are all coming with me," I said. "Once this storm ends, you can claim them from the State Patrol in town ... that is, if they don't arrest you for the horrible child abuse crimes you've committed. If anyone tries to stop me or gets in my way, I'll kill you. If anyone tries to put out the fire I've started here in the tree, I'll kill you."

Looking at the tree, I could see it was going up pretty quickly. "Most likely, this hall will burn to the ground. I don't know what that means in terms of electricity or heat once I've gone. Maybe some of the other buildings will still have power. I don't know. I don't care. But you can't go with me. There's a dead woman buried out there. You let this monster kill her. I'm betting there are a lot more out there, too. You all stood by while this monster abused your children, your women. You watched while he strung your people up on this tree ... to beat and kill them. So, whatever happens to you, now or later, I don't care. You can all freeze to death or burn or whatever. Just don't get in my way."

The tree was blazing now. The Gardener had caught fire and was burning like an effigy—the smell putrid.

One of the men with a gun shouted at me, "You ain't taking our kids."

Swiveling, I snugged the butt of my rifle into my shoulder and pointed it at him. "They're not yours anymore. You gave them to him, and now they're mine."

The man looked away. A woman beside him was hanging on his sleeve, trying to get him to continue the protest. He remained silent. The children, accustomed to obeying orders, had formed a line and were following the boy named Timber out the door and into the light snowfall. Before the door closed, Max walked into the hall and approached me. He sat in a perfect heel, watching the crowd with cold eyes. The two of us covered the children's retreat until they were all out and loaded in the trailer.

Addressing the crowd a final time, I said, "I'm sure you've heard from the townspeople about what Max here did to those who tried to attack me. Don't make yourself another example. It'd be better if I just shot you ... less horrific."

Max and I followed the kids to the snowcat. No one tried to stop us. The sanctuary burst into flame as we drove away, and I heard something explode. People were running in all directions, but they were behind us and posed no threat. As I gave my coat to the shirtless boy sitting next to me, I described the location where my car had crashed and told him that Toby was there awaiting my return. He knew the area intimately and showed me a much faster way.

We loaded Toby and Pilgrim into the snowcat and slogged our way into town. I stopped the giant treaded vehicle in front of Molly's place and unloaded the children. A snowmobile and a big rig without a trailer sat in the lot. We all went inside, and there was Pappy,

Trooper Wright, Molly, and another woman I didn't recognize. They turned as one when I opened the door, shock on their faces.

"This is Toby," I said, gripping his shoulders as the rest of the children flooded in around us. I pointed at Pappy. "And this man is your father's friend. He'll take you to him."

I looked to Trooper Wright. "You got some work cut out for you," I told her as I started for the door. "And Molly, pour me a coffee while I get Pilgrim and Max."

I paused, turning back, "Oh, and let the kids have whatever they want. I'm buying. After all, this is a business, right?"

EPILOGUE

Halloween came and went, as did Thanksgiving. Pappy shipped back to the Marines. Edward Ramirez and Toby, now reunited, were adjusting. Toby had a lot of healing to do, as did his father, but now they could do it together.

Tina took a leave of absence, and she and Billy went on an extended vacation to a Caribbean Island. Viper and the pups stayed with me ... or rather ... with Max.

Pilgrim, mostly healed, is acting as a surrogate grandfather, the pups nipping, chewing, and climbing all over him. He loves every second of it.

Max is teaching them all to be ninja killers.

There had been questions, of course. State and local authorities got involved. We'd left a mark at the compound and the base of the mountain where we'd crashed.

Four dead sentries sniped from distance ... bodies mutilated and torn ... a religious cult destroyed.

There were questions about rights violations, trespassing, burglary, arson, kidnapping, and murder, to name a few. There was serious talk of having me arrested and charged, but the FBI swept in and closed everyone else out. They did a comprehensive search of the grounds. They located documents and computer records pointing to bribes, donations, and favors—both to and from powerful political parties. They found over a hundred bodies—men, women, children, Toby's mother, and FBI Agent Peter Simon.

Shortly after they found Peter's body, I got a call from Special Agent in Charge Lance Kemp. He thanked me and told me the Bureau owed me a debt they could never repay. After that, all the questions from other authorities mysteriously stopped, and there was no further talk of arrests or charges.

The children I rescued were screened and given counseling and therapy. Some had been released to their parents, others to relatives. None of the men or women from the compound were charged or arrested, having accepted some kind of deal from the FBI concerning their investigation. Testimony from those men and women, along with the seized records, had led to a complete disbanding of the OTA. Several of the higher-ups had been arrested and were facing federal racketeering charges.

Rick's eyelid was repaired, and he went back to work helping people in need. Larry Gold was found unfit to stand trial by reason of insanity and is currently being held at the Colorado Mental Health Institute in Pueblo.

It was a week before Christmas, and Tina and Billy were due back the following day. I was sitting in front of Rick's office. The previous week had been challenging as I tried to fulfill Tina's request to disperse the pups before she returned.

I'd started several days earlier, flying to San Diego to meet with Pappy. He was surprised to see me but more surprised to see the puppy I handed him. He tried to refuse, citing military rules saying if the Marine Corps wanted him to have a dog, they'd have issued him one. I countered with the term Devil Dog and reminded him that the Marine Corps mascot is a bulldog. Before he could refuse, I gave him a rundown of his lonely life story and how this dog could be his saving grace. After much convincing and little *Dan Daly* chewing at his boots and laces, Pappy picked him up and stared him in the face.

The pink tongue coated in puppy breath flicking out and licking his nose did the final trick.

Pappy had lost his first war.

Next, I visited Edward Ramirez and his son Toby. I'd already phoned Ed, asking his permission to grant Toby a future protector and immediate helpmate. Toby's eyes filled with tears when I handed him the puppy. At first, he was too choked up to speak, but then he grabbed my neck while simultaneously holding the squirming dog. Afterward, he wrestled the ball of fur and teeth until they were both exhausted.

They would be good for each other. The puppy would distract the boy from what he'd been through while bestowing unconditional love as the boy mourned the loss of his mother. The responsibility of caring for the rambunctious pup would teach Toby about the need to be flexible in some areas while staying ramrod straight in others.

Billy was giving Irmgard her puppy when he and Tina returned, and of course, Tina was keeping one to train up for police work. That left Thor, the puppy I kept for myself, and one more.

At last, I knocked on Rick's door. The interns were there with him.

Rick beamed as he came to me. "And who's this?" he asked, reaching to pet the puppy's head. *Lightning fast*, it nipped his fingers before he could pull away. "Whoa, a speedster." Grinning, he shook his fingers, but he didn't try again.

"This is Anna," I said as I handed her to him.

He looked confused and backed away slightly. I shook my head, grinning. "No, Rick, here, take her." I handed her to him. He took her and held her awkwardly while dodging her needle-sharp teeth.

"What's this about?" he asked.

"Billy wants you to have her," I said. "Tina and I both agreed."

"I don't understand," he said.

"Billy destroyed your tree to save you—the tree your father gave you. He feels terrible about that. He understands the tree's significance as it relates to your dad, so he wants to give you this puppy as a replacement—a sort of proxy. When you look at this puppy, you will be reminded of the tree—the tree your father gave you."

Rick looked bewildered. "That's a very kind gesture, but unnecessary. It also doesn't make a lot of sense. I mean, this is a girl dog, after all. My dad was, of course, a man."

I laughed. "And your tree was a plant," I said. "It's symbology, Rick. It doesn't have to be the same. Whenever you see her, hear her, smell her, touch her, it will remind you of the day your father helped save your life."

"Saved my life?"

"Sure," I said. "The tree hitting Gold in the face saved you. The tree was given to you by your dad. You associated the tree with your father. Consider this—the man who wielded your symbolic father to knock out the man who was trying to kill you is giving you a replacement in the guise of this dog. It's simple psychoanalysis." I turned to Frick and Frack, his two interns. "Am I right, boys?"

They looked at each other, then back at me. In unison, they said, "Absolutely."

As with Pappy, Rick looked like he was going to say no. I backed away, holding up my hands. "You can't refuse. The man who saved your life has given you this gift."

I looked him close in the eyes. "And you know what, Rick? You need this—you really do. Added love in life—*real love*—is always a good thing. It will help keep you grounded. And, in those times when you wish you could ask your father for advice or you just want to be reminded of him ... well ... she'll be here for you. This is a good thing. Don't say no."

Holding her close to his face, just as Pappy had done, Rick looked at her as if searching for something. Instead of licking his nose, she nipped it. Rick grinned, nodding as a tear rolled down his cheek.

"This wasn't Billy," he said. He looked up at me. "This is you, isn't it?"

"Maybe. You've been through trauma, my friend ... something I know about. You helped me, Rick, and this is something you need. Let me help you."

He gave it some thought, then nodded before giving me quizzical. "Why Anna?" he asked.

"Named after Anna Freud—Sigmund's daughter."

Both of the interns clapped. "Nice," said one. "Well played," said the other.

After that, I drove home. Max was there with Viper. The rest of the puppies were growling playfully as they tumbled over Pilgrim. Sarah was there too.

And that was the best of all.

ACKNOWLEDGMENTS

Hello, dear reader. Once again, I would like to thank you for buying and reading the latest installment of the Gil Mason series, The Hand That Feeds. Cults are a weird part of the Colorado experience, and for some reason, the state seems to attract them like flies—a fact my wife brought to my attention. A couple of years ago, she heard about a cult in a Colorado town whose female leader was found dead, mummified, packed in essential oils, wrapped in Christmas lights, her eyeless sockets decorated in glitter. Even in death, her followers still seemed to worship her.

That story gave me the idea for The Hand That Feeds. In the book, I mention a few other cults that have landed hereabouts, but it's hardly an exhaustive list. I wonder if the radiation from all the uranium draws them here or if it's just the majesty of our beautiful mountain range. In any case, all or at least most cults and false religions are perversions of the true gospel, and the OTA is no exception. In The Hand that Feeds, I emphasize the difference between these belief systems and true Christianity, as Hollyweird and the secular world always try to conflate the two. I hope I made the journey distinctive, fun, informative, and exciting.

As with all of my books, I had a lot of help writing and finishing this one. I didn't find and catch bad guys by myself, and I don't publish books by myself either. All books require a team effort, and this one entailed effort from my wife (editor), my oldest daughter, Athena (she does all my covers ... and isn't this one awesome!), my dear friend

Barbara Wright (she and her daughter have helped me find K9s for the Sheriff's Office), and our wonderful editor Betty Fisher, who gave it a final review to fix everything we missed.

I thank God (not an expression of speech) for allowing me the enjoyment of writing, for encouragement from my fans, and for being able to introduce small pieces of His Word to reach and encourage others (iron sharpens iron).

Any incorrect, outdated, or misapplied information is wholly on me, either because it worked for the story or because I messed it up. Also, my editors give me constant grief for my use of ..., —, and italics. I break some grammatical rules while writing, but that's because I write to tell the story and make it flow as smoothly as possible. I apologize to those who find my use of these tools a distraction. I feel they add an effect for the average reader (me) that mere commas don't, and for me, it's all about the story experience. I don't claim to be a great writer, but I hope I'm at least good at spinning an entertaining yarn.

And finally, it comes to you, dear reader. Thank you so much for buying and reading The Hand That Feeds and making the Gil Mason novels a best-selling series. I hope to see you soon as the adventure continues in Silent Dog Still Water. Thanks for being a part of The Dog Pack, and please join me in our next hunt.

Until then...

ABOUT THE AUTHOR

Gordon Carroll is the author of GUNWOOD USA, Bone Hill, and The Gil Mason Sheepdog series. The Hand That Feeds is book 8 in the ongoing series, and book 9, Silent Dog Still Water, is in the works. Gordon grew up at the foot of the great Rocky Mountains in Colorado. He joined the United States Marine Corps at eighteen, served for seven years, achieved the rank of sergeant, and was selected for staff sergeant. Following his military career, Gordon became a police officer in a small (wild) city nestled snugly in the middle of Denver, Colorado. After leaving the police force, he became a sheriff's deputy and was eventually assigned to the K9 unit as a handler, trainer, and instructor. During his three decades as a K9 officer, he trained and worked four dogs (a hundred-twenty-pound German Shepherd named JR, a ninety-pound Belgian Malinois named Max, a fifty-six-pound Belgian Malinois named Thor, and a sixty-pound fur missile named Arrow). Gordon retired from police work in 2020 to focus on writing and spending time with his grandchildren. K9 Arrow retired with him.

f

ALSO BY GORDON CARROLL

Made in the USA
Middletown, DE
02 November 2023

41856154R00170